Praise for Lance Olsen's fiction:

"A major new novel from one of the more interesting new writers in
the genre and it's filled with enough ideas for an entire shelf of books."
—*Science Fiction Chronicle* about *Time Famine*

"Hell's still a-popping in these techno-parables, filled with surprising
insights and articulations."
—Samuel R. Delany about *Sewing Shut My Eyes*

"Relentless, savage, hysterically funny."
—Paul Di Filippo, *Asimov's,* about *Time Famine*

"The ultimate rock-and-roll novel."
—Brian Stableford, *Interzone,* about *Tonguing the Zeitgeist*

"A wonderfully funny, definitely unusual SF novel."
—Don D'Ammassa, *Science Fiction Chronicle,* about *Burnt*

"Reminiscent of the British New Wave Movement at its best."
—*Science Fiction Chronicle* about *Scherzi, I Believe*

Also By Lance Olsen

NOVELS
Live from Earth
Tonguing the Zeitgeist
Burnt
Time Famine

SHORT STORIES
My Dates with Franz
Scherzi, I Believe
Sewing Shut My Eyes

POETRY
Natural Selections
(With Jeff Worley)

NONFICTION
Ellipse of Uncertainty
Circus of the Mind in Motion
William Gibson
Lolita: A Janus Text
Surfing Tomorrow (Editor)
In Memoriam to Postmodernism (Co-Editor)

TEXTBOOK
Rebel Yell: A Short Guide to Writing Fiction

freaknest

Lance Olsen

Wordcraft of Oregon

2000

Published by
Worcraft of Oregon
P.O. Box 3235
La Grande, OR 97850
http://www.oregontrail.net/~wordcraft
wordcraft@oregontrail.net

Copyright © 2000
#22 in the Wordcraft Speculative Writers Series
First Edition: September 2000

Digitally manipulated cover image and cover design: Andi Olsen

Cover image: video still from Hollow Creature
Technical support: Barbara Ham

ISBN: 1-877655-35-X

Printed by Complete Reproduction Service, Santa Ana, CA

For Andi, fellow teratoid in the global exhibit...

I remember the old Brandenburgh Museum in Philadelphia where for the price of one dime—ten cents—you could see Jo Jo, the Dog-faced Boy; Plutano and Waino, the Original Wild Men of Borneo; Laloo from India with his twin growing out of his body; Arthur Loose, the Rubber-Skinned Man who pulled out his cheeks eight inches and let them snap back into place; and the famous Mrs. Tom Thumb. The popularity of the freaks carried the show, but various vaudeville performers, not yet good enough for the Palace or Roxy's in New York, were used as fillers. Among the people who got their start there were Al Jolson, Harry Houdini, Buster Keaton and Van Alsyne, who sang a little number he'd written called "In the Shade of the Old Apple Tree." Though these men did well later on, it was always the freaks whom people came to see.

— Daniel P. Mannix,
Freaks: We Who Are Not As Others

PART ONE:
FORGOTTEN HORIZON

1. THE DEMOGRAPHICS OF SUBAQUEOUS LIGHT

Dr. Jarndyce Mizzle-Sluggbury, the one-hundred-and-twenty-three-year-old Klub Med executive who'd wealthied himself fat and greasy as a bacon-wrapped chunk of filet mignon through his company's seminal investigations into cryonics (in 2021 he was instrumental in tugging back one Anna Tesler-Huntington from the brink of 2001 smack into a bout of spontaneous psychosis), debarked from the beetlish black cab outside his Knightsbridge flat at 3 Hans Crescent across the street from Harrods' counterfeit-gothic façade.

He slipped the brown-toothed driver his ebony cybercash slab and stood rubbing the side of his bearded face, loftily contemplating the deserted street, a good hundred meters of which he owned.

Safe-zone floodlights eradicating the night around him.

The driver returned the slab with a rotten-nubbed broken lampoon of a smile, and the doctor mounted the cement steps leading up to the massive heart attack that would drop him in less than nine-hundred seconds.

But Dr. Jarndyce Mizzle-Sluggbury had other matters on his mind at present ... nothing precise, nothing especially important ... just a gentle kaleidoscopic tumble of images and sounds from the last few hours ... laughter washing over the shiny table top at his weekly dinner with colleagues at the private club up Kensington Road ... approving quips about Great Britain's recent adoption of an isolationist policy spawned by the collapse of visa enforcement, the resulting population influx from Hong Kong, and the increasingly eerie sense those bleeding chop-chops had nudged the reals into something resembling minority status ... smoked oysters from the ponds south of London glistening on beds of crushed ice, rosy mounds of steak tartar garnished with capers and spring onions piled on a spinach-leaf carpet, lobster bisque, dab of Iranian caviar on a buttery biscuit, warm moist bread, a decanter of dark port, small sweet lemon sorbet intervals to cleanse the palate along the flyovers and roundabouts of this expansive gastronomical motorway ... and, finally, the honeyed sparkle of a slender glass of champagne raised in salute to Guy Fawkes Day, a refreshing breeze of general merriment despite this dreadfully humid November and dreary political wind blowing in from the Far East ...

Dr. Jarndyce Mizzle-Sluggbury loved food almost as much as he loved the idea of Great Britain. He loved to become one with food, merge its being with his, sense its wet mass peristalsize down the back of his throat, through his digestive tract, on its course toward uniting with his cellular mechanics, spirit and matter joined in a flash of alchemy.

He loved the smells of it. He loved the textures, the hues, the heft, the multifold recipes for its composition on the plate.

Food for Dr. Jarndyce Mizzle-Sluggbury was fine art.

It was also the reason he weighed as much as a Shetland pony ... why, with his short white hair and long white whiskers and rotund squat neck and capacious keg belly and pygmy thin legs, he reminded his colleagues of the main character in a Christmas pageant.

Genetic manipulation was why food hadn't murdered him. Dr. Mizzle-Sluggbury employed his wealth accrued from his cryonics work for Klub Med (as in Klub Medellin, as in the Medellin Cartel, an economic entity that diversified after most previously illicit drugs were legalized over the course of the first two decades of the new century) to extend his life in time in a method analogous to how food extended his presence in space. On a weekend holiday to a Swiss clinic on his ninety-eighth birthday, he had his genes twidgled to snip back his cholesterol-absorption capacity by eighty-nine percent while generating immunity to most airborne pollutants, many sexually transmitted diseases, most cancers, malaria, and TB.

With eight-hundred seconds left to live, Dr. Jarndyce Mizzle-Sluggbury halted before the slick white door to what used to be the Colombian Embassy, a six-story red-brick affair with white-trimmed bay windows and white wrought-iron balconies at each level. The overall effect was, he realized for the first time as he voice-activated the petabyte nano-puter that was his wool tie, wedding-cake-like.

The door awakened and asked him to step forward another four centimeters. He did. A thin red beam pinpricked out the peephole and flittered over his features.

"Face-recognition positive at three-thousand loci," a little girl's voice said in a polite Oxbridge accent. "Welcome home, Dr. Mizzle-Sluggbury."

The latch clacked. The door swung open. Dr. Mizzle-Sluggbury stepped into the soft yellow light and familiar music of his foyer. Gabrielli's trumpets emanated from the gray-green fitted carpet. An inviting scent of apple cider perfumed the air. The door swung shut.

Dr. Mizzle-Sluggbury, content and eiderdown snug, ambulated toward the kitchen, the notion of a cup of Earl Grey and an ultrasonic shower before bed waving primly to him from the distant borders of his awareness.

The tidy narrow foyer and hall were done in off-whites and olives and boasted a coat rack, two small indecipherable watercolors in gilt frames, a beveled mirror, and two cherrywood drop-leaf tables, on each of which sat a lace doily and an electric oil lamp.

The electric oil lamps sensed his presence, glowed brighter, and greeted him as he toddled past.

"Welcome home, Dr. Mizzle-Sluggbury," they said in unison.

"Thank you," Dr. Mizzle-Sluggbury replied.

In the kitchen the Wedgwood breakfast setting, designed to keep the meals it hosted at a steady temperature, heard his voice and chimed in.

"Welcome home, Dr. Mizzle-Sluggbury!" it pipped.

"Welcome home, Dr. Mizzle-Sluggbury," said the translucent fishbowl light on the ceiling as he appeared in the doorway and surveyed the small pink-and-white room.

"Welcome home, Dr. Mizzle-Sluggbury," said the Maracaibo microwave atop the white-tiled counter next to the Omsk coffee grinder next to the Malindi faucets, one for hot water and one for cold, which also saluted him, as did the miniature fridge, stove, dishwasher, juice-maker, and even Panasonic bubble hoover in the closet.

"No calls, no messages," the phone added after all the other appliances had quieted down.

The help had departed for the weekend and wouldn't return till Monday morning. These next hours were all his ... to putter about the flat, vada the telly, do a crossword puzzle or two. There he was, alone and glad to be alone, and there was Mr. Charles Dickens waiting for him upstairs in his library, and for these next twenty-four hours he could extract his self-adjusting monocle from his waistcoat pocket, slip into his silken smoking jacket, nestle into his recliner, and live as if his king and queen were something more than history, deference something more than memory, reality still built upon solid atoms with hard little bodies and predictable little trajectories.

"Tea, please," he said, with three-hundred seconds left to live, remembering for some reason the woman he had seen from his front window this afternoon, down on her hands and knees across the street in her one-by-two-meter garden, cutting her cucumber-green grass with shears, precise clips, and that component of the microwave which needed to understand the doctor understood him, filled a compartment of itself with water, agitated its molecules, and spritzed the boiling product into a waiting faux-porcelain cup at the bottom of which bobbed a tea strainer packed with Earl Grey.

"Cream, sir?" it asked.

"A bit. Yes."

Hot white stream hissed.

Dr. Mizzle-Sluggbury again rubbed the side of his bearded

features which didn't work anymore, consequence of the muscle virus that surfaced long before the holiday to Switzerland and took his wife, and took his son.

Humming along with Gabrielli, he removed the strainer, picked up the cup and, cradling it in his two hands, executed an exploratory sip.

His heart stopped.

His face turned red as if he'd just scrubbed it with a cheese grater.

The cup bounced on the tiles and yipped.

Dr. Mizzle-Sluggbury's mouth widened and his hands fluttered up to his chest.

Next thing he knew he was lying on his back on the kitchen floor, subaqueous light smarming around the blue-white ceiling, aware the status of his demographics was shifting.

The impressive fact was how little the shift hurt. In Dr. Mizzle-Sluggbury's imagination, heart attacks had always taken the mass of great lumbering elephants perching on one's chest. Only it wasn't like that at all. It was more like strolling into a blast-furnace and then strolling out again. Sensation vanished. Consciousness became a hairy fly, and the hairy fly whirred up and around the room, agitated, disorientated, banging into walls, bouncing off reflections, clambering for the cool light it sensed burning just beyond the frontier of existence, peering down occasionally through its compound perception at the well-dressed walrus peering back, palms flat on the floor, stubby legs spread in an unrefined V, mouth a pink orifice in a cumulus beard.

The fly flew backward in time—to this afternoon, to that woman clipping cucumber-green grass with shears in her garden—and zigzagged about her face. She was in her sixties. Her long gray hair was tugged into a braid that corded down the rear of her blue-gray Mao suit almost to her buttocks. Her face was plain, without makeup, without sunscreen, and gravitational entropy was well into speaking its language upon it, except for the neat slice of red lipstick she wore across her mouth. When she raised her head and hand to swat away the fly, she noticed Dr. Jarndyce

Mizzle-Sluggbury standing at his window, arms by his sides, observing her, and the smileless swat blossomed into the polite shadow of a wave before she lowered herself again to her business. Dr. Mizzle-Sluggbury nodded back, seeing, not the stranger across the street, but his wife, Cynthia, laboring in their own garden at their old flat in Chelsea the afternoon the doctor had told her her muscles were infected with the new viral form of muscular dystrophy that would gradually replace her healthy tissue with scarring and fat.

She was dying, the doctor said, and there was nothing to be done about it.

Jarndyce accompanied her home. Cynthia stepped out of the car and walked straightaway into the house and appeared in her blue-gray Mao suit and went directly to work in the garden, snipping, chopping, digging, patting, hewing, kneading. She wouldn't stop. The dusk came and she wouldn't stop. The dark came and she wouldn't stop. Jarndyce observed her patiently from the window, waiting, knowing she needed to touch everything she could.

Now Dr. Mizzle-Sluggbury became aware, as if from very far off, of a nibbling at the legs of his trousers. He attempted to employ his peripheral vision to determine what was happening.

The Panasonic bubble hoover, sensing an accident, had rolled out of the closet and released its cockroach bots to clean up whatever mess it might find. It had located the spilled tea and slurped the puddle dry. It had located the dropped cup and carried it back into its stomach where the maid would discover it Monday.

Then it located Dr. Mizzle-Sluggbury himself, lying motionless in an unnatural pose, and tried to raise him off the tidy tiled floor.

The hoover had never encountered such a large load of trash before and the lifting wasn't going at all well. So it ceased and, cooing and burring, processed this information.

A microsecond later, the cockroach bots switched programs and began their meticulous banquet.

It occurred to Dr. Mizzle-Sluggbury he could summon assistance if he could only open his mouth and utter one word: *help.* The phone would hear him and, comprehending the significance of the situation, ring up an ambulance.

Only it seemed his whole organic electrical system had short-circuited in one momentous thunderbolt.

His lips were numb.

His tongue was a lump of liver among his teeth.

Then he was that fly again, missiling from the stranger's head across the street and farther back in time … to the soggy interior of a hired orange-red Fiat alongside a road no wider than a footpath in northwest Scotland on the Isle of Skye.

Within the Fiat sat Cynthia, himself, and his son Jarndyce Jr. They were on holiday and had seen more castles, shipyards, and farm-shrimp ponds than they quite cared to. They were on their way to a remote eighteenth-century inn Boswell and Johnson once visited on a craggy precipice overlooking Loch Snizort to play croquet and watch gray birds. They had just passed a solitary white farmhouse with a black-tiled roof and stand of evergreens in a dense fog when they rounded a corner and thunked into the rectangular-bodied ewe.

Condensation clouded the windscreen. Irregular droplets bifurcated. Dr. Mizzle-Sluggbury heard his family breathing.

"Right, then," he said.

He looked at Jarndyce Jr., twelve and blond and cod-eyed, and swung open the driver's door.

He stepped into dank rimy air.

Jarndyce Jr. hesitated several pulses and followed.

They walked back over cracked asphalt to where the ewe lay. The impact had skidded her down the road and knocked one of her eyes out of her black mask. Bright blood globbed around her nostrils and mouth. Her rump was stained the color of thousand-island dressing. She panted rapidly. Her legs moved as if she thought she were still running.

Dr. Mizzle-Sluggbury loftily contemplated the animal, wandered off, and returned with a stone the size of a loaf of bread.

"Sometimes we've got to finish what we've begun," he explained to his son. He handed him the stone. "Sometimes we've got to do what we've got to do, and sometimes what we've got to do isn't a pleasant thing in the least."

Jarndyce Jr. looked at the stone, at his father, at the sheep. His eyes grew wider, intuiting for the first time how dangerous adults really were.

"Sometimes dying is part of not dying," Dr. Mizzle-Sluggbury said. He looked over his son's head: a ditch, an incline, moors sliding into silver light. "Go on now."

Jarndyce Jr. cupped the stone in his hand. He examined the ewe.

"Fast and sweet," Dr. Mizzle-Sluggbury primed. "Think of yourself in the same position. What would you ask if you could ask one favor?"

Jarndyce Jr. lowered himself onto his knees next to the ewe. Dr. Mizzle-Sluggbury observed his son observing himself. This was a moment, he knew, that would enter his son's history.

Jarndyce Jr. raised the stone in both hands and brought it down heavily on the ewe's head.

He raised it and brought it down.

Nothing changed.

The ewe scrambled horizontally, trying to rise. Its skull dented a little. More salad dressing appeared, this time around the exposed ear.

The boy looked at what he'd done, trying to organize his actions in his mind.

Dr. Mizzle-Sluggbury didn't let him.

"Again … quickly."

Jarndyce Jr. stared at his work.

"But it won't die, daddy."

"Of course it will. Go on."

"It just keeps living."

"You must hit it harder."

"I've hit it hard as I can."

Jarndyce Jr.'s nose sapped; he was about to cry.

"Put your back into it."

"But I …"

"Pick up the stone and put your back into it. Think of yourself there."

Jarndyce Jr. struck so hard the stone bounced out of his grip. The ewe flinched … and, snap, there came a clatter of two-toed hoofs on asphalt, a disgusted huff.

The animal was up, shaky, teetering, surveying its surroundings with its one good eye.

Before either his son or Dr. Mizzle-Sluggbury could internalize this, the ewe clopped in a half-blind half-limp toward the edge of the road, down into the ditch, and up into the tangled heather on the opposite side.

A moment, and it was lost in the fog.

Dr. Mizzle-Sluggbury came to understand that day just how much some things wanted to live.

Which was the kind of lesson he forgot soon as he could, part of his own complicated psychic survival reflex, till years later, in 2021, after his wife Cynthia was gone, and his son Jarndyce Jr., when, one amber afternoon in his lab on the top floor of his Knightsbridge flat at 3 Hans Crescent on the corner of Basil Street, Anna Tesler-Huntington's lids slipped open, and her eyes swiveled about wildly, trying to place herself in this future, trying to comprehend what existence held for her beyond death, beyond the long horrific series of icy nightmares that had structured her inverted reality for twenty-three years … and simply couldn't.

Her eyes rolled up.

Her body began to buck.

Insect-egg foam formed on her lips.

And Dr. Mizzle-Sluggbury saw something staring back at him from the bottom of her black terror he'd never expected to see: the bearded features of his own vaguely puzzled face.

19

2. MONKEY BOY

Next morning, a stagnant cinderblock-gray Sunday, a naked Japanese boy materialized on Basil Street across from Harrods.

He shot around a stalled double-decker bus discharging bio-diesel combustion, dodged a storm of bikes and three-wheeled tuk-tuks, and cut through the crowds shuffling down the pavement. He was twelve or thirteen. Skinny. His long tangled hair was the color of petroleum sludge. He sprinted past a microcephalic Pakistani beggar with the telltale tuft of fur atop her pinhead, back wedged against the building's counterfeit-gothic façade, knees to chest, and through the brass doors at the southwest entrance.

A guard lunged for him, but the boy ducked and veered, scurried through one of the metal detectors beneath the rock-candy chandeliers, and plunged into the cavernous Memorial Chamber.

Ever since Britain slid into post-burial chic, cemeteries across the islands pretty much used up, the death business had boomed.

Here was a room dedicated to it … clean, fast, respectful, thoughtful, space-saving mortality. Fake torches projected from gold-leafed walls and columns inlaid with full-length mirrors. A marble cremation kiosk, where you could place an order for your loved one or make preparations for yourself, rose at the center of a crisp perplexity of shelves jammed with diminutive mausoleum models for the family living room, garden, or business (petite Aztec temples, Muslim mosques, Greek sanctuaries), wax death-mask kits, holy books, and Grim Reaper action figures ...

"It's never too early in the race to think about the finish line," read the crimson holographic display fuddling near the ceiling.

Next to the kiosk, on a raised red-velvet pedestal in a plastic vacuum-sealed pyramid, stood the mummified leftovers of Mohamed Al Fayed, owner of Harrods from 1985 till a decade ago when the Turner Empire, Ltd., had blustered in.

Al Fayed wore a dark blue suit, light blue tie, and blue-striped shirt. He was bald except for a band of gray hair that began just above his ears and fringed around to join at the back of his head. Glassy brown marbles had replaced his eyes. The slight dried-skin tug on his cheeks and at his temples made him look a little surprised by his current position. His stomach cavity had been hollowed out and heaped with glittering antique pound coins enclosed behind a Plexiglas plate.

Lightweight armored airborne security cams hovering against the ceiling above the pyramid registered the Japanese boy's presence, a pale blur among a thicket of legs near Al Fayed's epidermal shell. They noticed the statistical anomaly of the boy's nakedness and rapidity of movement, and began to track him automatically.

He ran, the tape at the debriefing would later show, like a chimp ... stooped, sometimes even using his hands as an extra pair of feet.

He scampered, tiny scrotal sack and penis joggling, into the Food Halls ... past the floor-to-ceiling test tubes busy with lilac, white, and turquoise jelly beans, old-fashioned vegetable carts stacked with glazed-fruit baskets and marmalade jars and forty-five types of paté, coolers packed with huge pies of cheese ... and then through another portal, this bookended by immense carved cherrywood doors, past stacks of dark green wine bottles, mountains of golden coffee-bean bags, banks of emerald tea tins, through an ample room ringed by a white wrought-iron balcony trimmed with a live cropped hedge, and into the musky scent of uncooked meat ...

He stopped before a gigantic rococo fountain. A pair of sexy white-marble mermaids with lesbian overtones held a tray-sized clam shell on which the frilly scripted Harrods logo was engraved. They wore real shells in their cement hair, and below them cascaded a grottoish muddle of pink corral, stuffed herons, and a full Emperor snapper apparently sealed in a thin coat of plastic.

The boy stared at the trout, head bobbing negligibly, and five suspicious security cams in the vicinity armed themselves.

He reached out with his right hand and tore off a bluewhite palmful of fish, stuffed it into his mouth, began to chew, and the cam nearest the boy's head spoke.

Please maintain your present position, it ordered. *You are in violation of store policy. An arresting officer is en route and will be with you momentarily. Please hold. Failure to do so may result in prosecution to the fullest ex…*

Startled, the boy stopped chewing.

He glanced up at the mermaids.

In a single smooth move, he pitched sideways into a flock of black-robed, black-veiled Iranian women passing gingerly around him.

The smart-cam reflected for one one-hundredth of a second, refocused the click and hum of its luminescent digital thoughts, warmed its entrails, concentrated, and calculated the boy's trajectory.

A thin thread of white light squirted from its belly, kissed the boy's medulla oblongata, and retracted.

The boy's momentum carried his remains another meter, though he'd already been dead close to two seconds when he plunked down like a sack of bad tomatoes on the floor and slid, coming to rest at the feet of one of those boggled women.

Her cronies parted like a wide breath to accommodate her and the naked body of the boy who appeared to be kissing her sandals.

They looked down at this slash in reality's fabric.

They looked at one another.

Then they tilted their necks back and peered up at the silent lightweight armored airborne security cams hovering just above them like robotic hornets, seeming to understand they too were part of the film now.

3. DARK MATTER

Two hours later a woman walking her red-vested Pekingese stopped a pair of bobbies at the corner of Basil Street and Hans Crescent. She wore her long gray hair in a braid that corded down the rear of her blue-gray Mao suit almost to her buttocks.

"Sorry," she said, tugging at her panting dog's lead. "Hate to bother you. But I understand there's been a safety maneuver undertaken at Harrods this morning?"

"Right, madam," said the first bobby. His cosmetic harelip pursed, or tried to purse, in a stab at interest in the topic, revealing a hint of mucous membrane on its underside. "Doing up even as we speak."

The other bobby, a polite female waterbug with no chin, opened her mouth to add something and spluttered into a lengthy moist cough.

Her tongue was purplish black.

The three of them stood waiting for the waterbug's lungs to replace the bad air inside them with the bad air outside them. They all became aware of the ozone, rubber, methane, Chinese food, nitrogen dioxide, fresh-baked cookies, sulfur dioxide, frying mincemeat, grease, lead and floral soap they were inhaling.

"A little boy, was it?" the woman asked when the bobby had finished.

"A little boy. Right."

"Starkers?"

"Starkers, madam."

"Chop-chop, if I'm not mistaken?"

"Something of that. Right. You see him, then?"

The gray-haired woman peered up Hans Crescent toward Brompton Road and the McLenin on the corner. A giant holographic harlequin in a Communist cap, McLenin's registered trademark, protruded from the building in a frozen clownish dive into oblivion.

"This morning," she said, "half nine or so. I was working in my garden. I live just across the street. There." She pointed at a two-story brick flat cater-cornered to where they stood. Her dog made a little jump and turn in the air for no reason. "I happened to glance up and vada him climb out the window around the side. There." She pointed at the turreted red-brick flat with a white door and bay windows across Basil. "He disappeared up the block before I could quite take the whole thing in."

"You didn't call the police?"

The neat slice of red lipstick that was the gray-haired woman's mouth puckered.

"The occupant?" she said. "The gentleman who lives there?"

" … ?"

"He's something of a … not to put too fine a point on it …" A pale begonia blush tried to disseminate through the broken blood vessels in her cheeks. "He's rather a fruit-plate, really."

"A fruit-plate?"

"A Ganymede."

The bobbies exchanged looks.

"Homosexual, you mean?"

The gray-haired woman regarded the holographic harlequin. On either side of it flickered huge high-definition television monitors playing softcore porn interspersed with almost subliminally fast blipverts for the franchise: McLenin roachburgers, McLenin chips, McLenin colas.

A virtual Jane Austen in a black leather harness and officer cap, face bloodless as one of Dracula's victims, sucked a cherry-red iced lolly in the green English countryside, a strand of gooey cherry-red sugarwater spittling down her chin.

"Kid simple," said the woman. She looked back at the waterbug and harelip. "If I'd a pence for every lamb who strolled in or out of that flat in some form of peel-down, I'd move to Sussex and get myself a proper garden."

"Entertains children, does he?"

"I should think 'entertains' doesn't quite do the concept justice. Stares at me from his window sometimes like he's a sandwich short of a picnic." The red-vested Pekingese barked. The gray-haired woman gave the dog's chain an unexpected yank. The Pekingese yakked. "Shush now, Fopson," she said.

The harelip extracted his miniature recorder from the breast pocket of his short-sleeved khaki uniform and asked the woman to repeat her report succinctly and provide them with her name (Pollyanna Sorbate), her address (4 Hans Crescent), and her ID number (4.23.64.1616). He then told her how very much they appreciated her time and cooperation, and wished her a pleasant Sunday.

"We'll be in touch should we have any more questions," he said.

Pollyanna yanked on Fopson's gold chain again, Fopson gagged, and the couple trundled away down the busy street, the throng gradually absorbing them.

The last thing to disappear was Fopson's tiny agitated furry rump.

The waterbug, whose name was Sue Shih, squinted at the harelip, who's name was Henry-Higgins Hurlbutt.

Sue and Henry-Higgins stepped off the curb into that storm of bikes and tuk-tuks and crossed Basil toward the wedding-cake flat. They ambled through the noise and crowds, around a stalled black cab with a cracked windscreen that looked like a brick had smashed into it, past a group of elderly Asian men and women performing tai chi along the black-spiked fence bordering the white-trimmed bay windows, and cut into the passageway separating 3 Hans Crescent from the next flat.

The passageway was empty except for a north-African guy wrapped in a foil blanket. He slept in a fetal curl across the entrance. His dyed sulfur-yellow hair was done up in neat conrows and his sunken cheeks and sponge-nose bore the mulberry purple of a malfed skin-bleach.

Sue and Henry-Higgins discreetly stepped over him. Near a dented dustbin and aluminum pole atop which perched one of the neighborhood's powerful floodlights, they discovered an open window. Sheer white curtains shivered in the weak breeze.

"Have a look-see, shall we?" asked Henry-Higgins.

"Should do," answered Sue.

"Right," he said. "Leg up."

"Leg up. Right."

Sue hunkered down and interlaced her fingers into a stirrup. Henry-Higgins removed his hyperthyroidal khaki bowler, loosened his collar, and braced himself against the brick.

He rose.

"Little higher, if you don't mind."

"Not at all. Not at all."

"Good, good." Balancing himself, he palmed his way toward the cement windowsill. "You catch the morning news?"

"Can't say as I did. No." Sue's breath thickened. "Shite," she said. "Been doing up the bangers and red lead again, haven't you?"

He grabbed the windowsill and began hoisting himself.

"You hear parliament say we might be under attack?"

"We?"

"The islands."

"The islands?"

"Regular siege ... they say."

"Regular siege, only they don't know one way or the other?"

"They don't do. No."

"How can we be under a regular siege only we don't know whether we're under a regular siege or not?"

"Intelligence, they say."

"You're either under attack or you aren't, aren't you?"

Sue stood back, hands on plump hips.

"You'd ... oof ... you'd think so, wouldn't you?"

26

Henry-Higgins peeked his nose over the white ledge, Kilroy-fashion.

"I should do. Yes."

"Me too. Except there's ... funny stuff going 'round in banking, they say." He heaved and this time succeeded in locking his elbows on the windowsill. It took a minute for him to catch his breath. He nabbed at the curtains with a swipe of his left hand. "Viruses popping up on Friday's stock exchange." He fisted the curtains and pulled back. "Either legions of mercenary hackers arsing up the works on behalf of some foreign rinky-dinks, they say, or ..."

"Or what?"

Henry-Higgins's voice dropped a third of an octave.

"Or nothing," he said. "Load of lakesy coincidences." He blinked. "Aw cripes."

"What's that, then?"

Henry-Higgins blinked again.

It was a small bare room, two meters by two. Set into the wall across from him was a solid wooden door without a knob or handle. Beside it stood a pared-down crib on spindly legs, steel-framed and barred, with a clear vinyl covering over a beflowered mattress, a stained sheet, and a scrawny pillow rumpled into a wrinkled lozenge. In front sat a child's potty-chair, manufactured pine seat on a white plastic base. Tied to this was a yellow nylon tether. The tether looked as if it had been gnawed through. A pair of used nappies bunched on the gray fitted carpet.

Once white, the walls of the room had opaled with contaminates and smudged with fingerprints and olive-umber smears.

The smell gnatted in at Henry-Higgins with the tangible mass and texture of a strong tropical fog.

Henry-Higgins' sinuses dilated.

His throat closed.

"Down, down, down," he said, patting the air.

Sue stepped forward, stirruped her fingers, and eased him to the ground.

Henry-Higgins stood there, blinking.

His armpits were dark brown.

The cetaceous shadow of a dirigible dragged over them on its way to the new airport near Bri'n.

The response unit was made up of four NorAm-surplus Thai Khon Kaen urban light assault vehicles designed by the NYPD back in 2009 for the winter food riots ... primer gray, huge gripping steel-reinforced tires, parallel battering rams instead of bumpers, bullet-proof mesh over the squarish front ends and rectangular side viewing slits, hefty roll-bars arcing above those dual high-impact plastic bubble windscreens, machine-guns aft, grenade-launchers fore.

They looked like some kind of hallucinatory offspring of mutant cicadas, Big-Wheels jeeps, and military tanks.

The first two blockaded the street. The second two bumped onto the curb, hatches swinging open, and unleashed the SWAT team inside, Mylar anti-viral suits over bullet-proof vests, full-body riot shields raised.

The advance squad neutralized the smart-door with a concussion grenade fired from just beyond its line of sight. The next group, Putin-497 semi-automatics locked and loaded, full metal jacket, spilled through the narrow foyer and down the hall. The last, right behind them, avalanched into the stairwells.

By the time Sue and Henry-Higgins geared up and joined them, two attack troopers were already kneeling over a dark gray heap on the kitchen floor, brushing at something with rapid hand movements.

Sue assumed the thing was a load of dirty laundry.

Then she made out the contours of the old well-dressed dead man in the nice wool tie. His eyes were clinched shut and his mouth had widened into a half-yawn. His right leg was bustling with hundreds of cockroach bots. They'd chewed through his trousers and a good portion of his skin. Bone bits and white fibrous shreds shone among glistening strawberry muscle. Gummy black blood puddled on the tiles around his lower torso.

"No calls, no messages," the phone said. "No calls, no

messages. No calls, no messages."

Henry-Higgins walked over and slapped it.

The machine hiccupped and went silent.

Whenever the attack troopers tried to brush off a handful of techbugs, the things would just clitter across the floor, regroup, and rush back to finish the job they'd started.

The Panasonic bubble hoover chirped at everyone anxiously from the closet where it had retreated when the front door was slaughtered.

All the other appliances sat perfectly still, pretending to be inanimate.

The fitted carpet, too.

"What happened?" Sue asked, forearms folded over her chubby uterus like a pregnant woman.

"Flipping hardware misfire, looks like," one of the attack troopers said without turning around. "Read the sod as a load of rubbish and decided to clean him up. Won't stop, neither. Razz boys are on their way."

"They kill him?"

"Did that all by himself."

"Suicide?" Henry-Higgins asked.

"Aneurysm or such like. You the bloke called this in?"

Henry-Higgins nodded.

"Enjoy the paperwork."

"Upstairs," someone down the hall shouted. "We got an event, lads."

The cozy flush of the private flat gave way to the antiseptic gloss of a medical laboratory at the top of the first flight. Painted walls and carpeted floors blanched into virgin white tile. Rectangular bronze face-recognition smart-locks secured the doors lining the corridor.

The first had been kicked in. Behind it stood the room Henry-Higgins had seen from a different perspective less than half an hour ago. That awful muggy stench infiltrated the hall.

Behind the second door, now teetering on a single hinge, was a cramped storage room ... cabinets crammed with pharmaceutical derms, air syringes, medicine vials ... a gurney upended in a corner, black lasagna-noodle restraining straps dangling off ... piles of plastic beige bedpans ... something with the shape and heft of an aerodynamically efficient toaster oven.

Five or six attack troopers blocked the entrance to the third room, staring in mutely at what they'd found.

It was a small bare aromatic bog. On the gray carpet beside another pared-down crib sat Lieutenant Pierce O'Boyle, still in full bulky riot gear, stumpy legs stretched before him like a circus bear. He was tapping the carpet with his fingertips and talking in the effeminate voice a dog catcher might use to lure a stray mongrel out from under a car.

"Come on," he said. "There you go. Come on now ..."

Sue raised her gaze and pulled *her* into focus ... the underfed black girl in a pair of white plastic nappies ripped down one side and caught around her knees.

She was crouching a meter away from O'Boyle ... behind the potty-chair she'd been tied to with a yellow nylon tether around her thin ankle. She was twelve or thirteen. Her breastbuds had barely begun to rise from her wasted ribcage. Pubic floss fuzzed the scoop of skin between her thighs.

Knots of filthy matted hair extended below her waist.

A stream of urine trickled down her leg.

But it was those eyes Sue kept coming back to ... the beautiful overwhelmed methylene-blue eyes in the Caribbean café-noir face. They jerked from one attack trooper to the next like they'd never seen so many people in one place before.

She was cornered, Sue realized.

The girl sniffed the air for olfactory data like a cat for chicken gizzard on the kitchen countertop.

O'Boyle scooted forward, trying to edge up on her, only she spat and tried to retreat. The potty-chair was bolted to the floor, and the tether around her ankle tensed, so she was reduced to a kind of strange bunny-walk, hop-limping back and forth, those beautiful methylene-blue eyes spacious with panic.

"What the fuck is this all about, then?" the guy from back in the kitchen asked.

O'Boyle answered, still using that weird voice in an attempt not to spook the girl.

"Took out the door and there she was, all cringing and hissing and pissing herself."

"Squirrel, then?"

"Disorientated, like."

"Doesn't know who we are?"

"Doesn't know *what* we are."

A door blew off its hinges down the hall.

The girl cried out and dropped to the carpet. She began rocking on her heels, chin on chest, wash of infantile mumbles tumbling from her mouth.

"That's okay now, darling," O'Boyle said. "You're all right. We're all all right here. Just a little event going on, is all."

"Look at her," the guy from the kitchen said. "Hasn't a fucking clue. We're just so many bad dreams come jogging 'round to pay her a visit."

They studied her.

"Never been outside, has she?"

"Never been to the bleeding window."

"Geriatric's toygirl, you think?" said a short attack trooper with the distinct minuscule head-twitch of someone who'd sampled too much VR. "Keep her for the odd skin game?"

"Supposed to've enjoyed the young boys," Henry-Higgins said.

"What's he doing with the likes of her, then?"

"Testgirl," O'Boyle said.

"Testgirl?"

"Experiment, you mean?" Sue asked.

"Got ourselves a hermetically sealed system here, don't we. Nice bit of empirical method."

31

"Cripes," Henry-Higgins said.

"Look at the door. No handles on the inside. The crapper. The cord. I'd say we're witnessing some pretty disagreeable living research."

Another attack trooper stepped up behind the cluster of people in the doorway. The inside of his helmet had steamed over, but Sue could still see his eyes swollen with pollution.

"Begging your pardon, sir," he said.

O'Boyle didn't try to turn in his unwieldy suit.

The girl kept mumbling to herself, rocking on her heels and staring down at the carpet.

She'd pressed her palms over her ears.

"Appears our, em, our event here has like just expanded," the guy said. "Would you have a moment to check out this new bit?"

4. MIND CAVALRY

Down the corridor were four more rooms just like the first. In each was another child bound with another yellow nylon tether, a second girl and three boys.

The second girl looked Irish. Her hair was the red-brown of coffee held up to sunshine and her skin anemic as that virtual Jane Austen's on the high-definition monitor outside McLenin. She lay on her side on the gray carpet, a puppet with snipped strings, arms tucked between her legs, so wasted she didn't even try to stand when the door blasted open.

The first boy was Mexiental ... dark complexion, epicanthic folds, squat and sluggish as a tortoise.

The second was albino. His eyes were pink, epidermis smooth as a mushroom, thin hair so white it seemed transparent. He howled like a hound when he realized the attack troopers were coming for him.

But the last—leaf-brown, thick black eyebrows, slim bluish lips, distended belly, maybe Indian, maybe Middle Eastern—just stared at them as they invaded his nest, silent as a stone, fascinated by every detail of this new information arriving.

When O'Boyle bent over to have a closer look, the boy extended his fingers and gently touched the lieutenant's faceplate.

Two attack troopers took up positions outside each child's room and two began bodybagging the dead man on the kitchen floor, roach bots and all.

The rest collected out by the Thai Khon Kaens for an antiseptic-foam hose-down.

Bystanders assembled.

"Easy enough," O'Boyle said as he popped the seals around his helmet and toggled it off. His large earlobes were clipped into skin tassels. "Geriatric worm-buffets last night."

"Organs just hand over the lease," said the attack trooper with the swollen eyes, hoisting off his own helmet and glancing up at the hot cinderblock-gray sky.

A monk-robed Iraqi beggar with a wide cartoonish mouth like Dr. Seuss' Grinch stepped from the mob, pinched a centimeter of the lieutenant's suit between thumb and forefinger, and tugged.

"Poco dinero, poco dinero," he said.

"Maybe he only feeds the kids like once a day," O'Boyle said, shrugging out of the beggar's grip.

"Once every couple," said the attack trooper.

"By morning Jap boy's hungry."

"So he chews through his tether and climbs out the window, which is open to provide some air in the heat."

"Geriatric never thought they'd do it."

"Not in a million years," said the guy from the kitchen who appeared next to the others, fidgeting with a stuck seal. "Wouldn't of, neither, except for the hunger. Only kid's all confused once he's outside. Afraid, like. Not sure where he's going or why." The seal hissed and clicked open. He lifted.

"So the crowd carries him along," said O'Boyle.

"On the pavement. Across the street."

"Where the smart-cam reads him as a thief and smokes his hungry ass."

Henry-Higgins and Sue strode up, helmets cradled under armcrooks, suits dripping lather.

"Bang on," said the guy with the bad eyes. "Except for one thing."

"What about the kids?"

34

"What sort of shite was that old fucker pulling on them?"

"Brought them in as moppets, didn't he?" Sue asked. "Raised them from the get-go just to see what'd happen?" Her purplish black tongue prowled over her lower lip. "But what about the witness we spoke with who saw them coming and going all hours?"

"Harder things to get on the black market than a litter of pups, aren't there?" O'Boyle said.

"Only, well," said Henry-Higgins, "what was he after?"

O'Boyle inspected him. He raised his left hand and pulled on a shredded earlobe. A burglary alarm several blocks away began cycling.

"What if the guy was a ... what ... an urban farmer, say."

"Organ-grinder?"

"Raising a crop of backup kidneys in the larder, you mean?"

"Hearts, blood, corneas. Sure. Not necessarily for the open market, if you take my meaning."

"Spare tires."

"Bit of Mulligan stew for himself," said the attack trooper from the kitchen. "Bit of kate and sidney."

He laughed.

"Aw cripes," Henry-Higgins said, blinking.

"Didn't mean to offend, mate. But, em, you know. Organ ranches ... isolation tanks ... data ambushes ... Just more of more, i'n'it?"

He chewed invisible gum uncomfortably.

"Data ambushes?" Henry-Higgins asked.

The guy stopped chewing.

"Didn't hear, then?"

Henry-Higgins shook his head.

"Seems what's left of Cairo all of a moment wants payback for all manner of whatnot taken from the ragheads last century by the British Museum."

"Caught larging it with our bank records," O'Boyle explained. "London Stock Exchange, too. Whole Brit corner of the Other Side."

"Parliament in session as we speak. Threatening all manner of retaliation if they don't back off. Just another day in ..." He caught sight of something over O'Boyle's shoulder. "Hey. Look at what we have here."

"Mind cavalry to the rescue, i'n'it."

"About time," O'Boyle said, turning. "Well," turning back, "off we go, then, lads. Off we go."

The white-and-blue van's side door slid open and three orderlies, also sheathed in anti-viral rigs, hopped out with three double-barreled shotguns, each chamber loaded with a brightly feathered hypodermic dart rich with a strike dose of Rohypnol.

A quarter of an hour later, the van reentered the plaqued artery of traffic on Knightsbridge Road, an extension of that part of London where the governcorp preserved the well-kept building exteriors for the tourist trade, and crept past the perimeter of Hype Ark, red oxygen kiosks lifting like antique phone booths along the pavement. The flower gardens and trees beyond stood stripped and black in the dense silver smog.

Knightsbridge faded into Kensington, the wasted foliage into the dingy barracks and then, a few blocks farther, the phallic monument commemorating the great blaze at the Royal Albert Hall across from the acid-gnawed Albert Memorial spraybombed repeatedly in fluorescent green with the Swahili word for *unity*: UMOJA.

The memorial gave way to the compact brownbrick and whitewashed buildings of the Heistreet, nineteenth-century Neo-Gothic fronts, Georgian faux-marble skins, triangular Tudor plaster-and-beam busyness, a vigorous confusion of angles and shapes.

A righthand turn up Argyll Road, tailback tumbling off behind, austere flats mounting a small hill in increasing stillness ... and a left at the top onto Upper Phillimore Gardens, quiet row of symmetrical buildings that once housed the Jordanian Embassy and now the Aiwa-Benz Neural Orientation & Maturation Assessment Lab, numbers six to eighteen, some whitewashed, some with mustard-yellow brick veneers, each four stories tall.

The kids were carried to their rooms on the third story to sleep off the sedative.

When they started floating toward consciousness in the middle of the afternoon, the orderlies retranked them and wheeled them downstairs where the Uncle Meats waited.

The physical exams lasted into the evening.

All but the delicate girl with the red-brown hair was pronounced in good health. The Uncle Meats discovered during a routine scan she suffered from Severe Combined Immunodeficiency. Because of a defective gene, her body was unable to produce the enzyme adenosine deaminase. Her immune system had shut down, leaving her vulnerable to a flotilla of infections. The Uncle Meats began treating her while innoculating the rest of the children against measles, tetanus, meningitis, and assorted other diseases that over the last few decades had built up resistance to fifth-, sixth-, and seventh-tier antibiotics.

Next morning the psych team took over. They hooked the children to a wall of monitors to measure electrical patterns in their brains. Instead of normal activity, an unusually high occurrence of sleep spindles, or dense bunching structures, appeared. The children didn't speak. They seldom made any noise besides the occasional guttural grumble. They explored digestive biscuits, oven gloves, spanners and wallets tactilely, like blind people, bringing them to their lips, licking them, rubbing them across their checks and foreheads, expressions slack. They spat for no reason, shrank at touch, tried to retreat behind a gurney or under a lab bench when a new person entered their environment.

"They certainly haven't had a human childhood, have they?" Petrina Bogg, chief pediatric psychiatrist, a dainty floral-pattern-wearing bull with a click in her elderly throat, said at the staff briefing that afternoon.

She raised a red-and-gold porcelain tea cup decorated with Chinese dragons to her mouth and sipped, then set the cup down and browsed the countenances of her colleagues perched around the sitting room just off the foyer of number nine.

Painted paper scrolls, carved jade knickknacks, and stone Buddhas fracased across pistachio-ice-cream-green velveteen walls and on scrawny chocolate-red tables, impregnating the place with the sort of material agitation that made it almost impossible to settle your eyes on any single object for more than a flutter.

"They haven't, no," agreed Petrina's second-in-command, Devin Hung-chang. He had inserted his right forefinger to the first joint-and-a-half in his ear and tilted his head down as if he was expecting an important broadcast from his digit.

Devin, whose bland clothes smelled of mildew, was almost forty, unmarried, and terrified of dating, given the biological and psychological horrors that lurked on the other side of his office door. But this past weekend he'd met a kicking woman named Tymm Tai-ni at a party at their mutual friend and colleague Fiona K'ai-chuh's flat and was currently waiting for the results of Tymm's background check conducted by Sirch & DeStory, for which he'd forked out £150 Adjusted Pounds, which forkage would furnish him with her criminal, medical, and driving records, credit rating, job history, and marital status, as well as the statistical probability of emotional and sexual fulfillment on their first, second, and third dates.

So Devin was having a pretty hard time paying attention to this business with the kids.

"The spindles could mean droves," Petrina was saying, "or they could mean nothing. Brain damage from years and years of abuse … an inherited impediment … a traumatic response to radical social isolation … something else entirely …"

She ended her sentence with one of those clicks.

Devin thought of the sound his microwave made when the timer concluded counting down an instant before the beeper went off. This led him to think about Tymm sitting next to his microwave on the counter in his breakfast nook. In the morning. In the nude. Sunshine glowing pinkly through the modest cosmetic holes bored through her palms and feet for that crank crucified effect.

Devin extracted his finger from his ear and raised his head.

"I'm leaning toward the isolation thing," he said, plucking himself back from the brink of daydream.

"Isolation thing?"

"Think about it. Solitary confinement's one of the most severe punishments around, as our troops during the SoAm war learned. Want a bit of natter from an adversary, just pop him into the hotbox for a quick weigh off. Adverse symptoms frequently within fifteen minutes. Two, three days tops." He took a sip of tea, Piracetam-laced Darjeeling. "All right, then. Fine. Only now imagine a full year of the stuff. Six. Twelve. Multiply those two or three days by fifteen hundred." He reinserted his finger. "Ghastly," he said, reporting. "Simply ghastly."

"Meantime," Petrina said, "given their ages, our children's neurons would presumably be humming right along, wiring to accommodate the lack of stimuli in their cerebral configurations."

"Wiesel and Hubel," Devin answered. "Right."

"Wiesel and Hubel."

"Wiesel and Hubel?" asked Magda Karter, the new FeeMale head lab technician with a perpetual rabbit-nose cold who'd been raised in Armstrong City and come down the well five years ago for the transgender operation in Berne and televisual university in Oxford. Her face, à la the once-popular lunar flashtrend, was pockmarked with childhood afflictions she'd never in fact endured. She wore a conservative Moschino mesh suit with silver undergarments, shaved lilac hair, and a silver stud implanted two centimeters below her lower lip.

"Fairly obscure research from the seventies," Petrina explained. "Found that sewing shut one eye of a newborn kitten rewired its brain. So few neurons connected from the shut eye to the visual cortex that the animal remained sightless even after its eye was reopened." She savored her tea with a series of tiny schlucking noises. "The same, however, didn't occur in adult cats whose eyes received the same treatment."

"Conclusion," Devin said, "was that there exists an early period of development when circuits connect the retina to the visual cortex."

"Foundation of the current theory, then, isn't it," Magda said.

"Brain's born a neuron soup," answered Petrina, "with only a couple of neurons preprogrammed by genes into paths for breathing, heartbeat, involuntary reflexes, and the like."

"Trillions more just waiting for the grand upload," said Devin.

"But neurons only become integrated into the circuitry of the brain if they're used. They need chemical exercise to do their stuff."

"If not, they wither up like so many old grapes on a windowsill."

"And it's childhood experiences that determine which are used and how," Magda offered.

"Precisely," said Petrina. "No use, no hardwiring. Critical Period Theory."

"An average adult brain carries more than one hundred trillion connections," Devin said. "More connections than the number of galaxies in the universe ..."

"Math, logic, auditory maps, language skills, music, emotion, social attachment," said Petrina. "Everything that makes us us. All in one mushy kilogram-and-a-half hard drive system that stops increasing in size by the time we're fifteen. Only organ that tells us who we are."

"Although," Magda said, "chances are that virtually none of this networking occurs in severe social isolation."

"No use," Petrina repeated, "no hardwiring."

"We're talking honest-to-god feral children here," said Devin.

He withdrew his finger from his ear and stole a sniff before reaching for his porcelain cup and revisiting his sun-packed breakfast nook with Tymm Tai-ni.

"You can count the number of documented incidents on one hand," Petrina said. She turned to Fiona. "I believe Dr. K'ai-chuh's been reading up on the subject."

Fiona, wedged into a particularly lively corner of trinkets, became attentive. Like Devin, she was speeding toward her fortieth birthday and, like Devin, was unhappy about it. A large, triangular, aerodynamically efficacious nose occupied most of her flushed face. It looked like her robust olfactory organ had appeared first, sui generis, from thin air, and the rest of her features had grown in behind it. Her hair was bowl-cut short like Moe's in the Three Stooges and the muscles around her mouth always squinched, overly tight. When she wasn't paying attention she tended to sway with a telltale VR wobble.

"Yes, well, right," she said, gathering her thoughts.

She examined Petrina, then Magda, then the others sitting and standing around her—mostly lab-coated male and female nurses, one of whom, Dante Allegro, always unnerved her a little, what with those microchip implants in place of eyes swiveling somewhere behind his cataract-cream contact lenses—and finally Devin. She smiled weakly at him because, unbeknownst to the poor guy (who returned her smile over his tea cup, misinterpreting it as one of those amiable well-here-I-go-into-the-breech sort of expressions), Fiona too had developed a crush on Tymm at the aforementioned festivities and was also awaiting word from Sirch & DeStory about Tymm's profile.

At the exact eyeblink Petrina articulated her name, Fiona's mind had been occupied with an image of herself lying beside Tymm on a ginger-pink towel on a topless chalk beach on a remote Swedish island, Tymm's sunlotioned brown breasts (oily aroma ol coconuts and bananas sweetening the air) gleaming in the dangerous sunlight, animation-blue waves gurgling two meters away, chatter of bathers softening her awareness like Vaseline on the camera lens in an old film at the predictable leap into love.

She touched her nose and said: "Intriguing business. And business, I might add, that's captured the popular imagination with a vengeance for a good few thousand years." Her head rocked almost indiscernibly. "Em, if I may ..."

She bent over and removed a black plastic rectangle the dimensions of a cordless phone from her small beflowered handbag, pointed it at the middle of the room, and snicked it on.

White light sparkled from the Sega Morgan-le-Fay module and coalesced into holographic shapes: two human forms crouched beneath a lupine one on a three-dimensional Roman red-figure vase rotating at a slight pitch above the rattan carpet like a satellite in high orbit.

"So much so" she continued, "it's rather difficult to separate truth from fancy, really. The idea goes back at least to Romulus and Remus, and manifests itself in various stories seemingly disparate as Tarzan's ..." (Johnny Weismuller swung in jerky gray-and-white fastforward from vine to vine through a nineteen-thirties Hollywood jungle) "and Rousseau's myth of the natural man ..." (Weismuller dissolved into the delicate demure white-wigged Swiss-born philosopher abob in glimmering prissy rectitude). "In his book *Les Enfant Sauvages*, Lucien Malson lists no fewer than fifty-three alleged authentic cases since 1344 of children raised by wolves, panthers, bears, leopards, monkeys, gazelles, and even ostriches ..."

"Except they aren't authentic," said Devin.

"Can't be. No." Late twentieth-century footage of the last Kenyan game preserves rolled, beige grass and gnarled trees against a low orange twilight horizon, sexy swagger of lion hips, fast edit to a den's interior, feline cubs feeding at their mother's teats. "Granting a female wild animal might in actual fact suckle a human child—and that's granting quite a lot—the composition of her milk would be so different from human milk that it's extremely unlikely the child could survive very long on it. And that, it appears, is the good news. The bad is even if we say a child *could* survive by such a method, the animal would go dry long before weaning took place. The human infant would, not to put too fine a point on it, starve to death."

"Which is to say nothing," Devin added, "about how most non-human mothers drive away last year's litters before becoming pregnant with next year's."

"Right ... and yet what's interesting is that the stories keep on coming."

"Need for the primitive," Petrina said.

"Exploration of what a society requires in order for it to remain intact and functioning," said Devin.

"No doubt," said Fiona. "But some of these narratives have been quite well documented, haven't they? It's not all fiction and socio-psychological confabulation. Supposedly, for instance, there have been fairly inbred tribes like the Niam-Niams in what now forms the midwestern United States of Africa" (a nineteenth-century engraving propelled into view of an unclothed pygmied woman with a five-or-six centimeter fleshy appendage dangling from her lower vertebrae) "that possessed small tails, an inheritable disorder. They were captured and sold as the products of trans-species sexual union in the slave market at Constantinople. And many of the 'savages' shown in sideshows throughout old America and Europe, and advertised as having been captured in remote jungles and raised by beasts" (a sepia photo gathered of long-haired clean-shaven George Stall in furs, sporting ten-centimeter fingernails, circa 1898; Lionel, "The Lion-Faced Boy," more Skye terrier than killer cat, posing for his Barnum shot in 1907) "turn out to be everything from simple pranks to people suffering from hypertriochosis, a rather horrible condition whereby the individual is completely covered from head to toe with hair several centimeters long ... And then there are the *really* intriguing cases ..."

A scene from François Truffaut's 1969 film began looping, austere doctor in frock coat played by none other than the director himself, worried, unhinged even, introducing a mostly bare wadded-haired little boy to his own reflection in a full-length mirror.

Fiona overdubbed this with the tale of how hunters in the Aveyron Forest brought down an untamed pubescent child with their dogs in 1800. He was mute and his body scarred. He loped on his hands and feet. The hunters concluded he'd lived in the wilderness most of his life and, hoping to make a little extra cash off their discovery, sold him to a sideshow in Paris, where a young doctor, Jean Itard, saw him, heard and became fascinated by the chronicle of his detection, realized he'd stumbled across a specimen of what he referred to as The Forbidden Experiment, and, sensing fame, purchased him, took him home, named him Victor, and tried to educate him ... though Itard was unable to teach him to walk properly or even talk at all ...

Truffaut's anxious face liquefied into the sweet slow features of Bruno S. in Werner Herzog's *Every Man for Himself and God Against All*... and the gray misty Nuremburg square where, about a quarter of a century after those hunters brought down Victor, a cobbler leaving his shop at closing time came upon a seventeen-year-old bow-legged boy leaning against a wall. The boy was voiceless and nearly blinded by daylight. His skin exhibited a strange waxlike quality. The cobbler turned up two letters in the pocket of the teen's tattered waistcoat: one to the commanding officer of the dragoons stationed nearby, proposing he make the boy a soldier, the other from the boy's anonymous mother, saying she was unable to support him any longer and giving his name as Kasper Hauser. Not knowing what to do with him, the cobbler took Kasper to the neighboring home of Professor Daumer, who ascertained he wouldn't eat anything but bread and water and bore a sense of smell so keen he could identify different people simply by their odors alone. Professor Daumer gradually taught Kasper to speak in short sentences and thereby heard the story of how he'd been raised in a lightless cellar with only a single wooden horse for a toy, bread and water lowered to him daily till once he noticed the water smelled funny and, drinking it anyway, fell asleep. He woke next to that wall where the cobbler came across him. A year later, Kasper now coasting the lustrous edge of civilization, someone broke into the professor's house and stabbed the young man ... quite possibly, the police believed, those who had raised him, trying to cover up the potential scandal arising if they were found out.

That was usually how the documented narrative of the feral child unwound, Fiona explained ... be it of the speechless girl and boy who ran on their elbows, barked when touched, and preferred offal to ordinary food, found by the missionary near a pair of wolves in a rubbish heap at the brim of the jungle in Midnapore, India, in 1920 ... or of Genie, the break-your-heart-lovable girl uncovered in a room in the rear of a suburban Los Angeles house by social workers in 1970, her elderly parents having decided when she was three that she was backward and locking her there, where she sat almost completely alone for a decade, beaten for making noise, fed sporadically, then saved and whisked away to the Children's Hospital in the city where a team of scientists and psychiatrists tested their thesis that a nurturing environment can make up for a nightmarish past, only to falter, Genie ultimately falling into a long slate succession of foster homes and state institutions where she eventually succumbed to bureaucracy, solitude, and the antiseptic indifference of inquiry ... or, emerging with exponentially greater

44

frequency over the course of the last fifteen years, of those organ-grinder kids, often female, often imported from China, raised in isolation by various black-market establishments for the odd liver, lung, or large intestines, then butchered and dumped in some mews down by the Thames where what was left of their carcasses after those hasty operations were snatched up by various biologic inferiors for a little midnight snack, each victim a single component in the complex mechanics of the megalopolic ecosystem ...

Fiona snicked off her Morgan-le-Fay and slipped the black plastic rectangle back into her handbag.

"Nice work indeed," Petrina said.

She raised her tea cup to her lips and finished off the last of the Darjeeling.

Fiona nodded deprecatingly, Chinese-fashion.

"Yes, splendid," added Devin. "But, em," raising his chin, "I can't help wondering what it all adds up to. I mean, your report notwithstanding, in actual fact we continue to know almost nothing about these new charges of ours."

"Quite right," said Petrina. "Given their situation, I suppose we can say they're in perfectly acceptable health. We can point out that since arriving they've discovered each other and begun the bonding process. But, well, any more ..."

"Still sedated, are they?" Fiona asked.

"We're easing off as they settle in."

"That could certainly modify the equation, couldn't it?" asked Devin.

"No doubt. Though, honestly, by how much ... In any case, our current funding situation being what it is, I imagine we shouldn't want to invest too much fiscal weight in this particular project."

"Couldn't agree with you more."

"And the razzheads?" Fiona asked.

"Nothing on the old fellow's hard drives. Nothing on his backup disks. Whatever he was doing, he was extremely careful not to keep any records the likes of us might find."

"Certainly does elicit the rescue fantasies, doesn't it?" Devin said.

"It certainly does."

Petrina lowered her saucer and cup to a side table in her vicinity, nudging myriad oriental thingumabobs out of the way to create some space, and tapped the face of her Prada audio watch, which spoke to her from beyond the grave in an electronic rendition of George Harrison's sumptuous baritone.

She patted her hands together, indicating a conclusion to the daily briefing.

"Well," she said. "There we have it ... if there aren't any more questions ..." She browsed the countenances of her colleagues. "Remember," standing, "information is waiting to come off the dole. It's waiting for a nice durable rainproof roof over its head. It's waiting, in other words, just for us ..."

PART TWO:
KAMIKAZE MOTIVES
OF THE IMMACULATE DECONSTRUCTION

5. ELEMENTARY CHAOS

November shugged into December with all the enthusiasm of a univalve mollusk slinking across the floor of the English Channel on a crippled mucoidal foot. The nights remained sponge-soggy hot, the days chemical sour. London's atmosphere tinseled with so much bio-diesel and other grainy contaminants you could stand at one end of Upper Phillimore Gardens and be unable to see the neat block of flats down at the other through the metallic haze the media referred to as The Air-Quality Deficit. Every morning at their briefing, the Aiwa-Benz Neural Orientation & Maturation Assessment Lab staff found the barred windows in the sitting room encrusted with a henna-colored grime. Every afternoon the custodial team scrubbed those windows clean. And every evening, as the staff started putting the long day behind them, they found the windows useless as a pair of old spectacles misted with house stain.

Late one starless night, sky a luminous yellow-gray flush, Magda Karter stepped onto the back stone porch to blow her bubble-gum-pink nose, deep into another overtime shift in a lengthy necklace of them, and noticed the classical columns set into the sham marble blocks were blanketed with thousands of tiny dimples that reminded her, if she stopped to think about it a little, of the consistency of her own pockmarked face. Only these dimples had nothing to do with flashtrends and cosmetic semiotics. They had to do with pugnacious oxidation, the nasty rough junk of ravenous air out on a feeding frenzy.

Magda registered such specific fallout from the crummy weather infrequently, though, a pin in her existential hip that tickled when she'd almost forgotten it. She'd become far too interested in her new patients to pay much attention to such perceptual background radiation. Instead, she found herself progressively fascinated with the witchcraft of language. She came to understand from the inside out, watching the children try to learn simple human sounds, how special that business was ... how, as Dr. Hung-chang mentioned one day after the albino boy stopped howling long enough to surprise himself with the ability to utter the word *white*, apropos of nothing but a blank index card, and next break into laughter at his own revelation, you can speak a sentence of ten or twelve syllables right now, this minute, then look for it repeated just one more time in just that arrangement for the rest of your life, and chances are you'll come up empty-handed.

Language worked like phonemic pheromones. It was the receptacle of singularity, personality, the property that made people who they were, and it was why they could remember yesterday, blueprint tomorrow, cipher the metageometry of their lives, analyze some things, synthesize others, explain inconsistencies, reduce uncertainties, redouble them, construct a common social reality, give voice to everything from the concept of love to the dimensions of a zygote.

Not bad, Magda thought, for twenty-six letters and a couple dozen rules, most of which a guy who'd been using them all his life couldn't articulate if asked.

And the children acquired it surprisingly easily, much more so than the psych unit had predicted, even if at first it physically hurt their untamed mouths to pronounce its noises.

Human vocalizations rose from their throats like handfuls of ground glass.

Magda sometimes gathered the children in the observation room on the second floor. Sometimes she met with them one by one in their bedrooms on the third. She coached them with flash cards, acted out gestures and moods, marched and jumped and waved and pouted, fingerpainted and sang, introduced them to the world object by object.

Within two weeks, they could ask for shortcake after lunch and cheese and onion pasties for dinner. They learned what balls, blocks and beds were, then busses, biscuits and books. They became engrossed with the things around them, the sheer plenitude of the universe ... with the texture of walls, the coolness of tiles, the blue Hewlett Packard bubbles that whirred up one corridor and down the other, observing, patrolling, protecting. Sometimes the Indian, who seemed to think reality only occurred in front of him, would move to the barred windows, peer out, and point to the panorama, wanting to learn a new word for everything on the other side, a word for every shade of every color, till Magda came up short, ran out of language, realized there were only so many tints she knew, so many shades, beyond which all she could offer was a cuddle.

At first they hoarded things, glasses of water, tiger-eye marbles, bars of rose-scented soap, lining them up in soldier-straight rows on their bedside tables, caching them on the carpets beneath their metal hospital beds. They appeared disconnected from their own bodies, shocked by the soft soles of their feet or light touch of their hair the same way kittens are, over and over, by the sudden appearance of their own tails behind them. Petrina Bogg and Devin Hung-chang acquainted them with mirrors and video feedback loops, and the children began to learn where they ended and the rest of the cosmos commenced. Fiona K'ai-chuh taught them the difference between *I* and *you* by sitting them around a white formica table and pointing to one child, then the next, and reciting their name-numbers till they started to recite them themselves. Dante Allegro, the male nurse with those blue-milk contact lenses, slowly taught them how to walk without bunnying along: spines erect, arms hanging comfortably at their sides, ambulating at a well-mannered British gait.

One evening the black girl's features dissolved from affectless neutrality to sadness as Magda packed up her things to leave, and Magda understood she'd crossed an unrecrossable boundary from the country of therapist into the land of something dismayingly more blurry. That the children could form attachments meant they possessed the capacity to change. If they could change, they could change for the better. But that ability also meant, Magda knew, they possessed the capacity to change those intent on changing them.

In mid-December the black rains came, abrupt, explosive, deafening, oily with airborne impurities and the stink of fish. It seemed the atmosphere had turned so heavy with filth that parts of it had begun separating out and falling to earth. The street in front of ABNORMAL was pumice-dry and dusty ... and then alive with rushing sudsy water choked with cigarette packs, beer bottles, and hundreds of bloated bodies of blind mice that'd tried scuttering up from the swamped tube stations only to drown in the deluge above. Gardens marshed. Red-brown mud surged across pavement into avenues, clogging car brakes, uprooting bushes, generating sludge banks and muck flats where once there'd been only asphalt. The temperature remained constant throughout. The hot wet air started feeling like the humidity inside a shower stall. Windows steamed over. Paper moistened and curled. Tiny mushrooms grew like thousands of antennae among wilted khaki-colored grass in the parks. Airborne corruption started mating with water droplets, the progeny a mild form of sulfuric acid that bubbled paint right off car bonnets across the city. Downy mildew spread in yellow-green splotches along carpet in closets, inside shoes, across bathroom tiles.

And then the great gray slugs emerged, some ten-centimeters long, fat as thumbs, eye-beads pivoting atop stalks, silver trails of mucus with sexual connotations crisscrossing sitting-room floors every morning as dawn blanched into overcast contaminated daylight. The children toyed with them, crawled beside them, investigated their reflexes with pens and electronic pucks, intrigued initially, then only nominally committed to the things' relentless performance, and slowly bored in the confined corridors and offices comprising the labs, glances drifting up toward those barred windows above them, always ready for something novel, somewhere they hadn't traveled before.

To shatter the monotony, Magda assigned each child a birthday and celebrated the announcement with a week of party hats and pinwheels. The kids laughed more effortlessly, the sound they produced modulating into an increasingly natural part of who they were. They learned hide-and-seek and skipping rope. Their vocabulary dilated, grew into fifty words … primarily nouns, but also verbs, adjectives, and prepositions … lazed almost invisibly from concrete into abstract terms … emotions, simple ideas, notions of time and selfhood, possession and measurement. They executed unadorned math with toothpicks and tea bags. They heard their first music … cuts off the Pope's plasma-wrench album, *Textual Harassment*, which had been circulating three years now and was still firmly entrenched in the top twenty on the pop charts, catalyst for hundreds of thousands of the denominationally challenged across Paneuropa and Britain to convert to the true faith, including Dante Allegro himself, a little intoxicated on the happy knowledge always residing like your ID number on the slab in your breast pocket that you at least understood who the real boss was, who the good guys and bad guys were, what the cost would be of every petty sinful expenditure, everything predictable as the next round of cricket on a well-trimmed playing field in Cambridge.

Dante was humming a song from it as he steered the children back to the third floor after the bash for little 928, the sickly girl with Pre-Raphaelite hair and pallid skin, when they passed a ladder left till morning at the bottom of a staircase where the custodial team had been working to scour mold off a swath of flowery wallpaper, and the ladder spoke.

"Time to retire," it said with butlerian civility.

The kids had been doing what they could to sing along with Dante, mimicking the general progression of his gargles, but they all came up short when the ladder addressed them, never having heard an inanimate object speak before, except of course the stereo, and that had involved less speaking than making music and announcing cuts, which was a whole different affair.

The Indian boy reached out and fingered a rung, which stiffened a little beneath his touch. He retracted his hand.

The ladder spoke again.

"Please don't use me," it said. "I'm ready to retire."

The albino yipped.

Somewhere upstairs a rhesus monkey, member of another less mirthful research project at ABNORMAL, rattled his cage and answered with a high-pitched howl.

"Intelligent materials systems," Dante explained, annoyed at this interruption.

All that spiritual good feeling he'd just been experiencing vanished from his soul fast as a paperclip into a shag carpet.

He hulked there, milky contacts blank, a two-meter-and-then-some-tall crow examining a desiccated rabbit on the side of a motorway. He had better things to do, more interesting places to be, than with this bunch of mental defectives. Like down at his local pub, The Royal Knight's Mare, over on the Ease In, with his mates, tossing a nice goddamn round of darts, nice goddamn pint of nice goddamn lager resting in its own gooey golden afterbirth on a nice goddamn table.

Which is where he was planning to go soon as he got rid of these nice goddamn chuckleheads.

He took two steps back and two forward, suddenly bitched off once more at this stooge job he'd taken last summer to make ends meet because there just wasn't any other way, was there.

Made him sweat just thinking about it.

Give him a handful of darts, a warm lager, a roomful of the lads, maybe throw in the odd holoporn featuring that raunchy dead meat queen Elektra Geestring doing some felch and bunch punch, and he'd be chuffed as a pig in shite.

What was so fucking difficult about all that? Wasn't like molecular biology now, was it. Wasn't too much to ask. Wasn't too fucking much to hope for. But this git gag ... fucking food for chop-chops and kiwis.

He sighed through his gristle and phlegm, upshot a sort of muddy geothermal burble.

"Knows when it's fagged out, like," he said, sulky.

"Fagged out?" asked the black girl.

Dante didn't like the weird accent she was developing either. Wasn't right English at all. More like ... what?

Fucking yanks even weeviled into your vocal chords, you weren't careful.

"Pooped, like. Yeah."

"What's 'pooped'?"

"Oh, well, fuck," Dante replied, checking the Sony watch implanted in the skin of his wrist. "Broken, like. Unable to do its grind. You know. Takes its own blood pressure. Sets the results against other times it's done the same. Pressure too high? Remodels itself. Pressure too low? Remodels itself. Shape-memory, they call it. Only comes a point when it can't shape any more. No more memory. No more get-up-and-go. Then it retires, like. Gets the slingers."

"It's sick?" asked the black girl.

"Old, like. Used up. Busted its electronic arse. Same principle as works in the walls of this building in which we're standing in here, i'n'it, and bridges in the ritzy section of town, and aircraft skin, and such. Corrosion and stress sensors. Shape-memory actuators."

"Corrosion?" asked the albino.

"Actuators?" asked 928.

Dante audited them a couple of seconds.

"Right couple of little prats, aren't you?" he said.

He looked up the staircase and pictured himself testing a dart between his thumb and first two fingers, touch light as a hubbie's on his first honeymoon stretch of how's-yer-father with his cherry wife, lads going quiet all around as he wound up for the Big Toss.

Hiss. Clop. *Bull's eye.*

Applause.

Hoist a warm one.

Few more minutes of this, he'd be there, laughter and good cheer packaging him like … what? Like a nice goddamn cushy Venus Flytrap, is what. All a matter of finesse from here on out, really.

Diplomacy. Frills. Style.

"Enough of fucking Mister Ed for today, right?" he said, returning to Greenwich Mean Time. "Up to bed. Got a big one tomorrow, haven't we?"

928, still dunced in her pointy party hat, tilted up her face and opened her green eyes hopefully.

"Fun?" she asked.

Dante grinned like a Komodo dragon.

"Not bloody likely, luv," he said. He turned and started mounting the carpeted stairs, neck tucked into his shoulders, arms gathered at his sides like wings. "Not bloody likely at all."

Because next day the Uncle Meats began treating the cause of 928's SCID through the first of four series of painful jabs, removing white blood cells of the immune system from her body, inserting normal copies of the faulty gene into the collection, and returning the treated cells to her circulatory system.

Dante assisted Magda in pinning her down as the syringes descended like a flock of mean sparrows.

The grin that cracked his features the night before never diminished.

928 kicked and screamed. She cried out with such surprise each time a hypodermic punctured the skin on her buttocks that the psych unit quickly steered the other shaken kids, whom they initially thought might be able to lend the girl moral support, from the room. 928 wailed. She screeched with the hiccupped astonishment of betrayal. She tried to twist out of Dante's pythonoidal grip. She thrashed her beautiful red-brown hair the color of coffee held up to sunshine side to side.

And something in Magda's chest cavity collapsed like that fagged-out ladder at the bottom of the staircase was ready to do. She wanted to leave with the children, abandon this ship ... except she couldn't ... she knew what was at stake ... she knew what she had to do ... and so she did it: she held on to 928's soft sweaty left hand and squeezed and told her everything was going to be all right, which she knew in a sense it was, whispered every encouragement and promise she could think of, all the ones her mother never whispered to her in that Swiss clinic, and half an hour later, 928 sitting dazed and bleary-eyed on the metal gurney, lemon lolly in fist, sniffling and sullen, Magda said she wanted to show her something she knew she'd like.

She collected the other children and led them all down to her office. In place of walls or floor rose unsteady stacks of archaic books, many safety-wrapped in baggies, covers missing or bent, and ancient floppy disks, some in plastic cartons, some loose, and messy waterfalls of computer slabs, music-chips, readouts. In one corner a slight anomaly in the heaps of material suggested the outlines of a desk. On it sat a Sennheiser headmount and large-screen painting-thin Gateway puter console flanked by Altec-Lansing speakers that mimicked two Fujian puppets.

Magda and the kids side-shuffled over to the monitor which was busy screen-saving with a brashly colored cloisonné pattern of the assassination attempt on the last state-sanctioned British monarch, imitation of something from the Yuan dynasty.

She cleared some detritus off a swivel-chair wedged near the desk, took a seat, and tapped the terminal.

The cloisonné pattern fractaled into pixel fog.

A bantam version of chubby Mao Zedong in a clown's nose and drab jacket double-timed it out from the wings. When he reached the middle of the otherwise black display he turned to Magda, put his hands together as if in prayer, and, wide toothy smile overpowering a good third of his head, bowed.

"Hiya, sweetie," he said in a New Jersey accent. "So what can I do ya for?"

"Brought some friends in to meet you." Magda included all the kids in a hand gesture. "Say hello to everyone."

Mao scouted past her, squinting.

"Pleased to meetcha, I'm sure."

He waved a minuscule yellow palm. The children's features animated. They nudged closer through the junk for a better look. 928 waved back shyly. The Indian and albino boys said polite hellos. The Mexiental and the black girl ogled, delighted with this new entity.

"Meet Mao-Mao," Magda said. "He's my digital proxy. Digital proxies, actually."

57

"Digital proxy?" asked the black girl.

"He looks like one person, doesn't he? But really he's lots of people all at once, and each of him helps me out in various and sundry ways … don't you, Mao-Mao?"

"You bet, sweat meat," Mao-Mao said. "Regular buncha backseat drivers on the data expressway."

He cleaved into two of himself, then four, then eight. Soon the screen was thronged with a bustling morula of him.

"Some of him are teachers," Magda continued. "Some are guides. Some shop for me so I don't have to go to the store and shop for myself. Some try to figure out what sort of music I might like to listen to at a given moment by reading my facial expressions and body movements and then calculating what I listened to last time I made similar ones. Some are secretaries and check my email and phone calls and remind me who I know and what I've done and what I need to do and when and where. And some are my research assistants. They help me find things I'm looking for on the Other Side. They know all the roads in there. They've traveled a good deal of the global matrix. And some have no other job than to make me feel happy when I'm off my feed. Cheer me up. Give me something to chuckle about."

Some of the Mao-Maos jostled into a tumbling team and built an artificial-life pyramid that caved in on itself, Keystone-Kops fashion. The children shimmered into laughter … even little 928.

The proxies beclouded into a twinkling haze and resolved into jesters with caps and bells and huge cod pieces. A cluster of dolphins darting across the screen. Multitudinous versions of Santa Claus, some tall and thin and stately, some in broad-brimmed hats and breeches and pipes, some tubby with beards and red suits and black knee boots.

"Have a very Turner Christmas," one of them said.

"You want we should sing you a carol or something?" said another.

"No, no," Magda answered. "Thanks anyway." Then to the kids: "And they change over time. Evolve. Learn. Just like you, really. They know their kit. In fact, they're in school right now."

"They are?" asked 928.

"All the time. You see, they figure out what works and what doesn't. Then they throw out what doesn't work and keep what does. The Mao-Maos that help the most stay with me and make more of themselves. The ones that don't eventually move on to other puters run by other people where they might be able to assist with something else. Some learn to help each other. Some learn to work well on their own. Some form little villages and little cities in there, everyone performing a different activity … all at once. A software planet that continually renews itself."

"They help people," the albino said from under the hand scratching his pug nose.

"They do." Magda paused. "Or most of them, anyway. Some aren't very nice, actually. They're called rogue proxies. Sometimes they fight with other proxies and make them sick. Sometimes they leave my puter and give the information I've collected inside it to other puters without my permission. At any given instant there are thousands of them on the Other Side. Seven thousand new ones a month."

"They hurt good proxies?"

"Only the good proxies fight back, don't they. They send out bobby proxies to arrest the rogue proxies and put them in jail. So more times than not everything works out for the best at the end of the day." Magda looked from the albino to 928. "Would you like to talk to the Mao-Maos yourself? You can tell them how you're feeling. Ask them anything you want."

The Irish girl shook her head *yes yes yes*.

"Right, then." Magda faced the screen. "Say hello to 928, everybody."

All the Mao-Maos stopped what they were doing and turned their attention to the crowded room. Everything on the screen was yellow and pink with expectant teeth and gums. The Mao-Maos opened their mouths to speak.

"Buh-buh-but …" 928 said.

The Mao-Maos fetched up.

Magda turned and looked at her, encouraging.

"What would you like to tell them?"

Magda ran a palm over the Irish girl's hair. It felt like velvet and cashmere.

"That's not my name," the Irish girl said.

Magda's heart kerchunked in her chest like something alive in back of a car boot.

The other children turned and looked at their sister.

"What?" Magda asked.

"That's not it. 928. That's not my name."

"It isn't?"

"No." She deliberated. "It's Jada."

"Jada?"

"Jada," the Irish girl said. "Right."

"But …"

"My name is Jada," she said, testing.

Magda leaned back in her swivel-chair and raised her fingers to her lips. She felt like she was existing in two places at once.

"Hiya, Jada," all the Mao-Maos on the screen said in unison. "Pleased to meetcha."

6. PHASE TRANSITIONS

RYKKI

my name she said the one inside me the one who speaks when I am not speaking she said my name and I listened

because I have always listened because that is what I do because I am me and not others because I have been since the before-time when nothing happened forever and ever

dust sifting down in sunlight I could see it grain by grain count it in the before-time before numbers were numbers and I was me and nothing else existed in the room except air pushing in and out of my lungs

nothing happened forever and ever and then everything happened all at once the man with the loose gray face staring his sisters and brothers above me

sunshine winking in my head

he passed me food

he passed me water

I could count it grain by grain and then everything happened all at once the horror-men shouting my sister and brothers the word beginning to rise from inside me

from the one who speaks me when I am not speaking she began to say my name and I listened

because I have always listened because that is what I do because the voice won't be silent it tells me things about the part of me that isn't me scent of every word I use

my name she said

Rykki

VOX NOTES. MAGDA KARTER. 18 DECEMBER, 11 A.M.

Within an hour of patient 928 "naming" herself, patient 926 followed suit, thrilled when the digital proxies on my puter began applying the word "Rykki" to her. Within forty-five minutes the male patients had imitated this pattern. They became more animated than usual, then displayed atypically assertive behavior. Patient 927 adopted "Tris"; 929 "Oran"; 930 "Zivv." Difficult to understand the significance, if any, of these. Difficult as well to understand where and how such "names" might have originated. Or, given the patients' rudimentary proficiency at pronunciation, is it possible these aren't names at all, in actual fact, but inexactly mimicked sounds from their surroundings ... nonsense syllables, acoustic confusions? Could "Zivv," for instance, simply be a variant of "sieve" or "sift," "Oran" "orange," perhaps, or "aura" ... "names," in other words, appropriated from the environment and reinforced positively by the digital-proxy software?

RYKKI
everything happened all at once the big black bird with the cracked smile

the ugly man who smells of wet rot the one who used to be a man but changed her mind and speaks soft language like the fragrance of hyacinths I remember them

say your name they said as if I had a choice *say your name darling tell us your name come on now you can do it* on their knees lolly in hand but I saw him hold down my sister for the jabs I saw the black bird hold down Jada

silence blinking through flowers

the pigeon landing like a biplane in the garden

because she told me because she showed me because the pigeon touching down caught my breath in my throat what else could it do it was so beautiful the sound of its wings like air pushing in and out of my lungs in the room before numbers were numbers

say your name darling they said *there you go do it again*

what do I remember when I remember telling myself the stories

the words I hear

is it repetition recall is it putting together the voices that speak me in ways they don't know like the stained-glass fish we make in the afternoons rain at the windows they don't exist and then they do

when they laugh their faces squeeze with yellow teeth

come into us they say *come into the screen*

Zivv reaches out his hand to follow

because at that moment in the brilliance of the garden there was nothing more lovely than the final glide

I went blind I went deaf I lost my voice my heart stopped

everything became white cold became sunshine winking through hyacinths

gentle as the sound of my name

VOX NOTES. DR. HUNG-CHANG. 18 DECEMBER, 11:45 A.M.

I'm still not quite sure what to make of "Jada," "Rykki" or "Tris." Suggestions, anyone? Java, perhaps? Re-key? Trix? Tricks? Wherever they happen to have originated, the extraordinary fact is that they are here now ...i.e., that the patients have taken it upon themselves to further individualize themselves, separate themselves from experience outside themselves. They are, that is, continuing to stabilize their identities at a remarkable rate. In just over a month, they have evolved from Stage 3 prelinguistic babbling associated with the last half of the first year in an infant's life into the beginnings of patterned "true" speech, a nascent vocabulary of two or three words associated with a one-year-old into the thousand-plus vocabulary of a three-year-old capable of framing full sentences. Their motor skills have developed along similar lines ...Nurse Allegro reports that they have evolved from ability associated with 1.5-to-2.0 years (prehension and release fully developed; gait propulsive; creeping backward downstairs) to that associated with approximately 4.5 years (elementary skipping rope; hopping on one foot; walking on line). Their general socialization progresses at an astonishing speed. We must, it goes without saying, maintain a cautious approach, but we have, I should think, much cause for optimism.

VOX NOTES. MAGDA KARTER. 18 DECEMBER, 9:15 P.M.
Patients agitated at bedtime. Continue to ask to play with the digital-proxy software. Appear to be intrigued with the feedback loop that's been established, as if by uttering their names the digital proxies are validating who the children are. They asked how the digital proxies work and I found myself at a crushing loss. Can you imagine? Time was, I suppose, when technology was mechanical, all levers and cogs and wheels. You could see the effects of your actions. Now everything's become invisible and abstract ... magic, not to put too fine a point on it. There's nothing to see, nothing to guide understanding. What can I tell them?

VOX NOTES. DR. HUNG-CHANG. 19 DECEMBER, 8:27 A.M.
Tell them it's called headway, Ms. Karter. Seems our guests are increasingly interested in the universe outside the windows here. Time to introduce them to some larger concepts concerning geography and culture.

RYKKI

memories fly at me like black birds breaking their beaks against a window

they don't stop don't let me rest where do they come from the voice the one inside me the one who speaks tells me to look listen I do

they aren't mine are mine I've seen them before in dreams seen these people and things already

his bald head on pillow jowls swollen eye sockets lips faint blue arms limp legs like jointed canes what part of me am I remembering what part of the before-time the old life the one that isn't mine

the garden the sunlight winking in my head the pigeon landing the man with the blue lips waiting like I waited for something not to happen but then it did

because I have always listened always looked because that is what I do because I am me and not others because I have been since the old life since before that and this is what I hear what I see

he reaches up takes out his eyes tells me to put them in my sockets

see what I see he says

he palms bluewhite boiled eggs waiting I turn and run every night to my brother's room down the hall among the bubble police crawl up beside him he rolls over I climb into him

because Zivv stops the eyeman from digging in my brain

the horror-men

Zivv is me and not me my brother the one who watches like I watch because he can't help it everything's so fresh lime scent citrus soap on the back of the big black bird's neck

memories with cavities in them like a mouthful of bad teeth

oh well fuck the big black and white penguin says when Tris doesn't want to open his presents because Tris is Tris and not me he likes to be still *oh well fuck* he says

bit of the low bandwidth

Oran lives in words I live outside them Jada lies silent

every night monkeys scream

he reaches up and takes out his eyes and tells me to put them in my sockets and I run to Zivv who takes the eyes away from me

when I open my mouthful of memories to say them I see the monkeys crying inside their cages

bald pink heads growing wires like hyacinth vines smiling because they can't unsmile there's no fun in it anymore for them

Beijing is where you can become not-you Mao-Mao says so many people dragons pedicabs flying horses silk bicycles snakes puppets water bridges

once upon a time there was a city called Cairo-Egypt but a rock fell out of the sky

asteroid says Magda

asssssssssssssteroid says Oran

Cairo-Egypt went away but wants its statues painted walls jewelry back because it doesn't have any left

you could hear thunder in London as the rock changed to sound and light

once upon a time they used to put you in the ground when you went away but now you can't because there's no more ground left but that's what Cairo-Egypt wants

more ground the ground they gave us

what part of me am I remembering what part of the before-time

my father says the voice inside me

take these eyes he says

and look

what do you see?

VOX NOTES. NURSE ALLEGRO. 3 JANUARY, 2:11 A.M.
On night shift found Rykki girl in bed with Zivv boy again. Separated them. Third incident this fortnight.

VOX NOTES. MAGDA KARTER. 3 JANUARY, 8:37 A.M.
Rykki quite agitated. Tells me she doesn't want to sleep anymore, ever. She'll be all right, I'm sure ... just needs some TLC and a bit of distraction. Time, perhaps, to consider some sort of outing? This rain ... it's enough to give anyone the black dog.

VOX NOTES. DR. HUNG-CHANG. 3 JANUARY, 4:07 P.M.
Reluctantly concur with Dr. Bogg. Two caps sodium amytal tonight. I imagine we're dealing with some rather unpleasant recollections from the Hans Crescent days. Zivv watches her, hovers nearby during their waking hours, approaches almost protectively when others speak to her. When she's frightened she goes to him straightaway. I shudder to think what they must have gone through together. I feel like I'm trespassing in a land where nothing is what it should be. Giraffes grow from the ground. Time goes backwards. How can we talk about this?

VOX NOTES. DR. K'AI-CHUH. 7 JANUARY, 2:15 P.M.
Third round of gene therapy went off nicely this afternoon. Latest blood work indicates normal cells taking hold at a robust rate. Jada's energy returning. Nurse Allegro and Ms.

Karter report she's joining in on the others' games with increasing frequency, chatting them up constantly. We're making quite good progress on this front, and are well ahead of previous case subjects. The fates appear to be smiling down upon us, don't they.

VOX NOTES. MAGDA KARTER. 10 JANUARY, 10:25 A.M.
I remain disturbed by Rykki's temperament. Days following nightmares go hard on her. She wanders about distracted and solemn. Even little Zivv can't seem to cheer her up. But I have to wonder if sedation is really the solution. She seems drowsy, detached, fuzzy-headed.

VOX NOTES. DR. HUNG-CHANG. 11 JANUARY, 1:45 P.M.
Concur with Dr. Bogg. We need to keep Rykki as comfortable as possible while she works through her recollections. If she can model positive behavior for the others, perhaps we can make their journeys somewhat less grueling when their time comes.

VOX NOTES. NURSE ALLEGRO. 12 JANUARY, 5:40 A.M.
Rykki girl sleeping with Zivv boy again. Can't keep their hands off each other nights. Seems a bit unhealthy, like.

VOX NOTES. DR. HUNG-CHANG. 12 JANUARY, 10:45 A.M.
No, no, not unhealthy in the least, Nurse Allegro. Rykki's going through a bad spot right now and needs emotional support. One of her peers is providing it. The less heed you pay this, the better, I should think.

VOX NOTES. DR. K'AI-CHUH. 15 JANUARY, 11:00 A.M.
Vocabulary in the neighborhood of fifteen-hundred words. About eighty percent intelligibility. Grammar of utterances close approximation of colloquial adults'. Syntax systematic

and predictable. I'd estimate we're near the linguistic development of four-year-olds. Quite extraordinary. Oran a bit ahead of the others these days, Tris a bit behind.

VOX NOTES. MAGDA KARTER. 21 JANUARY, 9:25 A.M.

Rykki approached me this morning during playtime in Observation Room B and related that she'd had another nightmare. Horror-Father Dream, she called it. I asked her if by her father she meant the man who had looked after her in the Hans Crescent flat. She said no; she meant her father, her "actual" father, "the monkey man in the hospital bed." Tell me about him, I asked. "I only see him there, in the hospital bed," she said, "but I know he's other places in my head, too." How do you know he's there? I asked. "Everyone's in there somewhere," she said, "all you have to do is look hard enough." Why do you suppose he offered you his eyes? I asked. "Oh, he has so much to show me," she said. "My eyes just aren't going to be enough."

VOX NOTES. DR. BOGG. 21 JANUARY, 12:15 P.M.

Perhaps the false father is a surrogate for us all ... the people who wish Rykki and the others to see the world through our eyes. We are, from her point of view, colonizers of her consciousness. It sounds like she's having an understandably difficult time with our "psychic resettlement," as if she's quite frightened by what she's beginning to see. Who could blame her, I wonder.

7. THE IMPERIAL MALLMAZE IN THE DATA-BUSTING RUST-BELT OF HOMICIDAL HACKERS

Devin Hung-chang found out Fiona K'ai-chuh was deep into dating Tymm Tai-ni who, Devin thought, had really been deep into dating Devin Hung-chang who, it turned out, was dead wrong.

The transformational event occurred one morning while Devin stood in his breakfast nook, plastic bottle of Malaspina Glacier water in hand, chant by the Pygmy Children (who really were pygmy children, from various tribes along the equatorial region of the United States of Africa) on the sound system. The rainy weather molesting London since December all at once paused for thirty-five seconds. The cloud layer fractured and evaporated. Sunshine cascaded through the kitchen, photonic sea through a ship's ruptured hull. It glowed pinkly among the modest cosmetic holes bored through Tymm's palms and feet as she sat naked on the counter next to the microwave that made that annoying clicking sound like Petrina's old throat and dinged, announcing the completion of two McLenin Roachmeat McMuffins. Devin reached over, snapped open the door, inserted his hand, and his life modified.

"No time, pussums," Tymm said, hopping off and heading for the two-meter-square bedroom, which was also the two-meter-square living room, which was also the two-meter-square office, which was also the two-meter-square entertainment center. Her feet hit the floor and her firm breasts bounced exactly once: down, up. "Date with Fiona in an hour. Ta."

She actually used the word *pussums.*

"I, em … I'm a little surprised here," Devin said, a little surprised.

The clouds rematerialized outside the large oval high-impact plastic window. The sky slated over. The sunlight fled. The barometric pressure dropped so quickly Devin could feel it in his eardrums. A heavy rain began chattering in his cranium.

Oblivious to all the meteorologic symbolism, Tymm started gathering up her clothes around the rattan sleeping mat they'd snuggled on like teens less than twenty minutes earlier. They'd been doing a lot of that lately, having entered the circuit of infantile behavioral patterns associated with new love. They fed each other at Persian patisseries, extending arms across tables, fork tips loaded with almond croissants. They rocked on park benches, she on his lap, he with his face pressed against those hocus-pocus breasts of hers. They exchanged small gifts and undertook endearing preening rituals, almost unconsciously winnowing through each other's hair as they lay side by side beneath mildew-scented towels that passed for sheets while they compared backgrounds, interests, beliefs, and physical maladies.

"I'm shocked," Devin said.

Tymm wriggled on a pair of bruise-blue jeans.

"Yep," he said. "That's me. Really, em, filled with wonder. Awe, in actual fact."

He rubbed his freckled scalp. Devin was naked too. He felt his shaved scrotum tingle in response to the plummet in pressure.

Tymm stamped into one simulated-snakeskin boot.

"Boy oh boy," Devin said.

Tymm stamped into the other.

Tymm puffed a tangle of oil-slick black hair out of her face and glanced over at him. Devin still couldn't get used to this flashtrend where you wore clear instead of colored sunscreen. It looked so … menacing … in a discomposingly sexy way. Tymm bent from the waist, swiped up her loose silver pseudo-fishscale blouse, and clittered it over her head.

She walked to the door, unfastened diverse bolts, locks, hooks, and latches, opened it, and stepped through.

It shut unassumingly behind her.

"No doubt," Devin said to his empty flat. "Just really, really taken aback."

He put down his water bottle and muffin on the counter and reached for his phone on the other side of the microwave, called Sirch & DeStory, and asked for his credit back. A chipmunk-voiced digital-proxy avatared on the monitor as a fleshy blood-vesseled valentine and explained Devin had long since exceeded his three-date credit-back guarantee. Devin hung up in mid-explanation, which started sounding gradually more intimidating to him, rebolted, locked, hooked, and latched his door, human-wormed under his mildew-scented towels that passed for sheets on his rattan mat, took a fairly large hit of permeable jax off the inhaler buried in his music-chip collection, and lay virtually motionless on his back for twenty-four hours staring up at the ceiling, across which marched, if you squinted hard around the eighth hour, a fat black ant that took frequent breathers and had something creepily robotic in its gait. Devin developed a headache, he strained to see it so intensely. It was pretty small and far away and the light wasn't that great. He developed a spinal throbbiness, too, because he never got around to changing his position. The nerves in his fingers felt thorny and then shut off. Ditto his toes, his feet, and his legs below the knees. In the fourteenth hour, the ant entered a series of figure-eights, backtracked, meandered in a generally westward direction, took an obtuse angle that resolved into a scalene triangle, opened into a pentahedron, then put down anchor near the lip of a zigzag crack. Those breasts. Devin just couldn't get them out of his mind, the way they bounced exactly once: down, up. Or the way he couldn't take his eyes off those holes in her palms each time she'd raised her slender champagne glass spiked with an innocuous hallucinogen to her white cockeyed collagen-injected lips at Fiona's party all those months ago. In the eighteenth hour the ant took off again, this time at an insectile sprint, but backwards. Or how they learned they liked *exactly* the same band, the Pygmy Children, and *exactly* the same album, *Kombat Fatigue*, with those chants that were more like puerile moans than chants, induced, if you read the liner notes, by electrodes implanted deep inside the brains of those children and stimulated randomly by an external computer. Or how Tymm did that thing with her mouth when the birdshit splattered her shoulder at the picnic in the bandstand by the Round Pond in Kensington Gardens; it looked like she'd bitten into a ball of sealing putty. In the twentieth hour the ant arrested and embarked on what Devin interpreted as a staredown with him. This lasted till a dim luster brightened the bio-lit room. Then the ant just dropped off the ceiling, dead, and ticked against the concrete floor half a meter away from Devin's numb left thumb. He rose painfully and crawled over to make sure. Yep: it was dead all right. No doubt. Crackly dead. Dead as a yellow fingernail.

He chose to take this as another sign.

His crypt reeked of new beginnings.

So he stretched, yawned, pulled his knees to his chest in a half-hearted attempt at yoga, rolled onto his belly, rose onto his elbows, hoisted himself erect, aligned his back, shuffled down the hall to the sink-cum-chlorine-pump, washed up, brushed his teeth with a brush missing every third bristle, shuffled back to his crypt, ate the staling muffins and drank the flattening water, shrugged on some clothes, and limped off to ABNORMAL.

Not that he was in a wonderful mood or anything when he escorted the kids into the Big Television for the first time. He wasn't. He was nauseous, like he'd popped a couple of laxatives the night before and they didn't work, and didn't work, and all of a sudden did work in the middle of the daily staff briefing, but he couldn't excuse himself because he was the guy talking and he was right in the middle of making some important point about some important subject ... except he also felt removed from everything, as if he was living far inside the liquid curves and cavities of his internal organs ... except he also knew he had this job to do, this mission, and the kids had been looking forward to it for weeks, and by golly he was going to do it.

Magda was waiting with them on the front steps of the old

Jordanian Embassy when Devin, umbrella iglooing above him, limped up the block from the Heistreet bus stop. Magda had outfitted each child in a pair of fresh black Levis 5001's and a gray Versus-Gateway collarless buttondown shirt implanted with sensors designed to detect the presence of pollution in the air and dispense measured amounts of deodorant—Brook Shields Estrus for the girls, L. L. Bean Uzi for the boys—if sussing out the presence of perspiration. Chemical-rich raindrops spattered the kids on their trot down the checkerboard footpath toward the grumbling flat-gray Chaika with tinted windows in which Dante hunkered behind the wheel. Their shirts polka-dotted pale green and ocher, meaning it was going to be the kind of day that seemed like it was getting a good healthy aqueous scrubbing but in reality was suffering from a freakishly elevated Air-Quality Deficit.

Dante was listening to the media issue standard warnings between songs by Sekret Servix and Stock & Hausen on the Chaika's golden oldies station about how no one should stay outside more than fifteen minutes at a stretch, even with protected skin, and everyone should bathe especially seriously when back inside again. The elderly, the young, and those with respiratory complications or early-stage melanoma should remain indoors entirely except in the event of a genuine emergency.

Magda waved goodbye from the front steps, blew her gloopy nose against the bad chemicals, and disappeared through the imposing main entrance of number nine. The Chaika executed a cumbersome eight-point U-turn on Upper Phillimore Gardens, centimetered down Argyll Road, and eased into the busy crush of traffic on Heistreet, tuk-tuks and double-deckers, bikes and black cabs, mopeds and lorries, Asian compacts and American saloon cars all puzzled into an almost motionless mosaic.

Flooding had skrimmed the scene. Soggy scraps of cardboard and gray mice souped with red-brown mud along the curbs. Vendors had abandoned their fruit carts and kiosks. Shop windows were boarded up. A mesh gate closed off the wide low luminous tiled entrance of the Kensington tube station and the machine-gun-toting bobbies were gone.

A stray intrepid pedestrian decked out in respirator, goggles, rubber gloves, rubber mackintosh over Klub Med-tartan kilt, and LaCrosse biohazard boots recommended by the World Health Organization shot out of a newsagent's, jogged down the pavement, and darted into a Chinese bank past the deserted shrine where a weak feather of smoke rose from a smoldering pile of incense and paper money before a plaster likeness of the Great Helmsman himself.

The kids didn't mind any of it, though. After all, this was their first good look at the world outside the hazy windows of ABNORMAL, and it was the only one they'd ever seen, poison rain or no, and from their viewpoint it was the most beautiful and exciting place in the solar system. They couldn't keep still. There was just so much to look at. They fidgeted inside the used Russian limo, two in the front seat with Dante, three in the back with Devin, needing to palm every object within their reach to make it real. A few minutes into their trip, Zivv and Rykki caught sight of the on-board navigational screen on the dash next to the steering wheel Dante sat behind, arms folded, humming along to one of My Friend Noo and the Biohazard's ditties, and Devin explained from the backseat how it spoke to satellites and other cars, as well as to Dante, choosing and directing the limo along the fastest routes, warning of operator-fatigue or broken speed limits, and maintaining a safe distance from the vehicle in front by reading feedback from the infrared device incorporated into its headlights. Jada noticed the tiny face-print recognition cameras on the doors that activated or deactivated those red pinprick lights on the shoddy black leather armrests by the release handles and spent several blocks making them work. Tris, by the window across from her, fixated on the pongs that despite the air-filtration mechanism still osmosed into the car, sniffing the manufactured breeze for traces of necrotic hydroponic vegetables and wet hair, while Oran, pink eyes wide with admiration, wanted to know the name for everything in this increasingly dense multiverse … till he saw his first flying-wing plane, eight-hundred passengers belted into its movie-theater-like abdomen six thousand meters above them, and fussed till Dante, temper shriveling, pulled over next to a sweet-smelling Thai café so he, Oran, could roll down his window and watch the thing slide south heavily toward the new airport near Bri'n.

It took them more than an hour to stop-and-start across town to Victoria Station, a dull redbrick approximation of the pyramidal copper-faced Diacomm Labs mothership in Los Angeles, vast HDTV screens broadcasting softcore porn interspersed with blipverts for its subsidiaries twenty-four hours a day.

Dante's discolored teeth vanished behind a thin tight frown as he and the others pushed through the hordes of waiting travelers inside the station, including this jabbering pack of Catholic Pentecostals, seventy-five or a hundred strong, speaking in tongues into cell phones... warming up for their pilgrimage to Reading, where the Holy Spirit had recently incarnated in the bloody tears wept by a giant holographic harlequin protruding from a McLenin franchise.

The train was on time, its immense electric engine birring in its berth. It was one of those maglev tiltbod jobs, Devin said, shouting to be heard over the din of fundamentalists, sleek and low as an alloy lamprey, capable of cresting 500 kph suspended 1.5 centimeters above its tracks while inclining the passenger compartment relative to its wheeled undercarriage to avoid subjecting its occupants to uncomfortable lateral forces as it tore around curves at cheek-flapping speed. The choked humid tubular interior was all gray epoxy and foam save for a hint of Asian influence in its analog-bamboo jalousies and delicate dragons embossed on the plastic around the pretend rice-paper sliding hatches that separated cars. Devin, Dante, and the kids wedged into their straight-backed seats opposite a well-dressed Vietbodian family who'd replaced all their natural teeth with imitation ebony ones in a show of tribal unity, and across the aisle from a Dread Jester prinked out in a purple crewcut and cosmetic laughing mask, cheeks slit clear to the ears, gums laid bare, nose cauliflowered. She was deep into channeling on some album or maybe how-to chip, eyes closed, face angled ceilingward, fingering the silver aug behind her ear.

Soon they were jetting through the flat industrial wastelands north of London, everything brumed in mineral ash, rain relaxing into drizzle. Free from the heat island of the city, the temp fell four or five degrees. Silhouettes of auto factories discharging smoke and flames into the thick gunmetal sky shot past. Junkyards strewn with tens of thousands of crushed cars and dead machinery. The ominous stacks of a deserted nuclear power plant. Several grimy redbrick towns, each smooging the edge of a steaming pond, argon lamps burning even by day, air-quality-alert signs posted at intervals along the streets. They flew through Himmler Hempstead, Dumstable, Luton; Woeburn, Milton's Keys, Wolfton. Herds of emaciated cloned sheep, white fur stained by atmospheric lead, lifted their heads in pastures of withered clover and watched the train scud by. People began cropping up ... riding along narrow roadsides in tuk-tuks, sheets of plastic wrapped around their shoulders and over their lowered heads ... strolling through muddy commons with children in governcorp-issued respirators ... cooking over the pitchy blaze spewing from dented barrels lining a five-meter-high wall unfurling kil after kil across the landscape like a drab ribbon of concrete spraybombed into a solid commotion of day-glo delusions, skull-and-crossbones, powerfists, phalli, threats, curses, crosses, enormous cartoon female torsos with leg-stumps spread ... GIVE BRITAIN BACK TO THE BRITZ ... CHOP-CHOP WANKERS CAN SNIFF MY DOG BOLLIX ... FUNG PI, WITEBOY ...

Devin reached into his waistcoat pocket and tugged out a handkerchief, patted his forehead, and shut his eyes. He'd grown up there, on the other side of that wall in the safe-zone compound called New Guangdong, and the last thing he wanted to do these days was see it again.

Nine-year-old Devin, and children like him, became in British eyes the reification of everything that was arsed up with the place, an admonishment of what was to come if the reals weren't careful, which, they had a sinking feeling, they weren't ... which, it turned out, led to rising tensions in the vicinity of this and similar Chinese safe-zone compounds around the country, till the race riots erupted shortly after the turn of the century, and one morning on his way to public school just off the beige green Devin looked up to see the burning lorry bristling with camouflage-bedecked patriots blunder through the main gates. He only recalled smidgens from the next twenty-four hours ... the explosions ... the machine-gun pops ... the image of orange fire licking from the black-framed windows of what had once been his flat ... and his elderly neighbor, Mr. Kung Fu-Grenville, that nice old ex-prof who used to show him his library, every precious book sealed in a Ziploc, lying in the street, scalp balled into a juicy brownish wad next to him, head an abused rugby ball ...

Those memory streaks added up to who Devin would always be. His progens and he escaped to London with enough credit to start over again, his father now driving a double-decker, his mother working in a roachmeat market near their flat in the Docklands, and they got on well enough, Devin even finding himself eight years later attending the televisual university at King's College, drawn increasingly to kids like himself ... the lost boys and girls, the ones who felt childhood was just an extended waiting for something else, something more authentic, connected and healthy, that would, Devin finally learned, never arrive...

He winced awake, dislocated, the guy who'd just stepped off a plane in Melbourne after a thirty-six-hour flight from Stockholm.

The maglev tiltbod was thrumming beneath him, stationary, and Dante was gathering together the kids, and the Vietbodian family was shuffling down the aisle behind an Ozone Baby in a limp flowery dress with miscellaneous flashback beepers adorning his putty-colored flippers, and the Dread Jester was bending forward in her seat, shooting what appeared to be a good-sized dose of rapture into her nasal cartilage with a pressurized syringe.

Devin contemplated taking another hit of permeable jax off the inhaler tucked under the handkerchief folded in his vest pocket for a restorative disposition, but thought better of it and stood to join the others.

The stiffness in his legs had almost melted away.

The Imperial Mallmaze, its name a bit of a laff at the exiled royal family, started as a group of shops on a side street in Noneatin in the late nineties but, under the auspices of the Virgin-Disney people (under the auspices of the Klub Med people, under the auspices of the Diacomm people), cleaved, replicated, and grew like some sort of dream-time steel-and-glass transmutation, both above ground and below, spreading westward into Birmingham, chewing away at the city through the decades till it more or less replaced the city, supplanting some of the less economically solvent natives therein, while also creating a home for lots more, part office complex and part bazaar, part governcorp housing project and part conglomeration of innumerable faddish boutiques ... a stunted Sherwood Forest bisected by a stream rushing with holographic water (floating chessboards, pointillist fruit, vintage psychedelic stripes and paisleys) ... full-scale BosniaLand theme park highlighted with make-believe mortar attacks and ethnic-cleansing festivals ... manmade lake with Yellow Submarine rides ... tennis courts ... football fields ... even this forgery of a little corner of the Swiss Alps complete with snow and bunny slopes for the wannabe skiers in the family ... everything tumbling together into a clean, Brinks-Force-patrolled reverse Revolutionary War in pursuit of Britain's culturally receding hairline ... a one-roof haven away from the snipers and pedophiles, gangs and goofballs, carbon dioxide and diabolic ultraviolet gene-scrambling radiation outside ... except, well, maybe for that teeny-tiny outbreak of humidifier lung over by what had once been the University of Aston, result of micro-organisms, molds, and spores building up in the recirculated air, tissue damage same as that from asbestos, but ... WHY TAKE A CHANCE? the advertisements said, LOSE YOURSELF IN THE MAZE ...

The idea caught on. Soon Imperial Mallmazes sprung up across Norwitch and Plymuff, Holyhead and Scarsburrow. And the Brits loved them. Pizza Hut called, and they came. McLenin knocked, and they answered. In droves. Thousands of them, millions, mobbing the imitation public squares and Roman-pillared passageways, packing rides, squashing into stores, butting, shoving, jostling toward the merchandise and the jubilance, queues be damned, hajis to the Promised Land.

Rykki, Jada, Tris, Oran, and Zivv stayed bump-into-you close to Devin and Dante, rubbernecking at the three-hundred-and-sixty degree data-spill as they passed an Athlete's Foot outlet that featured StarTAC hiking boots implanted with global-positioning sensors, a Michael Jackson Co. retailer that sold hyperbaric chambers with built-in HDTVs for that oxygen-rich collagen-full mien, a Bausch & Boeing stall that flogged retro mirrorshades with face-recognition capabilities that'd take a look at who you're talking to and whisper his or her name into your ear while listening via word-spotting software for important phrases (*that humongoid contract thingie*, say) at which point it would project the relevant info—stats, images, text, whatever—onto the inside of your reflective glasses.

A brash voice out of TexMex interrupted the weak Chinese muzak by All This Useless Beauty on the PA system, brassy five-note singsong salmagundi of dissonant harps, flutes, xylophones and cymbals.

"Sorry to bother you fine folks," it said, "but we got ourselves a little bomb alert in Happy Hamlet Five. Best if you sort of just move on through if you're in the vicinity. Best, I repeat, if you sort of just move on through. Security's on the way ... And, by the bye, don't miss our blue-light special in Rue the Day, two kils south of Eiffel Tower Town, hear?"

The burgundy Panasonic robotic bubble-guards that'd been bustling among the shoppers' feet became vexed and ripped off in the direction of the purported danger.

Several minutes later the human Brinks-Force de-miners arrived dolled up in oversized Plexiglass visors, inflated kneepads, cumbersome Kevlar vests and clownish air-cushion shoes, leading razzed Alsatians before them.

Devin and the others detoured north, down a block of seemingly trashed storefronts in V-2 Village, plate-glass windows shattered, iron mesh buckling out of the split street, cute little controlled fire spuming from a broken gas main. They proceeded by a Circuit City highlighting those new Onkyo entertainment centers, teleputers with VR remotes, surround sound, and ostentatious data gloves that could break your heart with their rococo sense of aesthetics, everything viewable from an ersatz-leather recliner custom-sculpted to your shape and rigged with full-body heated massage, fridge, and catheter for those long weekend excursions to the Other Side ... then one of those oily-gray-film-windowed smoke rooms congested with muggle burners and tobacco fiends who could fire up at will inside the cubicle and simmer away in their own four-percent inhalations and ninety-six-percent side-stream waste.

Two doors down they entered a Gap, tiny uncluttered space, not much bigger than Devin's flat, with no clothes in sight anywhere.

"You remember our talk about custom manufacturing?" he asked, making his way over to one of the eight shiny translucent black plastic tube-booths lining the place.

"The cross-country cyclist," Rykki said.

"Brilliant." Devin smiled and squatted, pinching up his slacks. Rykki's incredible blue eyes always startled him. "The cross-country cyclist. Right. And where does our tired cross-country cyclist find a spare derailleur gear for her bike when it breaks down in that small IBM-Nevada town just south of Winnemucca?"

Dante, instantly bored by the stench of education, sighed a large punctured tire of air and wandered off toward the store's exit to see if there might be something more interesting there.

"In the floppy disk in her backpack," Zivv said.

"Very good ... and what does our cyclist do with the disk?"

"Brings it to the corner all-night copy shop."

"Where it's printed from a puter design file, isn't it? Clever. The program tells the machine tool in the shop how to deposit a thin layer of structural material by spraying droplets of liquid metal in a certain pattern, building layers into the new gear. Same principle with auto parts, boat parts, you name it, right?"

"And clothes," Jada said, stepping up beside Rykki and Zivv.

"Exactly. And clothes. In the olden days people mass-produced a standardized product. Now they mass-customize personal goods." He stood and pressed the hatch with his fingertips. It clacked open. "Shall we see what the Gap has to offer?"

Zivv entered first.

Devin told him to stand still while the others made some fashion decisions on his behalf. The hatch snapped closed and a screen on its outer surface rezzed up, displaying this week's catalog along with a rough eggplant-purple three-dimensional mannequin-grid of a boy with Zivv's scrawny build.

Jada, Rykki, Oran and Tris flipped through items in it, trying on various combinations, till they found just the right smog-colored t-shirt with The Imperial Mallmaze logo stenciled across it in copper, baggy prewashed pretorn blue jeans, white socks, and white super-hightop techno-sneakers with twinkling chartreuse lights set into clear polymer soles.

Devin tapped the banknote icon in the upper right corner. Figures tallied on the screen, a crimson thread of light jumped from what looked like a camera lens just above it to eye-scan him, and heavily encrypted digital A&Ps moved between the offshore bank housing ABNORMAL's account and the offshore one housing Gap Co.'s.

"Would you like to contribute to the Governcorp Tax Fund?" asked the screen in an electronically neutral voice in accordance with the Voluntary Dues Law.

"No, thank you," Devin said.

Rykki looked up at him.

"Time was when people paid the governcorp a little credit with each purchase they made. Called a 'tax.' Helped the governcorps afford diverse activities. Only you can't tax what you can't see, can you? Best they can do now is ask all polite if you'd like to make a bit of a donation. No surprise, really, most people don't. Had enough of that business ages ago."

He tapped the ENTER icon and a laser lightshow webbed inside the tube-booth, optical scanners taking Zivv's waist, hip, thigh, length, neck, chest, and foot measurements.

Four steps away, Dante hummed "Sweet Mêmes Are Made by Thieves" to himself. He raised and lowered his heft on the balls of his feet, crossed-arms-inspecting a puffy-faced teen in silver hair-plaits, snug gash-colored body dress and matching lipstick, utter lack of animation in her facial logographics, absentmindedly exploring the inside neck of her plastic Versace caffeinated artesian-well water bottle with her muscle-grafted tongue while waiting for a tube-booth to free up.

"That was fun, now, wasn't it?" Devin asked half an hour later when Oran, the last to use the machine, opened the hatch and stepped out.

"Crank," he said. "Yeah. How long before it's ready?"

"No time at all, I should think." Devin rubbed his freckled scalp. "Meanwhile, let me show you something I think you'll *really* fancy."

" ...?"

"It's called Vachuru Lane."

"Vachuru Lane."

"Right. VR arcade. You know how Ms. Karter's digital proxies sometimes come out to visit you?"

"Mao-Mao."

"Well, same thing. Only it's you who go in and visit them."

In the public square beyond the entrance, the crack of a controlled explosion split the nonstop low-frequency background noise.

Dante licked his lips at the puffy-faced teen who extracted her ant-eater's tongue from the bottle's neck and glanced up quickly, reflexes sharp as those of a spooked adder.

One minute Rykki was walking through the neon-lit mouth of Vachuru Lane with her brothers and sister, huge vibrant neon-pink teeth set into a stretch of plastic translucent-black wall like the tube-booths, into the vast tekked cavern shrill with electronic pings and chitters, dark except for the multicolored flickerings leaking out from behind the VR goggles of the rapt trippers nestled in what looked like a disorganized field hospital of form-fitting foam dentist chairs ... and the next she was here, swimming through *Atlantis*, the news and entertainment magazine, understanding why those people she heard about who spent just *way* too much time on the Other Side almost never went outdoors, hardly even to the bathroom, didn't know if it was day or night, didn't care, and were severely disturbed by anything with real weight, mass, or natural color... soothing sound of oxygen-tank bubbles and distant Chinese muzak (All This Useless Beauty back, not somewhere *out there*, but right *here* in the

84

middle of her skull) rilling around her as she wafted in an electric-blue cartoon-gel Mediterranean Sea among sparkling white ruins of the mythological kingdom ... tumbled columns, a wrecked temple, limestone blocks scattered along what once had been an impressive main road littered with broken statues and shards of terra cotta pottery ...

Only that stuff didn't interest her half as much as the cloud of yellow-bodied, black-and-white-headed, long-nosed butterfly fish in which she next found herself suspended.

She hovered among them, arms extended loosely from her sides, lallies parted and bent at the knees, discomfiting feeling of weightlessness in her lower abdomen. Seemed their scales reflected sunlight from above, but when she focused harder she saw that wasn't it at all. The lightforms were moving images, different on each fish ... sight-bites for the articles she could choose from. One involved those plutonium leaks in the Irish Sea from the decommissioned sub reactors dumped there ... another an interview with an Immaculate, skin-glam who didn't believe in the pornotechnics of the previous generation, nothing kinked, nothing barmy, just flesh-on-flesh Touch Sex.

There was a documentary about this runty nerd in a daffy mustache who'd executed all manner of ball-ups back in Germany almost a hundred years ago. A profile about Oleg Gorievsky, head of KGB operations in London turned talkshow host, and one about the newly formed Nano Klub, consortium of larger governcorps overseen by Klub Med intent on keeping smaller governcorps from developing nanotech out of fear such development might lead to barrages of micro-warfare and -terrorism. Something about the British fleet putting down anchor off the coast of what remained of Cairo in a pretty ominous show of force, and one about China's use of PNE's, or Peaceful Nuclear Explosions, to divert water into the Gobi Desert from the Brahmaputra River by blasting a twenty-kil channel through a mountain range, outrageous amounts of fallout notwithstanding, all under the patronage of Envirosafe Waste Management.

And—what was that?—something to do with what appeared to be an upside-down glassy white beanstalk several thousand kils up the well leading down, down, down from hundreds of space stations and orbital theme parks, where its pallid roots had fastened, toward earth's atmosphere.

Rykki reached forward and lay her hand on the fish flank televising this graphic, and her undersea universe expanded: she was inhabiting a different existence altogether, hanging alone far out in space, examining the white-and-blue sphere below her, that weird reverse-beanstalk descending ...

"Within fifteen years," an announcer's narcotic voice whispered over the muzak in her head, "nanotechnology will have advanced to the stage where a bloc of governcorp investors will be able to join forces to create this superstrong cable by manipulating carbon atoms with swarms of nanomachines. The diamond strands comprising it will possess fifty times the strength-to-weight ratio of aerospace aluminum. This forty-thousand-kilometer-high spar contains elevators that will lift millions of people and billions of tons of resources from earth into space for mining, colonization, and entertainment. Long after its completion, nanosystems within the spar will continue to monitor for weaknesses and strive to maintain structural integrity ..."

An unexpected sense of solitude rushed in at Rykki, the oxymoronic union of all this info and all this emptiness giving her a major case of the creeps.

Nor did it help that there weren't any smells here, either ... made the whole thing seem busy and sterile at the same time.

The cosmos Rykki woke up to one day in that horrid little room on Hans Crescent never slowed down, it occurred to her, never took a coffee break. It reconstructed itself every eyeblink, and the game of navigating it turned out to have a lot less to do with remembering than with learning how to forget, trashcanning hundreds of mental files every day just to stay on top of those sensations and facts surging at you. It made her feel perpetually light-headed, remotely anxious, like something really important was always happening across the street, on the other side of V-2 Village, on the flanks of one of those butterfly fish she *couldn't* see, only she'd miss everything because her attention was homed in on something else, on what would prove to be some dispensable thing, some wrong thing, always.

She extended her right foot, toed the planet earth, and she was back in that scintillating yellow piscine cloud. She closed her eyes, trying to steady herself. When she opened them again, some pixels flashed at the corners of her vision. She felt seasick, then sad. Way off she could just distinguish Devin and Tris flippering along like two indolent turtles. Far below, Oran and fifty or sixty other trippers, one in a tremendous black cape undulating like a jumbo jellyfish, explored the ruins which Rykki figured led to other articles or maybe even other virtual spans altogether ... science shows, say, or SinSim parlors, concerts, sports replays, fashion parades. Every once in a while a tripper would reach forward, touch a portion of stone wall or dark-green sculpted bronze bust, and plip out of existence. Rykki decided to follow, search for a less alarming province but, just as she raised her arm, a commercial interrupted her.

A long boulevard extended far into a bluish-gray haze of skyscrapers and pandemic housing projects, relentless percussive gongs and drums and clappers of the Peking Opera germinating in Rykki's brain pan.

Chang'an Avenue in Beijing.

Some part of her slowly recognized it, as if she'd been watching an old vid thirty minutes before it dawned on her she'd already seen it twice. Recognized, too, the glazed emerald pagoda with gold trim and straight-backed Buddhas on each level ... one of the Forbidden City's dragon sculptures, scaly marble claws reaching for a flaming marble pearl ... the commotion of Guanyuan bird market ...

Rykki wasn't sure she was viewing the real Beijing or a digitally enhanced version of it, the authentic article or some tampered-with copy of a tampered-with copy designed by an office-full of mucus-toothed ad geeks who'd never journeyed farther east than the Docklands, thinking *if you can make a jingle out of it, it'll sell.*

As she watched, the weirdest thing occurred.

That guy she'd noticed a little while ago, the tripper in the

87

tremendous black cape, undulated into her commercial. His head was shaved down the middle and hair moussed on either side like large black wings. Under his cape he wore a dark dapper suit circa 1890 with waistcoat and golden watch fob. He bobbed up in front of Rykki and rotated to face her. She saw he had that rouge-corpse look of late-stage alcoholism and his eyes weren't eyes, really, but polished rooster-comb red plastic shells that reminded Rykki of an exoskeleton, somehow. In each one sputtered a vid.

Rykki crooked her head forward to see better and picked out a foggy London street at night, gas lamps, a gaudily dressed woman walking along quickly, the dreamlike form swooping down.

"Jack the Ripper," she said out loud.

His mouth spangled into a smile and he turned, spread his cape, and leapt into the broil of the bird market, hands morphing into talons, and began shredding away ... not at the pedestrians and cages, the things themselves, but somehow at their electronic essences, tearing huge sections away from the commercial's surface.

Swaths of the illumined cartoon gel comprising Rykki's virtual reality went black. It wasn't that he'd somehow damaged them. He'd obliterated them, just like that. They didn't exist anymore.

Rykki turned around, flummoxed, trying to understand the nature of this antimatter binge ... the texture of her environment was tattering, coming to bits everywhere.

Something glinted past her. A silhouette. She turned again.

It looked to her like a bobby, his partner right behind, whistles screeching, billy clubs raised. Jack the Ripper glanced over his shoulder, saw them, and stopped his work. He grinned, mouth full of rubies, and evanesced into the pixels around him.

That's when Rykki tasted something rusty and slimily wet along her soft palate.

Blood ...

8. PARASITIC SINGULARITIES
OF THE DREAM-TIME GARDEN

RYKKI

A black carnation opening in my head, so broad the sky itself turns dark, and me shouting *go away! go away!*, only it doesn't go away, I don't go away, I'm still there, will always be there, half a year older than I am now, the girl strapped into the dentist chair in the nightmare clinic, blouse unbuttoned, yanked back, chest painted with iodine, incision that was once my breast spilling red and watery down my ribs, nurse with the teardrop rhinestone glued to her forehead between those abundant green eyebrows sucking at it with a vacuum tube, bald Uncle Meat with fur-tufted ears scooping out the last adipose tissue from my growing cosmetic wound ... and then my eyes fluttering aware through the wispy blear of diluted anesthesia, torso heaving in the nylon restraints ... this is how it comes to me, this recollection that can't be mine, black carnation spreading, it has to be a dream but a dream can never feel like this, the Uncle Meat loading another hypodermic with a milky fluid containing the infectious engines, bending over me, my mouth opening, pressing the long gleaming tip home through the gummy conjunctiva of my right eye, barbed wire down my spine, knowing my own body temperature will soon bring them to life inside me, digital homunculi lifting their skeletal heads, orienting, frantically propulsive mechanical spermatozoa swarming up my optic nerve along a string of blue electricity toward the fibrous core of my brain where they will nest like heat lightning gathering above the ruins of Trafalgar Square, fiery encodings beginning to construct a hive mind among the soft awareness that was me, wasn't me, mating, laying death eggs, memory eggs, penetrating my cellular architectonics, reconfiguring them into something both programmed and not programmed, organic and inorganic, larvae cocoons wriggling through my consciousness, my father and not my father dying in his bed, my language and another's, this other one's, me shouting *get out of my head! get out!*, only it won't, they won't, can't, because they are part of me, these silicon leeches growing inside me now, a kind of love …

VOX NOTES. DR. HUNG-CHANG. 6 FEBRUARY, 5:47 P.M.

Rykki's seizure characterized by nasal hemorrhaging and blackout. Upon awakening, severe headache. Disinfectant took appropriate countermeasures against the virus that set upon the magazine she'd been visiting. I imagine the incursion shook her up rather badly, poor girl. Advise sedative tonight and, beginning tomorrow, full round of neurological tests. Best to be on the safe side.

VOX NOTES. MAGDA KARTER. 8 FEBRUARY, 10:00 A.M.

"It feels like my mind isn't my mind," Rykki told me between lessons. I asked her if she meant the headache. "No," she said. "It feels like someone's living inside with me." Who? I asked. She answered by saying she heard screaming last night. I suggested our monkeys upstairs. She just looked at me, as if I were completely missing the point, and changed the subject.

VOX NOTES. DR. K'AI-CHUH. 15 FEBRUARY, 3:25 P.M.

Dr. Bogg and I, as you know, have been preparing Jada emotionally for some time for her stay in the artificial womb. We've explained to her what she can expect, how this is a necessary part of her eugenic reorientation designed to strengthen her cellular composition against airborne toxins that might affect her more adversely than the other children.

This morning treatment commenced. Panic attack upon initial
inhalation of the semi-intelligent perfluorocarbons. Sedative
administered. Liquid-breathing comfortably. Intravenous
nutrition, morphine drip, gene therapy initiated.

RYKKI

The moon is Dante's eye ... you can hear its circuitry whirr as he leads us on an outing across Upper Phillimore Gardens to the old girls' school, well-behaved white Georgian front ... Dante and soft Magda with the hopeful smile and pink nose, in a downpour that smells of printer ozone and office dividers.

We move through the long bio-fluorescent corridors at the Feynman Research Facility where they cultivate hearts hands kidneys livers for the sick people who can afford them in rows of small fishtanks ... human skin stretched over whitish gristle architecture, yellowish granular fat, cherry-red muscle ... a doll-pink cluster of female breasts ... background thrull of the bioreactor providing nutrients, exchanging gases, removing wastes, monitoring temperature, twenty-four hours a day, like my sister a floating octopus in my head ...

Within the decade, says the razzhead in the lab coat, *we will have realized the first reliable anti-cancer nanobot ... inject it into a patient's bloodstream in vast amounts, control it from outside via macroscopic acoustic signals, and these machines will each release one molecule of an enzyme that will weld a protein to the ribosome of a malignant cell and kill it, just like that ...*

Magda blows her nose and sneaks a grin at me from behind her Kleenex. I grin back.

Imagine it, the razzhead says. *Or you swallow them like treacle and they're in your system and say you suddenly have a heart attack, well, that's okay, because they're right there and so they can fix it, and you slosh them around in your mouth when you have a cavity and they'll do the dental work, and if your circulation is impaired and you need more oxygen they can provide artificial red blood cells, too, help revive bodies preserved in cryogenic storage by repairing frostbite damage to the organs, generate a vaccine that cures the common cold ... and outside your system? Outside they can make automobiles that change shape and function at will, or grow food in a machine in your home by rapidly culturing cells from a plaice to create your very own seafood dinner, or build you a puter, or create a starship out of seawater. Every manufacturing problem will become a software problem. We'll have complete control over our physical shape and the design of our minds. We'll be capable, finally, of making decisions about how we make decisions.*

What would we decide?

How would we go about it and why?

But I can't imagine it, no ...

I'm walking through the incandescent dream-time garden instead, passing over an arched bamboo bridge. At its apex I lean on the railing and stare at the chubby orange-and-white-mottled carps floating like my sister just beneath the surface.

Beyond, ghostly green terraces.

Flowers and trees sing to themselves quietly.

Families wander among the genetically twidgled vegetation and rock formations. Couples sit side-by-side on decorated cement park benches, heads bobbing slightly behind portable silver VR rigs, roaming different gardens in their brains.

A thin purplish man passes behind me. He's wearing an off-white silk-analog suit and straw boater. He halts, steps up to the railing next to me, stares at what I stare at, abruptly sneezes.

"Duì-bu-qi," he says diffidently, and dodders off.

After a while I lift my elbows from the railing and turn to leave.

The thin purplish man collapses on the path fewer than three meters away. Curls into a fetal comma, black blood trickling from his mouth. He trembles modestly, lying there, hands tucked between legs, ashamed his death is causing such a disturbance.

Pedestrians slow their strides, restive all at once.

"Jiào jing-chá," someone says.

A heartfluster later my legs become sponge, my arms boneless rubber hoses.

I open my mouth to speak and my head unexpectedly tips back. I'm standing gaping at the whipped-cream-colored sky one second, two … and then I drop as well, tang of blood on my tongue.

"It's over," a voice whispers.

Above me swims a bald woman with oculated scalp. Her hundred slitted bumps flutter open, sleepy, washed-out blue eyes following every possible vector of sight. She's wearing a candy-apple Vietnamese dress and slacks embroidered with golden dragons. She makes sure to keep her distance.

"Ebola," she says. "Strain 214-N. Inhaled before your body could think."

My throat makes a wet sound.

"Bad project design, ultimately, is the thing. It happens. Everyone's gotta know when to fold." Her natural eyes skid up, across the bridge. "It's, um … been nazi."

She stands, brushes off some pebbles clinging to her knees with the back of her hand, and strolls away.

I listen to the scrape of her feet receding on the pebble path, becoming the past … the agitated high-nasal chatter of the police approaching cautiously from the opposite direction … and I feel myself begin to go blind deaf heart stopping … this world blanching into one packed with cold sunshine, loud …

VOX NOTES. DR. HUNG-CHANG. 7 MARCH, 3:35 P.M.

Good lord, Dr. K'ai-chih. What do you make of the anomaly at the core of the brain stem in vid 13798-A? Coloring's just a bit off. Shape's almost imperceptibly irregular. Appears at first glance to be some sort of swelling, doesn't it, but … well … that isn't it at all, is it?

VOX NOTES. DR. K'AI-CHIH. 7 MARCH, 10:35 P.M.

I haven't a clue, Dr. Hung-chang. Not a clue.

9. LIVING STEREO: TELEVISION COBRA: ULTRAVIOLET HOLIDAY

Magda stood at a concession booth in the Beargardens just down the dirty redbrick block from the New Globe Theater, which hadn't been new for almost forty years, waiting for her lagers and watching the piss-colored bank of clouds bunch in the hot sky above her.

At first she thought the underweight ethnically vague guy behind the counter was whistling to himself. He was spiffed up in a pair of gas-chamber-door-green Spandex tights. The rest of his categorically hairless body was painted in florid Chinese arabesques with variously hued anti-sun pastes. Blues, greens, and yellows, mostly. Gold studs embellished the skin above each lip corner and where his eyebrows should've been. An oxygen tube ran from his left nostril behind his left ear and, presumably, down his back to a nearby Oxybuster tank.

Then Magda heard the band strike up, dentist-drill pulses broken with the yips of frightened children, sweet rhythm guitar kerchunging in the background, and, when the guy reached across the counter to hand her her liquid-oxygen-augmented drinks in flimsy plastic cups, Magda grasped the fact the skin over his biceps had been inlaid with thumbnail speakers.

He was a living stereo.

"That was Sarin Dreams," the announcer in the guy's biceps said, "coming direct to you from the heart of Chainsaw Central, final song beamed in from Nairobi off the Hendrix I last night before it was struck by a rubbish bolt traveling fifteen kils per second, oh yeah …"

94

The two lagers were warm and brownish-yellow like the afternoon. It was early April, which out of habit people referred to as spring, and it was Magda's day off. The previous Wednesday the rain had arrested as rapidly as it had begun. Now the atmospheric soppiness was intolerable. The world shimmered in a marshy mist tasting of insecticide. There was no breeze, not even a gentle urban-canyon updraft. Emissions had nowhere to go, so they just stayed put, discoloring the vapor and exacerbating everyone's breathing difficulties. Despite the respirators, sanitary masks, and Oxybuster canisters, everyone looked pallid, sick, a hint lavender around the lips and nostrils ... but it didn't overmuch faze them. Why should it? This was the effing weekend, Sunday, start of bear-baiting season, family holiday-and-good-cheer time, wasn't it, and no stinking lung pathologies were going to dampen the Eastertide spirit, were they? Not on your effing Nellie.

Magda furrowed through the kecking idlers. Sweat accumulated in her armpits and riveted down her ribs beneath her loose-fitting dull gray-and-green-striped Riccardi prison-inmate-replica top.

Her baggy matching pants stuck to her bumcheeks in a confidence-disturbing fashion.

If she wasn't departing, it struck her as she stepped over a clogged drain grate chlorotic with slimed-over water and mosquito larvae, she was arriving. If she wasn't arriving, she was departing. She wasn't here and she wasn't there. This was how she experienced things: as a kind of in-between-ness. She was always almost somewhere else, always in the process of translation.

Her sinuses drained precipitously.

She expelled a sinusoidal yerp.

A family of seven gathered around an emaciated snake charmer. He had erect pigtails and sat Buddha-legged beneath a charred gathering of amputated stumps that'd once been a tree. He wore a loin-cloth and played a carved-wood flute.

It was hard telling the real pigment of their skins, the clan was so sooty. The kids were sharing a texturally enhanced drink in a large plastic cup, a Millennial Napper, turquoise balls of edible sodium-thiopental jelly free-floating in an orchid-pink liquid. The charmer's body was tissued in a rough corrugated shale-gray growth that looked like the scales of an alligator. Magda couldn't decide whether this epidermal motif was elective or not. Beside the charmer burned a small fire of twigs and trash. Over it slanted a tripod from which hung three chains supporting a shallow caste-iron pot in which bubbled penis-fat slugs in lard. On a large blocky television screen next to the charmer swayed a cobra with outspread hood.

Magda slowed, despite the sour smoke from the fire, snagged by the image. She was a sucker for wavering light sources. If something displayed motion and lots of glowing colors, she was there.

The snake had two heads and its skin opalesced like oil across water ... thanks, surely, to Virgin-Disney, blokes who'd held the zoological patent on such things. The charmer's satellite dish was programmed for surf mode. Ten seconds, and the reptile scattered into a conniption of gray-and-white static. In its place, footage from the recent Disengaged Conflict with Egypt consolidated on the screen. Two days after the March 15 ultimatum, Britain fired a volley of long-range conventional missiles from its silos near New Dover, destroying what remained of its adversary's namby-pamby air defenses and infrastructure, then followed with a volley of missiles loaded with short-lived antimaterial microbes that ate the rubber from enemy vehicles and silicon from their puters, navigational systems, and command and control centers. Next the arsenal ships fifty miles off the coast, tankerlike submarine vessels heaped with hundreds of vertically launched cruise missiles, broke surface and unleashed their ordnance: rockets of neural-disruption bio-soup that brought down a mean seventy-two-hour case of dyslexia on the population. Thousands of tiny drone saucers swooped in behind them, dropping antipersonnel devices and location sensors across the capital, some loaded with superpathogens that rooted out specific members of the brass, verifying their identities by means of their DNA sequences. Thirty-five minutes after the remaining enemy AIs committed suicide, ground troops amphibianed in to mop and occupy, sporting microbe-grown body enclosures that held off not only poison gasses and chemical agents but most projectiles, and were jazzed with artificial musculature and night-vision capability ... all tucked under a layer of biocamouflage that changed color automatically, sensed ambient temperature and then harmonized with it, rendering the wearers imperceptible to infrared detectors ...

Back to the snake for a nod to thematic unity ... and, *zap*, this talking head. Not, mind you, a head-attached-to-a-body kind of talking head, as in say a news anchor, but the real deal: a head sans accouterments sunk deep in a maroon velveteen pillow, John-the-Baptist-at-Herod's-banquet-like ... except for the tubes and filters and things hanging out from where the neck used to fit. It was, Magda recognized, Neiman-Marcus Converse, famous NorAm EPA advisor, who in his twenties had injected too much of that anti-aging Blue Prime into his gullible arms before fully understanding its commerce with the mounting UV rays. Presently he was in his mid-forties, ever so popular, an agonizingly dedicated addict for the black bang he needed just to even semi-function on a quarter-hourly basis, and the only thing left of him was his head ... sort of: he was sightless, earless, hairless, lipless, and half-tongued, scarred to a lumpy sheen with a hodgepodge of cellular crapouts, a pair of big mushroomy slits gaping where his nose used to be, and a rich frothy secretion foaming like saliva from the sparse pores that remained distantly intact across his pate.

His mouth was futzing around at present, looking like it might be testing the tensile strength of his jaws, which gesture was what in Neiman-Marcus Converse's inconsiderable cosmos passed for speech.

This sorry visual was overlaid by a voice approximating what Converse might have sounded like four or five years ago if he'd spoken through a radio-phone from the moon with his mouth full of taffy. The photocopy voice was busy explaining how there was really nothing to worry about just because a dozen canisters of radioactive waste dropped into the ocean trench off the coast of DisCal with the idea they'd be sucked into the earth's mantle by the geologic process of subduction had rifted, oh, maybe thirty seconds too early, sending a country-large toxic cloud whang into the Equatorial Counter Current toward, eventually, all things being equal, the coast of Japan ... and this at a time when the first reports were surfacing there, Loch-Ness-Monster-ish, of sentient strips of ocean, handiwork (the theory advanced by the local fishermen went) of some of the those flushed-down-the-toilet black-market nanodevices ...

A hand with asphyxia-colored nails reached out and brushed up Magda's back, roosting on the occipital bump at the base of her nobbly lilac skull. It took Magda a millisecond to separate this sensation from what she was watching on the television.

"Not much of a tune, is it?" Fiona said about the charmer's song.

Fiona massaged Magda's cranium a moment longer, then reached for her drink. Heat blotched her pale face.

The tranked kids had been replaced by a covey of affluent African tourists in beflowered shirts and formless oversized white shorts. A holographic tatt of an extremely red spider skittered up and down one of the men's white-cobwebbed legs. He raised his palmed vidcam and began recording ... not the icthyosed charmer with the erect pigtails, but the television screen beside him.

"It's not, no," Magda said.

Fiona took a sip from her cup.

"Coming up on time. Shall we slog our way to the pit?"

"You know, I was just thinking."

They began walking.

"About the show?"

"About whether there might be such a thing as a cultural rewind button."

"The emergency eject, you mean?"

"The one that gets us backed up a smidge. So we can see the presentation over again. Pause now and then along the way. Admire. Critique. Check and see if we mightn't edit it a peg differently this go-round."

It had been a lark, the date. Magda had happened upon Fiona eating a farm-prawn sandwich in the sitting room at ABNORMAL. They struck up a conversation and before long Fiona was telling her the story of being unexpectedly given the bump by her latest girlfriend, Tymm Taini, who explained to her two nights ago over an otherwise quite fabulous dessert at a Libyan café that she, Tymm, was in actual fact just using Fiona to make the guy she was genuinely sweet on, Devin Hung-chang, jealous ... a plan which, it looked like, had one hundred percent botched, and so, this being the depressing outcome, there didn't seem much point in keeping up the put-on, did there? Plus Fiona already had these two tickets to the opening of bear-baiting season and all, so ...

"Oh, I doubt it," Fiona replied. "Unit's broken, I'm afraid. Bollocksed up to a fare-thee-well. Everything's set on fastforward with those staticky lines zapping across the screen."

"So we're stranded here."

"We're stranded *there*. In the future. In the day after tomorrow. Today's already yesterday. Yesterday's the stone age."

At the base of a ramp they displayed the wash-off bar codes stamped on the back of their hands to a bored Plughead busy palpating his glands.

"Great," Magda said. "That's the best we can do?"

"What?"

"The best we can do? Consider ourselves stranded?"

"With the hurling-precipitously-into-the-future business? I have two theories." Fiona was holding her cup of lager close to her chest with both hands, protectively, like a baby bird. "First, we're getting exactly what we deserve, the bosh our karma dictates. We dickered around with one too many things we obviously shouldn't have dickered around with. All for the sake pretty much of fragrant armpits and nicely packaged junkfood."

"Or?"

"Or we're getting just what we don't deserve. We're simply being blindsided by universal circumstances beyond our control."

"And this is what we tell the kids?"

"The kids?"

"At work. The kids. This is what we tell them ... that there's no going back, it's all downhill from here?"

"Oh, well, the kids. That's another story altogether, isn't it."

Their seats, half-meter portions of a long unsteady particle-board bench, were located on the third tier. Magda could, if she leaned a few centimeters to the right, see down to the orangish baked earthen pit between the heads of the drunken men and women sitting in front of her in IBM-tartan kilts. They had a picnic going and were deep into singing a governcorp anthem out of tiny blue substitute-leather-covered books. Their hands were stunted bitty things, puppet parts, bound tightly with cloth from when they were corporate babies in order to retard osteal growth, earmark of those destined for work on the sales end of things.

In the center of the pit stood a telephone pole driven deep into the ground. Off it dangled a heavy chain. At the top of the pole was fixed an industrial-sized clock that slowly rotated three-hundred-and-sixty degrees.

The air smelled sickly sweet, a combination of fishy seawater and vinegar.

Fiona bobbed, angling for a good view of the pit.

"You decided where to go on holiday this year?" she asked.

"I haven't, no. Corfu, perhaps. Perhaps just down to the coast for a fortnight. I've always wanted to see the flood ruins."

"Killer at sunset. What's left of the Burnmouth stretch after the Melt is really quite fetching when the light catches the windows in the abandoned buildings just so. But Corfu ... the VR parlors there are simply brill. Not so encumbered by the traditional standards of the appropriate, if you know what I mean."

"The, em, children?"

"The children?"

"The kids? The other story?"

"Oh, right. That." Fiona examined her plastic cup and then tightened her eyes on the pit. A man in a black executioner's hood and sumo thong was yanking on the chain with his full bodyweight. "It's rather complicated, actually."

"How so?"

White seagulls were stapled above sampans on the Thames. Through the haze lifted the outline of St. Paul's Cathedral, chunk missing from the dome where the IRA bomb had exploded, and, far to the left, almost invisible, the Post Tower amid urban clutter like some cheesy prop out of a bad sci-fi comic. Directly below, over the roofs of the begrimed redbrick inns, casinos, and Levi-Strauss sweatshop manufacturing imitation rattlesnake-skin ten-galloners for export to the SoAm pampas, the Bankside Walk was a hash of dented appliance boxes, in front of each a meater offering his or her services to passersby.

"You fancy a bet?" Fiona asked.

"Excuse me?"

"A bet. Do you fancy one? On the tourney? I believe they're just about to sound last punt."

Magda touched the stud beneath her lower lip and experienced a rush of head chatter. The liquid oxygen was kicking in. Everything took on a glassy sheen as if viewed through contact lenses that were too strong.

She finished her drink, then asked: "How is it complicated with the children?"

"I'm really fond of you, Ms. Karter," Fiona said. "Magda. I see how hard you work with them. How much they mean to you. They really like you, you know."

"Yes, well, they're quite wonderful."

"So I thought someone should tell you before the staff meeting tomorrow. Give the news some time to soak in. Only it turns out I'm pretty much a girl's blouse when it comes to all this confrontation dibble."

"Give what news some time to soak in?"

"I'm almost forty. You'd imagine these things would prove easier by this stage. That one would gain instead of lose assurance as the years rolled on."

"I thought this was about you feeling really awful about Tymm."

"I know you did, dear."

"But it's really about you telling me something I don't want to

101

hear?"

"It is."

"So Tymm didn't tell you to bugger off?"

"Oh, no."

"You didn't break up?"

"We're a crypt job, in actual fact."

"But you …"

"The Tymm thing was a bit of a sell, you see, dear." Fiona tried to steer her words using her nose as rudder. "Sorry. Didn't want to make this all quite so cloak-and-daggerish."

"Make what so cloak-and-daggerish?"

"The part I'm about to make so cloak-and-daggerish, it appears." She looked up at the seagulls. "Blast."

"What part is that?"

"When Dr. Bogg asked me to do this? I told her not to worry. Don't give it a second thought, I said. What was I thinking? Cloak-and-dagger gag."

"Dr. Bogg already knows whatever this is."

"Everyone already knows. Dr. Bogg. Dr. Hung-chang. Our financial backers."

"Except me."

"Except you, dear. Right."

"I don't understand."

"No, of course you don't. That's because I'm not making myself especially clear. I'm trying to, mind you, but I just can't. It's the confrontation dibble, you see. Bloody English genes."

"And you're here to tell me."

"Right. I'm here to …"

A great communal cheer heaved from the congregation.

Magda and Fiona looked up.

At the end of that heavy chain now struggled a bear … a huge cloned reddish-brown grizzly with huge shoulder hump, huge stumpy elephantine legs, and huge ten-centimeter claws. It threw its head back and forth, trying to shake off its iron collar.

The IBMers in front of Magda and Fiona raised their elfin hands in powerfists and hooted.

The amphitheater entered a fresh echelon of consciousness.

"What about the children?" Magda persisted. "What did you bring me here to say?"

"Sorry sorry sorry. This is just all so, well ... so *splendid*, isn't it? I mean, the spring ... the hubbub ..."

"The, em, children, Dr. Kai-chuh?"

"Fiona, dear. Please."

"Fiona."

"Nothing like a battle for survival to pep up the spirit after a spot of the winter blahs, is there."

The pack of starved Virgin-Disney hounds, eight of them, each two-headed just like that cobra on the telly, lunged from the wings and were on the bear in a breath. They ripped at its flanks, yelping and snapping.

The clock atop the pole began ticking off seconds.

The congregation roared.

"The thing is?" Fiona shouted. "The children? The kids?"

"... ?"

"It, em ... it turns out they're not exactly, well ... it turns out they're not exactly children-like, if the truth be known."

Magda turned and stared at her.

Fiona carried on looking at the pit.

The grizzly reared back on its hind legs and swatted one of the dogs across the skull as it leapt for its chest. The dog squealed and dropped in place, shuddering with neural spasms.

"That's it, you see. They're not ... well ... *juvenile*, exactly. At least not in any genuinely *anthropoidal* sort of way, if you know what I mean."

"I *don't* know what you mean."

"Well, dear," she said, snouting for the right phrase, "I mean their brains aren't—how do you say it?—well ... their brains aren't exactly *brainlike* anymore."

"Anymore?"

"They were, you see. Once upon a time. Good gracious, will you

103

look at that." Another dog squealed and went down. "When we first examined them. They appeared perfectly normal then. Apart from that rather strange sleep-spindle deal, if you remember, which should have put the word about, actually, that something was off-brand. But Rykki's episode last month? The bad dreams? The nosebleed? That seizure? Well, we began running some more tests. It took us a while to believe what we were seeing. Except, em, it ends up, as things go, there's all manner of … well … *stuff*… in there."

"Stuff?"

"That wasn't in there last time we checked."

"What do you mean … 'stuff'?"

"I'm not exactly sure. None of us is. That's part of what we're going to talk about tomorrow. We're flying without radar, actually."

"You're saying—what?—a tumor?"

"Anomaly, dear, is what we're calling it."

"Anomaly."

"And well, the thing is, it's not organic, strictly speaking. And it's not just Rykki. It's all of them." She peeked over. "Are you going to be okay?"

"It's all of them?"

"Every one."

The information finally arrived.

"You're trying to tell me they're razzed."

"Synths. Yeah. And the thing is? They weren't synthetics a couple of months ago. At least not discernibly so. Something's been doing some codswallop up there behind our backs."

Magda lowered her head and ran the flat of her hand across its bumpy granular surface.

"So her dreams …"

"Really *aren't* her dreams. She wasn't talking metaphorically. It's phenomenal, if you stop and think about it."

The bear's flanks were matted with spittle and blood.

"You're saying the children are, what …"

"You recall our friend at number three Hans Crescent? Well, it appears he took a few unwanted newborns off their strapped mums' hands in Ease In and, em, well …"

"Shot them full of bots ..."

"Rewired their brains from the stems up. Rather a slow process, if you're going to do it right. The ultimate download ... bytes into biotics. Hardly even notice it, if you're not looking."

"But what's all that have to do with Rykki's memories?"

"We've been thinking digital reincarnation."

"Memory seepage."

"Before injecting the kids? He jabbed his pet bots into the brains of some cryos. Neurosuspension deanimates whose funds happened to be running shamefully low ..."

"Rykki's remembering their pasts."

"A kind of fagged-out immortality, if you ask me."

"He figured how to execute destructive reads."

"Disassembled the neural tissue dendrite by axon to get the info it housed."

"Part of them is waking up in the future ..."

"Rather like waking up in Istanbul, actually. Not very scary, if you stop and think about it, for people who like to travel. When you go somewhere, after all, you want it to be different from where you live. That's why you go in the first place."

"But if you don't like to travel ..."

"Then it's a nightmare. Every night. Over and over again."

Another communal discharge rose around them.

Fiona disengaged from the conversation and turned her attention to the pit.

Once the grizzly's hind legs folded it was just a matter of seconds before the dogs reached its jugular. A tube of blood pulsed from the football-sized wound in its neck. Tremors ran along its flank. Its jaws eased up, strikingly pink tongue sagging onto the baked orangish earth.

The hands on the clock stopped when its body lurched and went limp except for the jerking where the hungry dogs continued to feed.

The entire event had taken less than seven minutes.

In front of Magda and Fiona, the IBMers put down their champagne glasses and stood, preparing to enter the common epoch of the approaching Wave.

10. MIDNIGHT CONFESSION

With his big feet Dante barged up the carpeted stairs toward the third floor on his night rounds. He didn't bend his knees as he ascended, but rocked woodenly side to side, neck forgotten somewhere between his shoulder blades, arms avian appendages pressed tight to his briskets. He threw one stiff leg up a step, tossed his body on top of it, followed with the other, then repeated the movement all over again on the next step. In his dark fake-leather vest, loose dark trousers, and loose white Indian shirt, he appeared more penguinal than crowish.

Night rounds, he thought. More like middle-of-the-fucking-sparrow-fart-hours rounds, i'n'it. What was he *doing* here anyway in this bore-chore while every other decent human being alive on the planet was down at The Royal Knight's Mare playing darts, nice goddamn pint of nice goddamn lager in their nice goddamn hands?

What was he doing?

He was babysitting a git gag of sleeping chuckleheads, that's what he was doing. Bunch of VCRs with a load of fucking toasters for brains. What sort of job was that? That's what he wanted to know. What sort?

His back hurt and his legs hurt and his big feet hurt and his eyes hurt. Especially his eyes. Too much bloody looking. Check on this, see about that, get a line on the other thing. That was his problem. Now the muscles around his implants had swollen to twice their normal size, so it was hard getting a good swivel right or left. Had to look straight ahead. Study the carpet, like.

Which would make for a bleeding sad game of darts when he called it a day here, wouldn't it, him unable to give the Wink to his opponent before he let the old spears fly.

Dante halted, huffing, on the first landing. He put his hand on his heart. He sweat a while. This climbing business certainly took its toll.

That was the ace thing about darts, wasn't it. None of that running back and forth. None of that exercise shite. You just stepped up to the line, took a nice swig of the old refreshing lager, and let the javelin fly.

Tradition. Long line of warriors in this sport. Give the Wink to your opponent, bit of a friendly belch, let the games begin …

Sportsman-like, like.

Game of gentlemen among gentlemen.

Except for that arsehole who put his eyes out. Except for him. There was that. Double-gutted guy didn't play by the bleeding rules, did he. Dante should've known. Strands of fucking fiber optics implanted in his bare-arsed head in place of hair. Glow-in-the-dark nose ring. He stepped up to the line and Dante decided to employ his standard strategy. His only strategy. Little round of friendly whispering. Little bit of the odd taunt, the offhand threat. Before the match, during the announcements, in between every leg and set. Dante was a dart man. A spear jock. He knew how to play. Been doing it since he was six. And he possessed exactly one course of action when in doubt: abuse your enemy. Kick him when he was down. Laugh at his bad shots. Cough at his good ones. Seemed to always get things sorted, always ring the right bell. Except this time. Except this once. Dante sauntered on up to the line of fire when his turn came, revolved his head atop his neckless shoulders, puckered his lips in his patented Fish-Kiss at Dudley Double Gut, gave him that famous little good-luck-you-sorry-horseshite Wink … and Dudley with the fiber optic strands for hair and green torch for a nose put his eyes out. Sssssssssssssss. Picked up a fistful of darts lying beside his pint at the table where he was sitting and let them fly right into Dante's surprised orbs. Into his cheeks and forehead, too.

Having caught his breath, Dante pushed off toward the second landing. Governcorp said it'd be happy as a chop-chop with a bowl full of rice to pay his medicals, long as he had a job. "A job?" Dante asked. Dante hadn't had a job in four years. Didn't need one, either. What's with a job? Guy could get hurt, like. Got along just fine without one, thanks very much. Wake up past noon, pop a top on a nice beer, catch a bit of telly from bed, slip in the odd holoporn, fastforward through all that acting bilge to the good parts, down a couple bags of vinegar crisps, rewind, fastforward, rewind, fastforward, head over to the pub, toss back a couple pints, plate or two of bangers and mash, warm up the old arm for the night's performance.

The wrist.

It's all in the wrist.

Wrist and forearm. Don't forget the forearm.

First he loses his eyes and then this. His luck was all bunged up. Boot it or shoot it, the governcorp number had told him from her cubicle at the unemployment office, peeling tiny bits of dead skin from her cuticles. Boot it or shoot it. What choice did he have? A guy like him. All that potential. All that untapped possibility. And there he was. It just wasn't right. It just wasn't right at all.

Dante halted, huffing, on the second landing. He sweat a while. He sighed through gristle and phlegm. Starting to sound like everyfuckingone else these days, wasn't he. When did that happen? When did that like fucking sneak up on him? Didn't fancy it one bit. No. Not one bit. Whole bleeding country had turned into one grand glorious outfit of oversensitive wankers. Call a dago a dago, they go all owlshite on you. Call a bull-dyke a bull-dyke, likely as not to find yourself holding your cods in an egg basket. Can't disbleedingsparage the cot-cases. Can't even remind people the Brits made bloody burgoo out of the rest of the backwards world century before last, god love 'em, brown-sliced the lot, because the rest of the backwards world were a bunch of undercooked, shit-eating, blow-gun-licking, dimwitted, woodhick bushers. When did everyone get so fucking tetchy? When did that happen? Your old man spears the bearded clam with your sis and all of a sudden it's weep gag. Everyone wants to be the victim. Everyone wants to've been knocked bowlegged, given the chop, gotten new arseholes torn for them. Makes them feel important, is what it does. Self-righteous, like. You're a success? Well, I've been abfuckingbused by my hubby for the last thirty years while shooting up the black meds on the dole and my son guts cats on weekends and sets them afire with a blowtorch and my neighbors call me like racial slurs and beat up my anorexic auntie who's tarting just to make ends meet she's so fucking poor and my bulimic uncie's a peeper at a girl's school and my best infected friend's sleeping with her overweight priest who needs a kidney transplant and I'm not a victim I'm a survivor.

    Yeah. Right.

    Whatever happened to the square Johns? Whatever happened to the regular guys?

    Which, if you have to choose, Dante considered as he pushed off toward the third landing, was at least a bit easier to swallow than those bleeding AquariFreaks, wasn't it, everything all new-epoch-dawning rubbish and let's-hold-a-fucking-seance-to-get-in-touch-with-our-inner-child-Pluto-squared-my-fucking-arsehole. Dublin University graduates, the lot of them. Oh, right, let's feel good about ourselves while experiencing spontaneous healing and a couple of close encounters of the like I-was-a-former-kraut-serf-in-the-seventeenth-bleeding-century kind while sensing in our astrological arse-cracks that all those NorAm bleeding Indian sods weren't like the biggest fucking losers of all time but really gifted seers, right, in touch with the sodding bunnies and toadstools and shite, soldiers on the motorway to enlightenment at the public convenience down the road from the karmic battle for third-wave yank-my-bollocks, thanks very much. Oi. Show me the Tenth bleeding Insight of Uranus and I'll show you my Irish fucking root. Show me the Pure Energy Fields of the Great bleeding Transformation of Taoistic Dimensions in the Grand Guilt-Free Moment of the Human Potential Movement and I'll show you my puckered fucking brown eye. One word for you, mates. Just one. Cut the crap, eh? Get like a fucking clue. Stand on your own two bleeding feet. And grow the fuck up. Go on now. Do it. Grow. The fuck. Up.

Dante halted, huffing, on the third landing. He sweat a while. He put his hand on his heart. He unfettered an oniony burp from deep beneath his solar plexus and took a few quiet seconds to relish its piquant aroma. So there he was. A nice guy like him. All that potential. All those games of darts to be played. All those pints to be tipped. And there he was. Doing what? Sodding about with a bunch of little kitchen appliances with legs.

He didn't, he decided, especially like children.

He couldn't remember ever having been a child himself and so had no idea how to act around them. Truth was, they made him feel... uncomfortable, is what it was. Spastic. Little Martians that just weren't like you or me trying to suck out your soul, like ... *I want your fucking time ... I want your bloody attention and I want it now ... I want every sodding second of your sodding day.* They moved lurky and they thought lurky and they talked lurky. You cracked a joke around them, they just stared at you. Tried to chew the rag with them, they had a vocabulary of like two words. Ask them what they did, they'd tell you not much. Ask them where they were going, they'd say just out. Turn your back on them, though, and the laffs'd begin, wouldn't they. One big party behind that closed door called their foreheads. They smelled funny. They acted funny. They asked too many questions. Their fingernails were filthy. They reminded you of what a fuckwit you actually were. They were disrespectful, too, like, annoying, loud, thoughtless. They lied. They stole. They cheated. They exhibited just way too much bleeding energy in public. They needed sedatives, the whole lot of them, a good handful of barbs. They had like no idea of the consequences of their actions and so always crapped things up and then started going all screamy and weepy *because* they'd just figured out what they'd just done because they had like no idea of the consequences of their actions and that meant they had no control over their world which in their eyes was run by an army of fascist cyclopean adults with chains and whips and electric cattle prods and things like that and they needed to take a fucking nap anyway. They lived in a different city, didn't they. A different country. They lived two galaxies over and one down.

110

Adults were the gatecrashers of the stronghold, is what they were.

Dante didn't understand children and they didn't understand him. Fine. Brilliant. But the look they gave him. What was that? What did they fucking expect? Dante knew. Dante knew what they fucking expected. They fucking expected his fucking essence. That's what they fucking expected. They had an eye on his bleeding soul. He could tell. Anyone could. Just look at them. They wanted to make his spirit theirs like a brood of bloody whatyoucallem suckerbees.

Pay attention to me, their eyes said, *play with me now, play with me NOW... I vhant to suck your blood... I vhant to suck your blood...* And then that terrible terrible laughter only children can assemble...

Having savored his inner being, Dante pushed off down the dimly lit early-a.m. corridor. He began to hum. Little medley of tunes off the Pope's album. Fucking fantastic sounds, too, mate. Bleeding nazi. White-robe fever all the way. Dante was hooked on that guy. Just couldn't get enough of the old pontiff.

Okay. Awright. Okay. Enough with the ballsaching. Right. Enough with the crushing sob stuff. Truth was, if he took a min to think about it, this was a pretty good deal he had going here, wasn't it, even with the bore-chore business, even with the aluminum-pated ankle-biters, all said and bleeding done. This'd just do. Yeah. Bite on that a bit. Go on. Truth was, he had more freedom than most, didn't he. More fucking potential, too, as a humanfuckingbeing. Dante was ... what? A man, mate. He was a man's man. He was a man's man's man. He knew where he stood, like. He knew what was what. He knew where he'd been and where he was going.

He knew, he told himself as he put his hand on the handle of the first door in the corridor, how to have a good time. He knew, he told himself as he rotated that handle, which end was up. He knew, he told himself as he pushed that door open and reached into his loose back pocket and pulled out his electric torch, this job was just a minor diversion on the great carriageway of life.

No, he told himself as he raised the torch hip-high, old Dante

111

was a winner. Old Dante was a go-getter. Old Dante was a …

"Oi," Old Dante said. "What's this?"

The lightcone illuminated an over-exposed eight-legged two-headed monster fidgeting among a commotion of pursed sheets and pillows. It writhed and reared up.

Dante's vestigial neck retracted half a vertebra.

"What's this, then?"

The teratoid breached and tore itself in half. It rendered down into two smaller teratoids, and the two smaller teratoids rendered down into Rykki and Zivv, huddling together, eyes wide with shock.

Those sodding eyes.

Their hands in the act of withdrawing from each other's bodies. Their lips in the act of parting from each other's lips.

"What the fuck's this, then?"

Rykki made the first move. She always did. She ducked and rolled toward the edge of the bed, arachniding toward the carpet, hands protecting her face. But Old Dante had seen that maneuver before, knew it down to the ground. It was just a bit of the Game, bit of the set, wasn't it, and another step and he was there already, hulking, penguin-turned-crow, another step with his big feet and his own open hand was flying through the air like a white bird, yeah, that's it, like a beautiful javelin… like … like one of Dudley Double Gut's darts, and, *whump,* it kicked her back like a jolt from British Electric, didn't it, *whump,* right back into the headboard, *whump,* right into the other fucking little perv's chest, and then Old Dante's open hand was flying again in the nervous lightcone like a superhero on a world-saving mission smack into Zivv's left ear, *whump,* careful to keep those knuckles out of the picture, you bet, keep the old dope to a minimum, and the shite's sodding metal-packed pate snapped right, *whump,* and snapped left, because it's all in the wrist, isn't it, the wrist and the forearm, the wrist and the forearm and the triceps, and Old Dante couldn't help himself, mate, just couldn't help himself, as he slid into the fun stuff, had to give a bit of the old Wink to the kids, didn't he, had to bare his brown-rimmed teeth in the old patented Fish-Kiss, had to start flat-out, well, laughing, really, from right down where the oniony breath is kept somewhere below the solar plexus, because this was just up in the paints, wasn't it, *whump*, this was the pearler here, *whump*, because it just didn't get any better than this, *whump*, the golden information arriving.

11. BRAIN WARS

TRIS

they think I'm slow say *Tris take your time* but it's not that it's my mind
won't stop it's I can't shut it off can't slow it down in the space between
words this spill of language there's no sleeping and that's how I heard
them through the wall how I hear them every time his footfalls coming
down the corridor but they're too busy to pay attention the door swinging
back the fright in the air like static everyone thinking I'm slow but I can
hear it thrumming *oi, what's this?* the long blare of silence quick bumps
of footsteps the fall of hand through dark air *and me so fucking good to
you bleeding little sods this is what you do to say fucking thanks a lot
mate isn't it* clunk of bone against plaster *you fucking mentals* clunk of
bone against bone *after all I done* words teething through the pillow
tucked over my head no matter what *who was it took you to the bleeding
to the bloody zoo* and he did he took us there he took us to see the splice-
monsters the Virgin-Disney bio-copyrighted products of cellular-
mechanics Goofy part human part elongated pathetic dog-thing hands
too big white-glove tissue mutant feet unusable except to drag back and
forth Mickey mega-rodent with a chimp's disposition skull almost too big
to hold erect without the brace buried below its flesh smile burned into
its chromosomes with just enough intelligence to know how sad its life
really is the fat woman the whale woman thirty-meter-tall invertebrate
drooling and incontinent nothing but folds of living adipose tissue piles
of adipose creases pleats crimps of adipose tiny head buried where the
bellybutton should have been tiny Asian eyes stretched by glut that said

114

kill this thing I've become and the families throwing shelled peanuts through the bars though she had no arms to catch them trying to prod the white dimpled mass that was like them and not like them Jada standing beside me crying you could hardly hear her because the others were laughing pointing tipping back biodegradable cans of cold foamers come on down and have a little peek at the aberration-creations so you can feel a bit better about yourselves your own skrimmed lives unable to articulate who you are or why you're here because you know after he leaves that room after he throws her back into the room across the hall my sister my undone sister and closes the door behind him he's coming to visit me

VOX NOTES. MAGDA KARTER. 10 JUNE, 9:00 A.M.

I disagree vehemently, Dr. Hung-chang. I can't believe we're even discussing this. They're not some pack of unmanageable dogs, you know. I urge you to reconsider.

VOX NOTES. DR. HUNG-CHANG. 10 JUNE, 3:10 P.M.

I quite understand your concern, Ms. Karter, and to a good degree sympathize with it, but, as you know, beginning last week Dr. K'ai-chuh and I began to note the first signs of sexual awareness among our charges ... the increase in those special sorts of questions, to be sure, but also those quite physical manifestations, those public and private displays of intimacy. It's clear that psychologically they've embarked on the road to adolescence, perhaps presenting its markers in heightened form. I know how much they mean to you. They mean the world to each and every one of us here. But we must all remember the larger context in which we're working. Otherwise, we are doing them a great disservice.

ORAN

Ohhhhh-rahahahahahahan, she says to me across the table in our classroom at the commencement of daily lessons. *Ohhhhhh-*

rahahahahan. Oran. Sphinctering of lips into a tight *o* that pushes forward, stretching, and almost shuts the mouth into an *r*, tongue retracting like a snake up and back … and then the release of the *a*, the slide into the grimacing *n*.

Oran.

Me.

Tell us about mining, about space mining, she says.

Right, I say, touching the top of my head. Right. Well … the Space Age began to fizzle in the eighties, didn't it, as NASA started collapsing following the Challenger explosion, and the Russian program began collapsing following the failure of the Soviet Union, because … because the grand dreams turned out to be too … too pricey, didn't they.

Pricey? asks Magda.

The Russian program budget was cut by ninety percent, says Rykki, chewing blue bubble gum. The Baikonur/Tyuratam launch facilities fell to Kazakhstan. The Kazakhs turned off the electricity.

Fires, I say. Tumbleweeds.

The Gagarin Cosmonaut Training Center northeast of Moscow became a tourist trap for Westerners. Up on Mir they found instruments they no longer knew the function of.

Because? asks Magda.

Because you need an opponent to have competition, takes up Zivv, leg joggling under the table, all that energy waiting.

Brilliant. Magda raises a Kleenex to her nose and snuffs. Her forehead purples. It's not just the cold. You can see it in her limp blurry look. And so … ? she says.

We all exchange looks.

I nibble at my thumb.

And so, Rykki says, funding becomes increasingly chancy. The National Aeronautics and Space Administration gives way to the Global Space Administration.

She blows a bubble that cracks and glues blue to her lower lip. She sucks it in with a reverse hiss.

Small, cheap and practical, says Zivv.

116

Unmanned, says Jada.

She squeezes at something behind her right ear. Jada is scared of what the world will do to her, every breath quick and tense.

Tris doesn't say anything. He sits splayed in his bucket seat, arms folded across chest, as if the chair's too small for him, looking. He looks so hard you can hear it.

Unmanned? asks Magda.

Circumspection, I say, isn't it.

Cir-cum-*spec*-tion. A full, buttery word.

They observe me. I observe them ... but see instead an aerial view of Beijing sparkling through haze of an aluminum-lit evening, 3-D video game glittering red-and-white light strings below, just like Rykki says it will be, every night in bed.

On the other side of the gritty translucent window behind me an emphysemic car gripes along Upper Phillimore Gardens. Someone drops keys on the pavement ... *ka-chink.* And, somewhere on the other side of Beijing, Rykki's voice explains about robots, replacing the flesh that doesn't belong in such desperate provinces, constructing the first greenhouses and barracks on Mars, preparing for human arrival in five or seven years aboard a solar-sail-driven spacecraft traveling several hundred kils a second, here to there in less than a month when the time comes, the whole solar system as accessible as earth was in the Age of Steamships ... and maybe by the end of the decade on to the asteroid belt for mining and population, thinning the overcrowding here and providing resources, a tube-full of nanobots rocketed ahead to fully equip habitats for living colonists genetically enhanced to fight off calcium depletion, heart shrinkage, memory loss, space disorientation, claustrophobia, badlands desolation, techbugs using indigenous carbon and metal ores to make billions of copies of themselves, fabricating tanks and charging them with oxygen, sewing bionic gardens, forging small cities whose buildings appear more organic than anything on this planet, crooked, flexed, squashed, accrued like barnacles on the hull of a sunken galleon.

The bots know only two things in their silicon souls: *reach* and *flourish.*

117

That's all they are, really, just these two impulses, everything else an environmental impediment to overcome ...

My skin is the color of flatworms, my irises pink like the walls of a ladies'-room.

I look at Rykki chewing, at Jada squeezing, at Zivv joggling, at Tris who can't think of things to say because his head is bolting with word-noise, and smiles edge across our faces, unobtrusively, another biomorphic stain smudging Magda's forehead.

VOX NOTES. DR. K'AI-CHUH. 29 JUNE, 11:15 A.M.

The problem with immunocontraceptives, it seems to me, is that at best they will function for about a year. After that their effectiveness drops off rather precipitously and matters turn iffy, as you know. And who can guess where our charges might be by then, under what agency's jurisdiction? This, coupled with my concern that we simply don't know how the inoculations' induced immune responses will interact with the diagnosed neural anomalies, leads me to tend to favor other means to attain our ends.

VOX NOTES. DR. BOGG. 2 JULY, 3:35 P.M.

We have been instructed to treat said anomalies not only as potentially transmittable digital diseases but also as possible incubating pandemics until we can determine otherwise. It thus strikes me that our course of action has become quite clear.

VOX NOTES. DR. HUNG-CHANG. 3 JULY, 2:10 P.M.

Dr. K'ai-chuh: would you please prepare our charges for surgical castrations and hysterectomies, respectively, and address the question of which sex-drive suppressants might best work given current circumstances?

VOX NOTES. DR. K'AI-CHUH. 3 JULY, 3:45 P.M.

Certainly. Dr. Hung-chang: would you please relieve Ms. Karter of her duties with respect to this case and reassign her upstairs?

VOX NOTES. DR. HUNG-CHANG. 3 JULY, 4:30 P.M.
Done.

ZIVV

She's like all *Zivv if you want to watch just sit still,* and I'm like all *Okay okay okay,* me this gnome stuffed under a bridge made of baggied books and folders and such in her shadowy office ten in the stale p.m., chin on knees, cuz I don't know how to say it … it's just like she's a totally cool lady … and so when she asks me to come down after dinner I'm like all *I'll be there* and she's like all *Fant.* She hasn't even extracted her head from that Sennheiser headmount since she slipped into it at seven and my left foot won't stop that thing it does. Sometimes trying to live inside your own body is like trying to live inside someone else's space suit. Magda's *rapt,* like, like some race-car driver tubing into the curves with his eyes shut and his brakes fugged but it doesn't matter cuz he's got finish lines to cross. She's punching air with her data-glove, but I can't figure it, cuz she's like all *Zivv if you want to watch just sit still, this is really important,* and I'm like all *Okay okay okay,* but the space she's cramming into that thing is pure white-robe fever, is what it is, has to be, cuz she reaches over just now and flicks the manual on the shiny black plastic thimble-box hooked to her unit and *zap* she's into DNA-memory add-on now, the Mao-Mao force working like oil-burners for a long-overdue fix cuz you can hear the electronic whispers and purrs flowing up into a really crank electronic symphony, and Magda's cruising the ether wave … except then I like flash on that other sound and such? The subsonics of Mr. Cabbage-Head of the Lime Aftershave, Esq. You can tell he's on his way up, rounds a little different every night, *Bit of the old surprise tactic, eh?* Well, I'm like all *It's time, Magda, it's time,* only she can't hear cuz of the channeling and headmount and I'm like all *Let's go let's go let's go* and she's like all *What is it now, Zivv?* and but so I'm up on my knees shaking her shoulders to bring her back into the Big Television and she's all like *Huh?* and I'm all like *Party's over*, out from under the headmount, and the Mao-Maos are doing some sweet indecipherables, and everything's a skorry just in time cuz then the door like opens and he's all like *Oi, what's this?* But Magda is totally *good*, is what she is, totally like calm-and-what-seems-to-be-the-problem-here-sir, *Just going over a bit from the lesson this morning, aren't we, Zivv*, and but then I surprise myself cuz on the outside I'm like all *Yah, right, showing me some vid of the Royals giving their last little farewell from the balcony of the Palace before the Final Abscondence and such*, and he's all like *Yeah, well, YOU* (pointing to me) *don't belong here and YOU* (pointing to Magda) *shouldn't be like guffing with the toys, now, should you, so why don't we all just move it along, eh?* and she's all like fuck-you-very-much *Right, we're all done here anyway, ta*, and I'm all like my armpits just turned into the Irish Sea and I'm *leaking*, my body has actually sprung a thousand *leaks*, I'm like dripping sweat out of every pore and orifice on every centimeter of my epidermis. But inside my space suit? It's a whole different story in there. Cuz inside I'm like flipping Mr. Cabbage Head of the Lime Aftershave, Esq. the big one, wishing him with a cute little harmless babe-in-the-decompression-tube grin a go-fuck-yourself-a-dead-horse kind of evening, jumping up and down in there and yelling like every obscenity I can think of, cuz the yutz? The yutz is like the cheesiest of the cheesy gowks I've ever seen, and but then that's okay, don't you see, cuz like he just lost, is the thing, the fuckhole, and we just like won ...

12. VAMPIRIC LESIONS
IN THE PSYCHIC DELIVERANCE

On the Picadilly Line, Magda reached into her fraud-suede knapsack and extracted her laptop with built-in wireless modem. It was the size of a thin handbag, only looked more like a shellacked mahogany box with brass fittings and trim, remotely nautical and Victorian, with her name carved in sober Roman letters across its face.

She opened it and brushed first the backlit display on the left and then the backlit display on the right.

The tube clattered and squeaked rodentially around her as it lurched from outside air into tunnel, shifting tracks so abruptly Magda jerked into the anabolic dweeb beside her. He'd razored the back-half of his head and cultivated a cotton-candy pompadour on the front-half. He flaunted extracted fingernails and exuded a vitamin-B stink. But Magda could feel if not hear her puter activate and decided to pretend, like most people on tubes usually decide to pretend, that she hadn't really just bumped into somebody else, wasn't bumping into somebody else right now in what in other circumstances might be construed as a possibly lewd gesture.

Soon she was talking to the Gateway in what would legally cease being her office at 12:01 this morning. Before she left, she'd vox-noted her resignation to Dr. Bogg, who would receive it at eight, but would presumably be too busy with other matters to actually hear it till well past noon, at which point Magda would be in juridically fluid low-orbit on her way home to Armstrong City ... somewhere again between departing and

121

arriving, some amphibious state not quite here and not quite there ... only somewhere that just had to be a lot better than this.

The tube rattled and shook and skreeked and clanked and jangled. Magda couldn't hear Mao Zedong ask what he could do her for, so she pressed the TEXT icon from the menu running along the bottom of both displays and a comic-book word-bubble appeared over his toothy smiling head.

Above and across the car hung a queue of posters. The first explained what to do in the presence of an unmarked package, especially if you smelled anything even vaguely chemical or biologic around it. The second was for the Chungking acupuncture franchises and showed a happy white-haired eyebrowless Asian woman with a face pinned like a spiny sea urchin. The third and fourth were unreadable because someone had graffitied over them the Swahili word for *faith*, IMANI, in day-glo green, and someone else had added a couple Arabic words most likely about the advancing global Jihad in day-glo yellow since they were accompanied by a little stick-figure infidel hanging by his testicles from a little burning stick-figure tree.

Magda typed commands and believed she sensed the moon exerting its gravitational force on the earth, braking it, slowing it down a minuscule jot every instant, so each day would last just a millisecond longer than the day before.

The tube wrenched tracks again and dropped another level below ground. A row of caged safety bulbs whizzed by on the other side of the till-now-black-reflecting window. Magda worried about losing the modem signal with all this concrete between her and her Gateway. Across from her, a walnut-skinned guy in cash silver-blue VR mirrorshades swayed his head like a blind man next to a woman Magda's age who was so black she was almost purple next to a pale emaciated teenage girl with raccoon-mascaraed heroin-chic eyes and glue-on neck scalds who was gazing straight in front of her and unselfconsciously performing a series of maxillofacial stretching exercises.

Magda's nose drained.

She expelled a reflexive adenoidal honk and felt instantly

embarrassed, then realized most people would be extremely surprised to think how few other people around the globe were paying attention to them at any particular minute.

The anabolic dweeb with the vitamin-B stink leaned into her for maybe the hundredth time. Magda pinkied ENTER. Mao Zedong's face froze in that signature smile while it received her new data. The tremendous noise around her sounded like a building continuously caving in. Mao Zedong's face thawed. He put his hands together as if in prayer and bowed, then straightened and waved a teeny palm goodbye.

Magda waved back.

Petrina Bogg farted almost subaudibly in the midst of a nearly bottomless sleep in her Knightsbridge flat just down Pavilion Road from Harrods' counterfeit-gothic façade, one-hundred-percent satisfied with her life even in unconsciousness, with her successful career as chief pediatric psychiatrist at ABNORMAL, with her forty-year marriage, and even with the delicate floral-pattern sheets under which her expansive corporeality—with whose magnitude she had made emotional peace years and years ago, learning to love her excess as if it were the children she'd never had—formed a sort of rubbery dune.

She chased the fart, a bitter seeping febrile maroon affair, with a Morse code of clicks in her elderly throat, which would have awakened her husband, Fenton LeBonk, the puny excitable MP who reminded everyone who ever met him of a terrier on bams and always spoke without moving his jaw … *if* Fenton had been asleep, which he hadn't, for what felt to him like weeks, since he was instead busy planning his escape from this desiccated sarcoma called a mate first thing in the morning. He'd been planning it for months. His left foot vibrated with impatience beneath the sheets, willing the night to get a move on. The tip of his left forefinger tried to rub the prints off the tip of his left thumb. And when the acerbic maroon fart-haze hit him, he almost leapt from bed and sprinted around and whacked the grotesque, arrogant, miserly, priggish, self-infatuated, sexually stillborn seal known as his wife upside the head. But he didn't. He couldn't. His eyes watered with the fart's stench. His foot trembled with such rapidity the sheets slowly slipped off it. Just a while longer. Just a few hours. Then he'd be free. His throat burned. His heart thonked. Petrina would, clicking and clearing her esophagus of a semiliquid clot, rise at 6:30 a.m., shower, preen, eat like a malnourished hippopotamus in an especially fecund lily-pad-laden swamp, and leave for the office at 7:20. At 7:35 Fenton would be in a taxi on his way to Victoria Station, where in front of the Chungking acupuncture franchise he would meet his lover, Aki Pella, the mind-rattlingly ginchy eighteen-year-old blonde with those to-eat-nails-for cosmetically enhanced milkers, muscle-grafted arse, and pheromone-garnished bacon sandwich, who had worked one week and two days as his secretary before he got up the nerve to shoot her a line and give her a bit of the horizontal rumble on his desk, and who would now accompany him with the remainder of his not-at-all-insubstantial credit-line (thanks to his grandfather, who'd invested wisely on the ground floor of the Air Pyrate Muzzik skyscraper) to a little increasingly tropical island off the coast of Sweden where they would lie lavishly on the breezy beach and brown like waffles next to the neon-blue Baltic (recolored every morning by servants who tip-toed beyond the NO SWIMMING: BIOHAZARD signs with massive plastic barrels of cheerful-looking dye strapped to their backs), he thought, but where he would in fact three months hence suffer anaphylactic shock alone in his cottage after eating some bad borscht and drinking a fifth of single malt the day after Aki, bored to a state approaching snail-consciousness by the flaccid little high-strung rotten-mouthed dictator Fenton had become in her eyes the second his not-as-substantial-as-he-thought-it-might-be credit expired, left him without even a perfunctory vox, electronic, or hardcopy note saying adios, amigo, and he would lie there twitching on the terra cotta tiles like a severed power line in a hurricane, unhealthy white foam drooling down his once clean-shaven chin, remembering that last interminable night in bed next to putrid Petrina, and be simply amazingly ecstatic to have gotten away from her even if this was what it finally took.

But was incorrect.

For when he awoke from his coma six months later,

vegetablized, unable to so much as semi-bend his big toe, the first thing he would see would be none other than said miasmic not-so-little woman, throat clicking along like a ticker tape, having forgiven and forgotten, heart aflutter with love and relief, waiting to take care of her honeybunch (the guy who no longer had the ability even to modestly quaver his own incontinent eyelids, let alone attempt another thought about exodus), for the rest of his leafy-greens life.

Petrina would raise the small clear vial of shell-toxin in her pudgy paw, once, barely long enough for him to focus on it and manifest comprehension by a little flaring of his left nostril, tuck it away in her floral-pattern dress, and smile at him with very real affection.

Splayed tummy-down across her king-sized futon, which when unfolded took up all the floor space except that occupied by her fridge, microwave, sound system, and sex-toy collection in her eighth-story governcorp-subsidized flat which overlooked, if you craned your neck to the nerve-tweaking brink, Hype Ark, Fiona made sluffing sounds into the dental dam spread across Tymm Tai-ni's hooped and studded pudendum. Somewhere above her, Tymm Tai-ni made sluffing sounds back. They'd been at it for almost an hour, Fiona having awakened Tymm from a profound sleep by means of her aerodynamically efficacious nose, herself having awakened from a profound sleep by means of an extremely randy dream in which she was pretty much doing what she was at this moment in reality pretty much doing. Tymm opened and closed her white cockeyed collagen-injected lips in the mindless manner of a pithed frog and shifted position ever so scantily to further emphasize her clitoral nub, which had taken on the hue of a tightly-squeezed fingertip. Her breasts bounced exactly once, down, up, as she executed this. The Pygmy Children's just-released album, *Kujichagulia Guntz*, a present this afternoon from Tymm to Fiona on the occasion of their four-month anniversary together, played in the background, soothing puerile moans adding to the general sense of acoustic gratification in the flat. Someone far below in the street yelled something in Chinese. Someone else answered in Russian. A toilet flushed and water tore through pipes in the walls. Fiona reached up and gently inserted a pinkie through each of the holes in Tymm's palms and tugged. The couple was still at that stage in the early days of their relationship where every act of virus-sharing was an involuted experiment the dimensions of which would make Victor Frankenstein shudder with respect and apprehension. The futon was their almost-nightly laboratory, their fingers, tongues, noses, toes and hips their petri dishes and parabolic antennae. A car horn chirped. Every intimate act was an act of discovery ... an understanding that, as Fiona grubbed into her partner's dam, hurled an epiphany into the center of her consciousness and set it off like an exploding satellite in the night sky. The hottest chamber in hell, Fiona realized sometime past two in the morning in this soggy little corner of this cruddy little city, should be reserved for all the complainers in the world, the kvetchers and gritchers, the morose, the despondent, the never-ever happy no matter what they or anyone else did, the figurative can kickers and party-pooping naysayers, the forever too foot-draggingly tired or face-rubbingly blue or mean-spiritedly suspicious to get up and *do* something, those who didn't comprehend that the goal of every day was to achieve something and enjoy something and those who would remain forever dissatisfied with the hand fate dealt them no matter what hand that might be and those who believed along with certain ancient bumper stickers that life sucked and then you died and those who had become one with their couches and those who waited for someone else or something else or the hope of someone else or something else to initiate even the teeniest action on their parts and those who belligerently bought into the cynically arched single eyebrow or existentially stooped shoulders and those who never forgot and those who never forgave and those who couldn't care less and those who said *whatever* and those who let their hormonal dips guide their progress through becoming and those who never listened to their hormones at all and those who blamed an amoral universe for everything that went wrong in their lives and those who blamed their parents and those who blamed themselves and those who therefore drank too much or smoked too much or shot too much shite into their tattered veins and those who were just incredibly transcendentally content to barely slack by doing the least they possibly could 24/7 instead of relishing their potential and the potential of others and those who believed love like God was a moribund concept and those who somehow just never had the energy to cherish every respiring second as if they'd just been diagnosed with a terminal disease and those who had an excuse for everything and those who had an excuse for nothing and those who believed it was just never good enough whatever *it* was and those who believed confrontation was somehow more healthy than compromise and those who believed all human relationships were doomed to failure and thus made sure all the ones they were involved in failed and those who believed people could never really communicate with one another and thus made sure they didn't communicate with anyone ... but most of all those who had tricked themselves by all kinds of psychic presdigitations out of these unutterably special redemptive spans where there was nearly too much to touch and smell and taste and hear and see and think, and but most of all to touch.

Magda's Dracula program spread its black cape and opened its yellow eyes.

It hovered in vapors of zeros and ones almost two hours, gradually coming alert, before teetering and falling forward, dropping batlike into the mind of ABNORMAL's AI in the form of a piddlingly bad idea you dismiss before you've even finished having it.

The AI scanned itself, distantly cognizant of some disturbance in its matrices, then moved on to other business while the virus rotated its pointy-eared head so slowly the AI never thought to look back and scrutinize the insignificant motion within itself, and deliciously sank its fangs into the necks of the Panasonic robotic bubble-guards that rolled through the third-story corridors at night, convincing them as it sucked away both that they were deaf for five minutes and that upon regaining their auditory capacity they wouldn't remember ever having been deaf. It repeated this process on the window-latch programs, persisting till it didn't matter to them whether they were latched or not.

Done, it unhurriedly inserted its left hand into its mouth and began masticating. Over the next seventeen minutes it consumed its left arm, its right, and both legs. Next it curled forward in a series of almost intangible gestures and started eating its own torso.

When all that remained was its pointy-eared head, its tongue spurted from its mouth and whipped around till it had enshrouded the residue in a translucent pink film that itself began to feed.

Devin, terrified, lay flat on his back under the mildew-scented towels that passed as sheets on his rattan mat and tried to focus on the ceiling in the mercury-colored urban midnight light. Two hours earlier he'd taken a fairly large hit of permeable jax off the inhaler buried in his music-chip collection, but it had been a bogus hit from a spoiled lot, which Devin learned too late. Now the ceiling was swarming with fat black ants. It seemed, in truth, that the ceiling didn't even quite exist anymore, that it had been insectivally devoured, the ants had somehow *become* the ceiling in the act of ingesting it ... a vibrant black undulating mass. Which would have been really unpleasant in itself, no doubt, except that wasn't all. The ants? The ants weren't just *above* his head. They were *inside* his head as well. He could feel them skittering over the bones that comprised his skull where all that facial and cranial skin of his used to hang. He could feel them seething in place of the tongue in his mouth. They rushed through his sinuses and over the backs of his eyeballs. They migrated up his otic canals, nibbled through his ear drums, made burger of his hammers and anvils and stirrups and cochleae, single-filed down his Eustachian tubes, and blasted up his auditory nerves in a screech of B-film noise. They assembled massive ant ranches in the creases of his cerebral cortex and the queen, fat and gloopy and gnarled like a big white turd, excavated his cerebellum and wrapped her starched napkin around her horrible neck that joined her horrible cyborgish head to her horrible cyborgish thorax and picked up her mandibular knife and fork and went to gustative town while birthing thousands of larval rice-eggs every minute, which was awful, godawful, but not as really godawful as when her troops forced their way down Devin's esophagus in one big ramrod and then branched out into his lungs, ripping their way through mealy tissue and planting hundreds of larvae in some of the smaller less important semi-mucusy lung sacs, meaning Devin began to cough, feeling like he couldn't catch his breath, till he forgot about that slight discomfort because they had also made their way into his heart, at which point he lurched into a full-blown grand-mal seizure, or what from his perspective felt like a full-blown grand-mal seizure, but couldn't have been, honestly, since he still retained consciousness. Those breasts. Except what *really* scared him was when they got into his stomach, which felt like he'd just gargled with a liter of Sani-Flush laced with drawing pins and kirby grips, this flaming mass of damnation erupting into volcanic steam clouds when it hit meaty bottom and pretty much vaporizing his gall bladder and liver, and you didn't even want to ask about his bile duct or poor little fried knot of duodenum, before whooming full-speed-ahead into his intestines, both large and small, like so much superheated plasma, causing him instantaneously to go liquid, simultaneously projectile vomiting blood-ants from his mouth, on the one hand, and spewing them in a hot muddy red jet from his anus, on the other, before what *really* spooked him happened, which was that he then just sort of went ... supernova. One second he was there and the next he detonated, ka-*blam!*, covering the ceiling, which had become ants, and the walls, which had become ants, and the floors, which had become ants, with, well, ants and more ants and chunks of organs and flaps of skin and wads of hair, *his* organs and skin and hair, or at least that's what it felt like, only he maintained a certain essential third-party awareness throughout all this, an occurrence which has to shake you up, but not as much as when those organ-chunks and skin-flaps and hair-wads that used to be him sprouted compound eyes and six lallies apiece and antennae and almost imperceptibly small stingers on their bottoms and started tooling away, single-file, a miniature battalion of buggish body parts marching in different directions, merging with the ant-soup all around them, the ant sea, and Devin lay there, terrified, flat on his back, just watching his shredded selves disappear into the deep, into the dark, into that huge black nidus of bloodcurdling selflessness.

*   *   *

Rykki sat up telephone-pole straight right out of a bad dream in which she had just inserted her father's gifts into her head and looked around and seen Nothing. Not the nothing special with small *n* and small *s*, but the Nothing Incarnate with a capital *N* and capital *I*, existential nish, the kind of absolute nonexistence you experience ten kils deep in the ocean, in a cave, at night, if you happen to be a sightless frail-bodied parchment worm living in a mud-filled burrow, and the sun way above you happens to have burned itself out, and the sky happens to be clouded over, and the seawater happens to be the same temperature as your skin, or what passes as your skin, so you can't tell where you leave off and the rest of the wholesale darkness begins.

She sat there panting till she was ninety-nine percent sure this wasn't in actual fact the dream part, then bicycled her damp sheets down with her feet, slid out of bed, and padded her way toward the door.

Dr. Jarndyce Mizzle-Sluggbury, the one-hundred-and-twenty-four-year-old Klub Med executive, rubbed the side of his bearded face which didn't work and rezzed up his phone by voice-activating the petabyte nanoputer that was his wool tie, only the screen remained blank black.

"Blast," he said.

Last remnants of the plaguey Egyptian forget-me-nots after the Disengaged Conflict, he suspected ... terrorists hacking in and shutting down vast tracts of the British Telecom Network till the razzheads caught up with them and brain-stewed them over the wires.

He decided he'd try back again in five.

Meantime, he rearranged himself in his plushly padded recliner, closed his eyes, and took a sip of dark port from the crystal snifter in his right hand. Gabrielli's golden trumpets emanated from the gray-green fitted carpet around him. The recliner, sensing the statistical probability of his needs, activated its heater and massage unit. The bio-lights in his climate-controlled office on the twenty-first story of the Diacomm headquarters above Victoria Station dimmed. The explosives-proof screen retracted from the full-wall high-impact-plastic window that appeared from street-level to be part of the building's redbrick exterior.

He opened his eyes and saw London's low skyline glistering before him like an upside-down country night sky from his youth all the way to Grosvenor Bridge, the Thames, DungeonLand, and beyond into Battersea and Clapham.

He felt full.

He blinked and Anna Tesler-Hungtington's lids slipped open in his recollection. Her eyes swiveled about wildly, trying to place herself.

Dr. Jarndyce Mizzle-Sluggbury shook his head.

He tried to zero in on the Abbey Business Center in the far distance.

He raised his glass to his lips and took another sip.

He contemplated watching a few minutes of *The Final Summons*, that euthanasia gameshow broadcast from off the coast of Thailand, but ultimately decided against it.

As Magda adjusted her worn gray elastic g-net pouch around her aboard the British Airways shuttle on its launch pad at Heathrow, and the flight attendant with fishy webbing between her fingers and no discernible pause between her shaggy eyebrows provided safety instructions on a large-screen puter at the front of the cabin, the last byte that had been the binary visitor to ABNORMAL popped out of existence.

Dante cupped the handle to the door leading to Rykki's room in his palm and experienced this thought: *Before the game of darts, every man is small.*

An hour earlier, the last child, Tris, had slid down the slippery white plumbing pipes designed to impede burglars' ascent on the outside of number nine Upper Phillimore Gardens and clumped to the redwood-chipped ground amid the enormous globoid shrubs hedging the building.

He stood breathing with the others, hands on hips.

The air tonight smelled like tomatoes that had passed their freshness peak and been marinated in a light paraffin-and-cat-piss base. A car rolled grittily by on Argyll Road. Everyone took in their new condition. Somewhere on Heistreet a two-note emergency-vehicle siren dopplered by. The children were wearing the clothes Devin had bought them at the Imperial Mallmaze. Zivv's smog-colored t-shirt with the logo stenciled across it in copper appeared to glow in the mercury-colored light.

Several blocks east, deep inside Kensington Gardens, an outrush of drumming, wooden sticks on oil barrels, became discernable ... Somalian tribes communicating with each other by a method that couldn't be traced easily or tapped electronically by the law.

"Right, then," Rykki whispered. "Ready?"

"As we'll ever be," said Zivv.

Oran mouthed the words *as we'll ever be*.

Jada continued to squeeze that thing behind her right ear.

Tris stood breathing.

Another car rolled grittily by on Argyll Road.

Then they were over the meter-high ivy-tangled fence topped with silver arrowheads, trotting down the pinkish checkerboard footpath toward their future.

PART THREE:
ORGAN-GRINDER ART CRIMES

13. NO LIGHT: DENSITY

Three minutes after the Royal Family gave their farewell address from the balcony of Bugging'im Palace on the evening of November 5, 2023, their chopper lifted off toward Heathrow and exile in their Tudor-themed sanctuary on Erewhon One. The concept of the monarchy had come down around their ears over a long-winded and arthritically gnarled course that in retrospect probably hobbled all the way back to Edward VIII's marital-rapture-induced abdication in 1936.

A splinter cell of the Demopublicans, the sort of terrorist organization that pretended an anti-monarchist political agenda but was really comprised of a bunch of thugs who just liked to blow things up, promptly started plunking mortars into the courtyard from the roof of the Governcorp Offices Building on the opposite side of Sin James Park, their little way of saying have a good one.

Across town, a napalmic airburst above Kensington Palace bleached the purplish twilight sky a magnesium-flare white.

The nose cone carrying the polystyrene, benzene, and petrol broth had been delivered aboard a Russian Army-surplus Ufa 240 missile fired from what passed as a rubbish barge near the mouth of the Thames.

The initial blast leveled the south wing and a fair stretch of gold-ornamented perimeter fences. The ensuing fire-mist set the structure itself, surrounding trees, grass, gardens, and nearby pond aflame, then churned west into the embassies and east through Hype Ark, burning two days despite the sincerest efforts of the nearly bankrupt fire brigade. In the end, it depurated the royal digs down into a charred, leaky, patchily roofed pesthole with lots of terra-cotta chimneys that wasn't inhabitable by anyone except the hundreds of squatters who started turning up by week's end, whom the National Trust pretty much shrugged its collective shoulders at, having with The Final Abscondence run out of credit and motivation to even contemplate contemplating the resurrection of such an unpopular tourist attraction.

The squatters set up a complicated medley of cage-flats throughout the ruins, gloomy corners separated from other gloomy corners by nothing much more than a meter or two of chain-link fencing, each cubbyhole housing that squatter's entire collection of meaningful worldly paraphernalia, which usually boiled down to an olive-green sleeping bag and grocery sack full of useless tidbits procured during crusty-eyed day after crusty-eyed day wandering the nearby streets or milling around the scorched flora and fauna of the park.

You could hear them ... the Somalian tribal drums thumping inside the ruins, chainsaw-rip music emanating from the odd solar-powered blaster ... ceaseless titanic mumble ... pop and tinkle of the occasional smashed bottle ... and those laughs, high and zooidal, the sort of thing that puled up a flight of stairs in your most disturbing dreams in the really depraved hours ...

And you could see them: shadows fluttering cicada-like behind blown-out windows and through jagged sections of collapsed wall illuminated by sputtering cans of Sterno and red-hot coal splashes.

Which gave Rykki a major case of the jim-jams as she skirted the wreckage with her brothers and sister and stepped over a brownbrick fence into a thicket, residue of one of the gardens that'd grown back with some mutational vengeance, ankle-twisting undergrowth everywhere, thistles, dry prickly bracts, and loads of leafless palsied trees, everything so congested and thorny she had to slow her trot almost to a standstill and barely edge along.

She looked down to avoid what might have been a lumpy

pinkish-gray spatter of human vomit and when she looked up again *he* was standing in front of her staring at a point just behind her head.

He was talking so fast it sounded more fluvial than linguistic, eyebrows forming a single arch over his pug nose, Irish freckle-busy skin belied by that weird mottled accent, part Caribbean and part Asian and part cortex-fried NorAm black-med rant, palming his turkey-waddle-red dreads with a hand sans even the distant memory of one finger, clothed in nothing but a yellowish-brown jockstrap and necklace of small bones, clutching to his twiggy chest with his other hand (this one boasting something evocative of a thumb and a middle finger) what might have been the opal phone-sized outline of an electronic notebook.

"Ya go round tinking accidents occur at random, mon, don't ya, and all, but ya want ta know sometin' real?" he said, as if they'd all been strolling together hours.

Rykki backed up a step and bumped into the glowing albinic ghost behind her that was Oran.

"Ya want ta know sometin' straightout-straightout? I got de Top of de Universal Pops for ya, now, if ya listen to de one dat listens to de Big Tune, ya know what I'm sayin'. De Great Shake, mon, nuttin' else but." His head twitched with some disquieting myoclonic spasm. "Cuz ya know, don't ya, yah, ya all know it in de tips of dose little dendrites furballin' in your head, xiè-xie, ya know it like de back of your hinked *brain*, it be value and worth like to give Airdaddy de ear ..."

"Oh, *man*," Zivv said.

"Look," said Rykki, "I, um ... we just ..."

"Airrrrrrrdaddy," Oran whispered.

Airdaddy flicked Rykki's language off with a backwhip of his fingerless paw. The night-heat came washing up on them. He shifted the notebook a little and Rykki saw the screen. On it was one of those stupid chia-pet-like marginally AI kitties you adopted off the Other Side cuz you were painfully lonely in the Big Television and then fed, loved and played with like a real cat till it won over your better judgment when you were like four, only this guy was downright past it, geezer in his thirties if he was a day.

"I kinda think we oughta be like going right about now," Zivv said under his breath.

"Couldn't agree with you more, clever boy," said Jada, who stood next to Rykki, who stood next to Zivv, who stood partially in front of Tris.

Rykki heard heavy dogs barking in the park, someone leaning into his horn on Bayswater Road like he'd died at the wheel, some small animal sibilate through the undergrowth near her sneakers.

"Cuz wipe it if ya do, gwielo girls and boys, wipe it full. Cuz here's de deal. Here's the real. Here's the Number One Hit from Yesteryear: it don't matter what you believe, don't ya see? Not one gnat's ass. Not one teeny-tiny fuckola, my little ones. Bù. And ya know why? Eh? Do ya, now, little gwielo girls and boys?" Rykki could only make out three teeth crooking from his mouth, one on the bottom and two on top. He continued to look past her, even though he seemed to be winding up to make his central argument. "Cuz ain't no *Ran. Dumb. Ness.* Ain't no *iffy* on the Cosmic Top Ten. Every tune's a lock. Every stat's been checked wit' de local autorities." His head twitched again. He took a handful of dreadlock and yanked. "People? *People?*"

"Look," Rykki said, as interested as her siblings in what she might say next.

"Ain't no maybe dis, maybe dat. Ain't no even steven, my little black-skinned nü-háir. Name dat tune. Pick a door ... any door. Add dose figures. An' know what you get? Know de Final Resolution? Eighty-fivers and older? Know who I'm pointin' to?"

Rykki heard an ample exhaust fan whir to life somewhere north, Oran repeating Airdaddy's ramble a second out of sync behind her, a woman or young boy somewhere in the upper rafters of the palace who might have been screaming or might have been singing frag-opera.

And then this realization hit her.

Airdaddy wasn't the guy in front of her. Airdaddy was the guy in front of her's cat. He was relaying, or under the impression he was relaying, psychic dispatches from his electronic pet.

"Dey twenty-two times more likely to die accidentally den kids

138

five to nine. Dat be a fact, mon. Read it an' sleep. NorAm Indians? Four times more likely den Asian folk. Men twice den women. TexMexicans twenty-one den Exxon New Jerseyites. Accidents, mon. Just de way of the world. Way of the Way, ya know?"

"Uh-oh," Zivv said under his breath.

"Accidents happen more often at de poor. Rural folks, too. Scientific reality, mon. Airdaddy knowledge."

Rykki heard a chuffing sound to her right. Another joined it behind her, behind Oran ... big, cumbersome, the sort of sound immense people make when they're trying to be quiet.

"De poor? Bad meds, mon. Bad heating. Bad wiring. Dey cars be all Annie an' Dominoes. Beg dem an' beg dem an' dey *still* won't use seatbelts. Wipe it. Wipe it all." Another twitch and yank. His necklace rasped. It was fashioned out of bird bones. "Such a pity. Such a loss. An' ya know how, don't ya? Ya know how, xiè-xie?"

It struck Rykki they were surrounded.

"Well watch out, gwielo girls and boys, cuz forty-seven percent, dey take de last roll-call in motor vehicle collisions, ya know what I'm sayin', an' fifteen fall right down to dey Maker, an' eight poison deyselves by mistake, an' five go for dey tea in fires, an' four choke, *hooooo-gahhhh*, an' three call it a day when gettin' op-rated on, an' seven light de Roman candle in de middle of recreational activities, an' five try on de wooden kimono due to occupational fatalities beyond dey control at dis very instant in de world-time ... but *you*, my little gwielo girls and boys, *you* ..."

Zivv must have arrived at the same conclusion the same second Rykki did, because he suddenly said *fuck this* in a normal tone of voice, took a giant warm-up step forward, and punted the freckly guy in the jockstrapped groin as if he was going for a penalty kick.

The guy released a wheezy batch of air, dropped his notebook, cupped his crotch, melted to his knees, and tilted over backward.

His pals, eight or ten of them, rushed in from all sides.

Events came on like some kind of strobe effect. Rykki dodged left, Zivv right. Oran clambered directly over the downed guy, who had shut his eyes even though his mouth continued moving and begun to excrete what looked like marmalade.

One of his buddies grabbed Tris by the slow collar ... but not two seconds before Jada was up on his shoulders, steering him with his ears, which made him yodel and reach up to slap her away, giving Tris plenty of time to fully ruminate about his status in the galaxy and choose to follow Oran, who'd become a diminishing pale blur among the branches, while Zivv made a pass at the Jada-saddled cultist, a huge lunk with a head so small it seemed it was pasted onto him with some chintzy graphics program, mountain-goating him in a kidney and causing him thus to crumble into himself like a house of cards as Jada straddled off and hit the ground bobbing and weaving, Rykki and Oran and now Tris providing cover by zigzagging out of range and shouting to each other, which made it nearly impossible for the cultists to concentrate on any one of them, or anything else, for very long.

The kids sprinted through the thicket and burst into the open, forearms scratched, jeans and t-shirts ripped, knees bruised, stealth-jet of adrenalin leaving chemical trails through their minds, fanning out, mongoosing by a brick building with once-white-trimmed French doors hanging off their hinges and around corpulent expired trees and across brittle-grassed clearings and right through tiny camps that shot at them from the night where deros had circled their shopping carts, NorAm pioneer fashion, and the kids whooshed through, overturning those carts and trampling fires and spronging above clueless drunks, trying to create as much chaos as possible and succeeding pretty well, then pressing on along what was left of a fissured walkway with hunks of weeds fisting through gravel and off across another heath poled haphazardly with more deceased trees and expanses of waist-tall grass growing through burned-out car corpses and two old Pakistani men playing with a beanbag hackysacker under the moon that wasn't looking at all healthy ... but the whooping and yipping behind them continued to close in and it occurred to Rykki as she raced toward a modest incline, legs starting to sear, the Cat Cultists knew this park better than any place on earth ...

A system of perfectly rectangular manmade ponds welled up,

scummed surfaces glinting green-black in the lunar light. Zivv and Tris aimed for them, then pulled a sharp left and flanked a low warped black-iron fence in front of a gray-blocked shelter toward a breach in another mass of brush.

Rykki instinctively followed.

Out the corner of her eye she saw Oran and Jada bank tersely and do the same.

Two meters down a leafy tunnel came the perimeter gate with several spikes bent or missing and the kids were out on Bayswater Road among honking horns and braking cars and astonished shouts and blinding clouds of headlights, and Zivv was briefly on an orange-red Infiniti's bonnet beneath halogen street lamps, scampering across, Oran hopping onto a Honda assault vehicle's mudguard and off, the others eeling around exposed engines and through a pigeon-teal billow of bio-diesel, mouth cavities filmed with a lamina of grit ...

The cultists swarmed into the street right behind them, clattering over car roofs and thunking on pavement and gaining like fire across alcohol, and Zivv took off for the narrow entrance to the Lank Astor Gate Underground, Rykki right on his heels, and Oran and Tris and Jada next, tearing past the machine-gun-toting bobby before he'd finished lighting his cheap roll-your-own and through the alarmed metal-detector and into the flood of shiny custard-yellow tiles, across the speckled-tiled floor, over the robotic turnstiles.

The kids didn't go for the industrial-sized passenger elevators, but through what might have been a knobless steel door to a utility closet, only wasn't, that led to two flights of waffled iron stairs.

They clacketed down, ratt-a-tatt-tatt, one crowding right up on the sneakers of the next, never looking back.

At the bottom they hustled along the tubular white-tiled passage by a ventilation fan behind a partition of intricate grating and bars, and some more knobless steel doors (these marked with yellow-and-black DANGER RISK OF ELECTRIC SHOCK stickers), and a smashed plaster madonna veiled with cheery plastic flowers in a small grotto chipped out of the wall, smack into a second world below the first.

Naked bulbs lit the concrete cavern every ten meters.

Small food fires smoldered here and there among hundreds of deros.

Rykki thought a fog had seeped in from the sewers at first, then understood it was the dense metallic smoke from auto exhaust wafting down from the street.

Most of the deros wore sanitary masks. Those who didn't were making noises from way in their chests and intermittently hacking up flu-yellow loogies. The loogy-splattered floor squeegeed like neoprene when you walked on it, which made Rykki stop chewing her gum.

Some of the deros watched miniature battery-powered liquid-crystal television sets, vintage wireless earplugs projecting like little antennae from the sides of their heads, tuned to the Sports Network featuring replays of the Olympic Games from before humans came to run and jump pretty much as fast or high as they were going to run and jump, at which point the eensy-weensy spread between one athlete's time or distance or whatever and another's became naff to worry about. Some watched Magilla Gorilla reruns, some the Entertainment Network. And some watched nothing at all, just blank staticky screens, their televisual jones so intense they'd rather ogle gray fuzz or maybe even a broken microwave for hours than have to raise their eyes and have a vada around.

Some talked, some to their mates and some to the panoply of psychic phantoms fussing about their heads. Some loitered, scrawny hands in trousers four times too large for them and worn backwards. Some partook of a sort of ambulatory Brownian motion.

Behind a fridgelette lay a teenage girl with a face guttered with purple scars and cash multicolored stelliform hair. She sucked freon through a snapped pipe, deep into feeding her environmentally friendly addiction. Beside her slept her lover, one of those toyboys Rykki'd read about who as an infant had been stuck in a vase-like contraption with only his head and legs protruding so he grew into the shape of the vase-like contraption and was sold to the rich as a cute curiosity to keep around the mansion. He assumed a floating-in-a-formaldehyde-jar pose and was hugging a ceramic Viper automatic to his chest. It seemed like a fat ugly fly was crawling up and down his cheek and beneath his nose among his pollution sores, but when Rykki looked harder she saw it was only a not-all-that-realistic holographic tatt.

She next became aware of the glandular signature of various area tribes burning her sinuses … a stench more pungent than the most concentrated territory-marking pee sprayed on tree trunks in the Doberman-tiger chimera's cage at the zoo.

Rykki kacked.

"What sort of shite is this?" Zivv asked beside her, bent, palms on thighs. He was trying to get some oxygen into his lungs.

"Access tunnels," she said. "Utility tunnels. Storage tunnels." She swallowed her gum, extending her jaw forward.

"Tunnels connecting tunnels to other tunnels," Jada said.

A wind speckled with black granulets gusted up. A train racketed in behind it, headlight smashed, screeching and banging and clitterclattering past, vanishing down the other end in mini-tornadoes of smog.

The floor trembled several seconds after the sound had turned from aural to corporeal sensation.

"Hey," said Tris. "Look."

He nodded in the direction of a tube rat that had waddled into the loogy-opulent open.

Everyone in the neighborhood went silent, appraising.

The freon-sucking girl, who appeared to be channeling way too keenly on the gas to notice anything, popped her head over the fridgelette. She slowly wiggled her grimy toes forward and prodded her toyboy's bum.

In a single motion his eyes snapped open, his Viper snapped forward, the detonation sprawled through the cavern like a four-star general's command and the rat hopped into unintentional flight.

Its darted carcass skidded to a stop in a red smudge two meters from where it had been sniffing.

Cordite mixed with other aromatic ingredients.

The toyboy was dragging the thing by its fleshy tail back to his doss.

As he whumped it down someone yelled behind them *Dere dey be, my brethren! Dere dey be!* and someone answered *Airdaddy rule de Big Diàn-shì-ji!* and Rykki glanced back and saw the guy with the necklace and dreads highball into the cavern, loping over the sleeping, the singing, the experientially stunned, his apostles right behind. They kicked over televisions, slammed into loiterers, charging at the kids who themselves leaned forward prepared to run, and would have, had not the toyboy swung the heavy rat carcass into Oran's knees just to see what'd happen, causing him to plunge forward onto his elbows.

The toyboy's gas-sucking squeeze clapped in admiration at his trick.

Zivv scooped his hands under one of Oran's armpits and Jada the other. They hoisted him straight onto his unsteady feet. Tris dropped into a body ball which a cultist in the lead tumbled over into a clique of generally-hacked-off-at-the-universe-particularly-when-it-was-a-caucasian-universe ski-capped tall black teens from probably a Watusian gene pool who didn't so much rise as discharge from their sitting positions into a thunderstorm of ill-will and switchblades while Rykki effected something approximating a power dive she'd once seen in an old Ester Williams vid off a nearby fridgelette head-first into the exact same groin region of the cult's commander-in-chief as Zivv had punted earlier, sending the guy into an immediate catatonic horizontal rictus as his mates came up heartwrenchingly short when confronted by the towering black dudes wielding what seemed to be machetes ... which gave Oran plenty of time to shake off his fall and Rykki to scrabble off the ringleader and Tris to compute what'd just happened, what the appropriate responses might be to what'd just happened, and what they should all do about it, which was to decamp as fast as possible by throwing themselves into the congregation of the raggedy-assed down-and-outers around them who'd by now taken an abiding interest in what was going on ...

14. THE COLLAPSED LI-YUNG

Rykki poked her head out of the Lesser Square tube station on the west side of Charring Cross Road the next morning and without hesitation entered the human rapids sweeping by her.

Zivv, Oran, Tris, and Jada waited for breaks in the crush as if they were waiting for open slots in a revolving door and followed.

They were yanked up and carried along into the narrow fumy lanes of Chinaton which over the last thirty years had swelled and radiated through the Wessin, translating most of its economically ailing theaters into Buddhist temples, Mongolian wrestling arenas, and popular venues for Peking Opera.

The kids had spent the last couple of hours making their way through the concrete burrows below the city, too creeped out by their pursuers to slow down and with almost no idea where they were going. They'd navigated tunnels still in regular use, tiptoeing over live third rails to hug cabled walls when trains clamored by like giant mechanical pythons sparking bluely no more than six centimeters from their hunched backbones. Every passageway had been choked with chalky air that had spawned ulcers at the rear of Rykki's throat and around her nostrils.

She turned randomly down a mews and scuttered by a plate-glass window heaped with smashed-in TV sets. Paper lamps hung outside bamboo shop fronts lacquered burnt orange and jade and overwritten with gold mostly Chinese characters. A guy wearing brass-colored lipstick and a hemp black-belted jujitsu suit skinned a green snake outside a Cantonese café. Three steps down, a prehistorically aged

145

pot-bellied woman about as tall as an upright hoover in a backwards LA Gear baseball cap and colorless silk muumuu scissored the hair of a businessman.

Here, it occurred to Rykki, the city had reverted to its medieval roots. Everything was crammed, winding, contaminated, aggregated, a continuous sensory jacuzzi. For a brief stretch last century these streets had unclogged, even cleaned themselves up a spot. Now they'd slouched back to the M.O. they'd maintained pretty much since the first century A.D. London had shaken off all that progress bosh and returned to its good old self, an entity that protoplasmically sopped up everything that bumbled into its path and made it its own. Enough of the straight and narrow. Enough of the all-wool-and-a-yard-wide nonsense. London never met a culture it didn't ingest.

Rykki caught sight of a pub with a sign in gothic lettering under the Chinese that read The Collapsed Li-Yung, and caught scent of fat-fried farm shrimps and chips mixed with ginger, soy sauce, and lemon rinds, and she thought about trying to convince her brothers and sister to give it a try, even though they didn't have a pence of credit to their names, or even workable ID numbers, but then she began thinking better of it, just as the undernourished shiny-silver-bikinied mermaid leaning in the doorway pointed at her with a spindly white arm and appeared to read her mind.

"Blue Eyes fancy a bit food, yes?" she asked. Her voice was squeaky and off-pitch. "Blue Eyes fancy eat? Come in, come in. Blue Eyes full of sad. We get you eat. We get you plenty scrap out back. We make better. Make happy happy."

She'd peeled the insides of her legs and bound them together to graft them to each other, then complemented the resulting fishtail effect by shaving and oiling her scalp and having some large purplish slightly sexual mushroomy make-believe gills implanted below each ear.

Rykki's brothers and sister braked and clustered behind her.

Rykki laddered down her decision tree and opened her mouth to tell the mermaid no thanks only the woman had already taken her by her wrist and Rykki was zigzagging inside the dark wood-paneled pub muggy and breezeless as a summer locker room, half-foot-dragging and half-jogging to keep balance, her sister and brothers tagging along, the mermaid jabbering and gesticulating as she shuffle-hopped among small round wooden tables at which mostly elderly people huddled slurping away with chopsticks at bamboo steam pots heaped with noodles and chunks of orange squid, reddish-brown glazed chicken, and duck tongues the color of makeup Michael Jackson wore to his own funeral.

Sometimes someone leaned sideways and spat tiny bones on the floor, and sometimes someone whined or skreaked, apparently to themselves, hands rock-climbing into the air, discomposed by what someone else was saying to them in their ear plugs on their pate-mounted cellulars.

Above them on the walls on either side of the fireplace hung stuffed heads of pure-breed dogs: Irish setters, Welsh collies, English springer spaniels, Scottish deerhounds, West Highland whites ... first tacked up, Rykki supposed, when they'd been almost eaten out around this part of the city, and good stock came to be considered a real delicacy among the indigens.

On the green-carpeted floors below the shelves sat angry erect backed poured-concrete dragons with jade inset eyes.

Rykki recognized Musikal Olestra tinkle-dinking on the sound system.

"Not worry, not worry," the mermaid was saying. "We watch for own. Watch for small one like you, me. Kojak find you ... snip snip. No babies. Cut you tubes." They banked down a hall, past signs for the gents and ladies and a governcorp poster reminding passersby to PRACTISE SAFE SUN, to a cramped cobblestoned passage where urine foamed in the shallow gutters along either side. "Every people city forget. City have short memory." She laughed. It sounded like a stepped-on magpie. "Very bad outside. Very bad. Every people huài. Every people yí-dìng shì gao cuò le. You come here. We feed. Make better. Make happy happy." The oceanic sound from the pub faded. The mermaid's fused feet made a schluffing noise across the wet stones. "Mu-qin want meet you. I know. You meet Mu-quin, then eat, okay? You be happy happy. Full.

147

Everything good. Mu-quin make you Mu-quin's children. Make you jia-shu. Family. We all family here. We belong like one. You channel on my legs, Blue Eyes? You channel on Mu-quin's work? Every people artist here. Mu-quin artist of artist. Princess Hacksaw ..."

The spittly damp room they entered possessed a bare weathered uneven wooden floor. Drying herbs dangled from clotheslines, horizontal bamboo poles, open cupboards. They were scattered across long rectangular wooden tables flocked with mortars and pestles and a TV set. On the set's screen looped a vid of a man's head resting on the sandy bottom of a fish tank. Neon tetras flitted around it. The head was alive and its eyes were wide and the guy was holding his breath. The effect, Rykki knew, was some sort of optical illusion, but she couldn't work out how it'd been done.

There were no windows anywhere. Or maybe there were windows, only they'd been shuttered. Either way, besides the door looking out on the dim passage and the blue mist radiating from the telly, virtually no light inhabited this space.

Rykki had that immediate uneasy feeling which arrives when you can't tell where the walls of the room you're standing in end.

"Wait here," the mermaid said. "Mu-quin come. Every people eat." She pirouetted on her feet-tail and shuffle-hopped out the door. Rykki heard her laugh again as she made her way back down the passage. It didn't sound at all wholesome.

The kids waited.

Rykki and Zivv exchanged looks.

The head on the television opened and closed its mouth. A single bubble floated up from its nose.

Jada scratched the middle of her forehead.

"Come to think of it," she said, "I'm maybe not quite as hungry as I thought I was."

"Me either," said Oran.

"I think I'm missing the plot here or something," Zivv said. "I was doing fine till like ten minutes ago. All of the sudden I'm lost. Could someone please fill me in on what just happened?"

"We took a wrong turn," Rykki said.

"No shite."

"A *really* wrong turn."

"Several of them, in actual fact," Oran added.

"Turns so excessively wrong," said Jada, "I'd correct them this very second, if it was down to me."

"So," Rykki said. "Right. Okay. What we do is this …"

A low growl rose from the darkness.

"Lovely," said Jada. "Just lovely."

Rykki took a step back and rotated her head minimally to engage her peripheral sight and saw a little stooped Mao-suited woman form from the shadows. She was so ancient she made the pot-bellied barber back on the street seem like a smooth-skinned rouge-cheeked babe. She didn't so much shamble as wheeze and heave herself forward, swollen sandaled meaty blocks of feet never leaving the floor. Her neck stuck osteoporotically out of her shoulder blades at a ninety-degree angle in a way that made it impossible to see her face till she tilted her head to one side and peered up. Rykki then got a peek at those cataractal eyes and the long tapered mustache that gave her a catfishy look.

While Rykki and the other kids vetted her, another little stooped Mao-suited woman stepped from the murk and joined her chum. By comparison this second made the first seem peppy and girlish. The notion of moving her head any way at all had seen better days. She contented herself studying her clawed yellow toenails like a Roman oracle bird entrails.

A low pneumatic droning commenced behind them … a clacket … a hydromechanical whiz … and Mu-quin Li-Yung, proprietress and namesake of the pub, rolled into view.

She was slumping in a wheelchair, pet ocelot in lap. Then Rykki realized Mu-quin Li-Yung *was* the wheelchair. Her naked withered upper torso emerged from a mechanistic conglomeration of bicycle tires, blinking red Christmas lights, another TV set looping that same image of the fish-tanked guy's head, a car battery, length of coaxial cable, old-time digital clock with green numerals, small spinning bowtie antenna, and

149

cyber-fruitcake of unidentifiable coils, vacuum tubes, and spark-plug-looking things. And the ocelot wasn't sitting in her lap, either. It *was* her lap, or more precisely her abdomen, black-spotted toast-brown feline head and shoulders sprouting from amidst appliances and just starboard of the stoma bag where Li-Yung's vitals should've been located ... and fully mobile, too, or as fully mobile as the situation allowed, its eyes glowing redly as if surprised by a flashbulb and its neck craning side to side as if trying to birth itself from the machinery that comprised its host, growl from its throat almost subsonic.

Mu-quin Li-Yung drew up between what Rykki now understood were her bodyguards and braked. She scrutinized the kids through eyes so runny and sappish it was difficult to tell what color they were. The parts of her that were flesh bore the pigment and composition of greasy steak. It appeared all the glandular substance had been lipposuctioned out of her breasts. Their nipples looked like wide bad bruises and the deflated sacs constituting their remnants sagged flatly down her ribby chest.

There were a good six centimeters between the base of her gaping nostrils, whose corners attached themselves to her face somewhere far out among the wrinkled frontier that maybe a century ago had been her cheeks, and her thin inverted-V lips. But there was almost no distance from her thin inverted-V lips to the knuckle of her chin. Her forehead eructed into a huge knot that conjured in Rykki's imagination a single protruding tough-skinned buttock which modulated into a bald ridge where her eyebrows probably once lay.

Mu-quin Li-Yung took some time for respiration, consulted her artificial pancreas, a watch-like device half-buried in her right forearm, and finally spoke, her toothless mouth moving gummily while her voice emanated from an antique Toshiba radio mostly hidden by her left armpit.

"Gwielo find Mu-quin foxy babe, yes?" she said. "See it in eyes. Gwielo know why? Gwielo guess?" She unhurriedly ran the fingertips that had just palpated the stoma bag under her nose. "Bag of earthly delights. Sack of plenty. Can eat, still maintain figure. Diet of champions.

Life big jet-boat tour on Thames. Retro all broke. Every people enjoy ride. Embrace speed. Gwielo come here want Mu-quin's bang-zhu? Mu-quin's help?"

"Well, em," Rykki said, "the lady who brought us said you might be able to spare us a bit of food. Maybe just the odd ..."

"Dao-piàn say that?"

"Dao-piàn?"

"Fish doll. She say food here? Plenty eat?" Mu-quin Li-Yung laughed, gaspy and moist. The body guards produced some gulping noises that indicated they might be in on the joke as well. "She right, gwielo girl. Plenty plenty. Everywhere food." She raised her palms. "You name. We take care gwielo kind. We take care little one."

"We don't want to trouble you or anything. But if maybe you could see your way clear to spare us a little something, you know ..."

"Gwielo run way, yes?"

Rykki looked over at Zivv, who couldn't take his eyes off the ocelot.

"We'd much appreciate it," she said. "Whatever you can afford. We're very hungry. We'll eat and be off directly."

"Mu-quin take care little one. Hack into company puter. Phone. Bank. Don't matter. Encrypt file. Put bite on company to decrypt. All sort bang-zhu. Food flow like river."

She petted her tummy. The cat leaned into her strokes. Mu-quin Li-Yung slivered her eyes contentedly.

"We don't want to be a bother or anything," Rykki said.

"Every people eat. Every people part of family." She unslivered her eyes. "Look." She raised her pincers and swept them across the room.

Rykki did.

Her eyes had become accustomed to the dark. She still couldn't see the perimeter, but she could make out movement in every direction. Under one table rocked what seemed to be a phocomeliac man well over the seventy-year mark, hands sprigging directly from his shoulders, fingers fused into seal flippers, beside his partner tugging absentmindedly at her elastic facial skin. Under another slept a pair of middle-aged conjoined twins merged at the chest, thumb-sized translucent mole connecting their foreheads, four arms and legs shivering in REM, while near the table with the TV crouched one of those gray-haired Gargoylers Rykki'd once read about with a bumped back and head pushed in on one side, his pregnant mother having strapped herself with a corset so tightly her child had been born deformed and thus capable of bringing a good price from the underground bio-dealers.

The place was weirdly kinetic.

Rykki made out other humanish shapes leaning against what might have been a stretch of wall or some sort of partition, squatting on tables, scrunching on the planked floor just outside the blue photonic cloud from the television screen.

She'd never seen so many old people before.

Mu-quin saw Rykki seeing and laughed.

"Gwielo know '64 World's Fair? Seen pictures?"

"I have done. Sure."

"Awesome science. Happy clean moonhouse. Shiny monorail city. Tidy white flat. Flying car. Smiling homemaker."

"I guess."

"Only one thing."

"… ?"

"Only one problem."

"… ?"

"Got future all cuò. All wrong. No flying car, no tidy moonhouse. End cold war instead. Every people immune system arsed up. Earth shit itself. Designer drug replace happy homemaker. Urban tooth rot replace shiny monorail city." Her chest inflated and deflated. Air chuffed through her trachea. "Know one thing boss gwielo got right, eh? One thing future give bang on?"

"What?"

"Nice television."

Rykki craned her neck toward Mu-quin as if the gesture might compensate for her inability to understand.

"Nice television?"

"Future give great set. Hen duo channel. More than we can watch."

A short oval-faced woman with no angles whatsoever associated with her body squeaked a medical cart into the half-light from the passage. The front wheels clacked in circles rather than revolving forward. The woman's bloated skin was white and each limb so cylindrical they created the impression of a collection of water balloons tied together.

Instead of meds, the cart was loaded with bowls of henna-colored soup and mugs of stout.

"Eat eat," Mu-quin announced. "Good food. Make strong. Give healthy. Mu-quin feed family have no family."

The kids helped themselves. Rykki noticed something not completely departed at the bottom of her bowl seemed to be blowing bubbles, so she went for the stout. It tasted warm and corky and overran her nervous system immediately.

"This is awfully kind of you," she said.

"Who need pure air for breathe? Bio-engineering rock, eh?"

Rykki drank. Foam mustached her upper lip.

"You're saying tomorrow will always be different from what we can imagine."

"We got satellite receiver. We got news twenty-four seven." The ocelot stretched itself across Mu-quin's thighs, purr revving, third lids curtaining satisfied yellow-green eyes. "Except boss gwielo forget something. Forget something big."

"What's that?"

"Boss gwielo forget us. Forget here."

Rykki looked around. Her brain felt smeared. A scratch on her right thigh itched.

The Gargoyler crouching by the television blew his nose daintily, one nostril at a time, into his palms.

"The down-and-outters you mean?" Rykki said, feeling simpatico.

"Not you." Mu-quin's tone changed. "Us. Here."

153

"Us?"

"Every people with suì-shu. How you say? Every people with years. Governcorp give special somebody life-extension service. Important politician. Scientist. All sort white med. Somebody keep governcorp keeping on. Rest of us? Forget. Rest of us governcorp leave to body running down. Say we diversion economic force. Make room for young somebody like you." Her chest rose and fell. Her dedented mouth started to move. "Know what this called?"

" … ?"

"This called Politic of Age."

"Doesn't sound quite fair, does it."

"Gwielo know what we say to Politic of Age?"

She shook her head no.

Mu-quin leaned forward.

"We say fuck that, Charlie," she said. "Sod off." The ocelot's eyes popped open. Its head raised, low growl barely audible once more. "So much fung pi. Law don't mean jackshit here, you know?"

"Right, but …"

"Age is rage," said the phocomeliac's partner beneath the table, now busy rubbering the skin below her jaw.

Rykki tasted something steel-like on the back of her tongue. It brought to mind the electric version of the color blue.

She blinked and the world quantumed ahead in a film with missing frames.

"See man there," Mu-quin said, aiming a pincer at a perfectly normal-seeming guy in hemp pajamas with scanty yellowish pollution-burned hair that'd once been maybe black. Arms crossed, he leaned on the table with the television on it and gazed at the fish-tanked head gazing at nothing. "Familial dysautonomia. Neurological skrim. Hold flame to skin, can't feel. Stick needle in thigh, think you being sexy. Woman sitting at feet? Anosmia. Loss of smell. Don't know if flat on fire. Nose gone to smash. We got skin disease here. Tired organ. Boil. Know all off by heart. Governcorp say fuck you. Say no treat cuz we leftover. Make room for next somebody. Gwielo know what we say? We say fuck

154

you back. Don't give toss what you want. We want what every people want. Take shit on death. So gwielo know what happen? Know what leftover do?"

The steel-like taste advanced into Rykki's sinuses and she assimilated the data that she couldn't fully feel her fingertips anymore. She wanted to be anxious but the pharmaceuticals in the stout wouldn't let her.

"I can't do. No." She shook her head. "I'm feeling a bit mashed up, actually."

"We go guerrilla. Declare war. Intergenerational conflict."

"Think maybe I need to, em …"

"We say fuck governcorp. Fuck young. Fuck you."

Rykki's mind unclogged fleetingly.

"Fuck us?"

"Fuck you."

"Why us?"

"We soldier now. Soldier of elder. And you …"

"Us?"

"You POW in battle of age."

Jada sat down gracefully like she was wearing an elegant hoop skirt she didn't want to crease.

As if on cue, Oran joined her.

Tris let the bowl of soup he was working on and aluminum spoon drop from his hands.

"Kojak find toyboy body in passageway, you know? Overdose. Knife. You name. Pack up. Ship to crematorium. Only toyboy body no arrive." Her fingers returned to the stoma bag. "Turn up here. Make good supper for leftover. Yum-yum. Food come from where food come from."

"You gave us the fast shuffle," Rykki said.

"Leftover take little gwielo girl and boy for walk. Cross Thames. We visit clinic. Soldier clinic."

"Soldier clinic?"

"Pet shop. Borrow this. Borrow that. Every people department store inside."

"Organ-grinders."

"You not so clueless, gwielo girl." She raised her chin and studied the darkness above her. "Know what? Baboon endangered specie. Wolf. Plenty little gwielo girl and boy. Animal need your help. Every people have heart, you know? We help animal. POW help, too. Lend hand. Eye. Liver. Skin." She stroked the ocelot's head. "Welcome to bio-farm, little gwielo girl and boy. You top-line crop."

"Run," Zivv told Rykki, speech slurred by the drugstore in his soup, then fumbled forward into the bodyguard on Mu-quin's righthand side.

The room cattled to life.

But the room was already behind Rykki, falling away, and Rykki was already running, or at least taking a stab at the general concept of locomotion.

Problem was she didn't have much sensation left in her legs anymore, either, so her progress quickly deteriorated into a kind of stumbling lumber. She found herself groping through the dim cobblestoned passage beyond the doorway, unable to hold to a straight course, shoulders slamming walls, feet plashing in that urine foaming along the gutters.

Her body came to her in a series of segments, some of which she sort of felt, and some of which she saw wafting up like a flock of detached black birds around her.

The film she inhabited pounced ahead several more frames. She jumpcut to the dark muggy wood-paneled pub, the wooden tables at which mostly elderly Chinese men and women twiddled with their chopsticks and whined on their pate-mounted cellulars.

Outside on the choked pavement she collided with a male bobby who'd gone overboard with metallic silver mascara, lipstick, and fingernail polish, and a female bobby whose face was a Strawberry-Quik miscellany of skin graftings connected with prominent sutural scars.

"Help me," Rykki said, or thought she said, only it occurred to her her oral musculature had gone slack and the phrase had come out sounding a lot closer to "Hulma" than what she'd intended.

She tried again.

The female bobby stared down at her with small black glinting seal-eyes, the graftings having veneered all expression out of the rest of her physiognomy.

"Who do we have here?" she asked.

"Chinese, you think?"

"Bit more African in flavor, isn't she?"

"Could be. African. Sure."

"No no," said the undernourished shiny-silver-bikinied mermaid leaning in the doorway behind them. "No African." She raised her spindly white arm and pointed a finger at her forehead and smiled. "Blue Eyes—how you say?—not all ready for people."

"Not all ready?" asked the female bobby.

"Bit dim, you mean," said the male bobby.

"Wall paint. Lead baby."

The female bobby meditated on Rykki.

"Mothers do have 'em," she said. "She belong to you then?"

"Indenture."

"Got the papers, do you?"

"Inside. Yes yes. You see?"

Rykki concentrated very hard and said: "They snatched my brothers and sister and me. Back of the pub."

"Easy, Star," said the male.

The bobbies met each other's look.

"Won't be necessary," said the female to the mermaid.

"Sorry to bother you, madam," said the male.

"No no. Never be too careful." The mermaid's face brightened into obsequiousness. "Kojak maybe want cup herbal tea for take-way? Good for healthy. Good for robust."

"Much obliged, but we've got to be on our way. Cheers."

"Kojak come again. Always welcome. Law every people friend."

"Right. Well."

"Ta-da," said the female bobby.

"Cheers," said the mermaid, settling her hands on Rykki's

shoulders, revolving her with a certain degree of practiced tenderness, and aiming her straightaway into the enormously anti-hygienic arms of the jockstrapped Cat Cultist who was waiting just inside The Collapsed Li-Yung, bird-bone necklace rattling in excitation.

15. THE CITY OF DIS

Rykki couldn't tell how many hours passed. The film she inhabited wasn't only badly edited; it was also out of focus and large segments of it were over- or underexposed.

She had to go to the loo. That part she knew. But she was too dizzy and fagged out to even think about standing up, so she opened her eyes, ready to tell someone about her problem, only she discovered herself sharing a grubby bronze-spotted straw-stuffed mattress smelling of sneakers and prepubescent farts with her brothers and sister plus this legless genetically wangled rooster with cephalic palsy twitching in front of her nose.

She closed her eyes and opened them again and found herself standing at a zebra crossing, right wrist in someone's grip, waiting to ford a wide avenue jammed with bicycles into a drab stained-glass window of smoke-gray triangles.

One of the osteoporotically challenged bodyguards was attaching a derm to Rykki's arm.

The dark room smelled like an ashtray.

Rykki's mouth stung with raw pollution sores. They felt like she'd gargled with iron filings.

"I have to go," she said.

The hydraulics in the osteoporotically challenged bodyguard's neck engaged and she rotated her head to one side and peered up. Her foggy eyes met Rykki's.

The brownish complication that passed for skin around the abrasion that passed for a mouth crinkled and bunched. A long wispy spiderwebbish filament of drool bungied off her lower lip and quivered midway between there and the grubby mattress.

A hoarse whistling vocalization freed from her throat. It reminded Rykki of a broken airlock.

It took a while for Rykki to comprehend this was the bodyguard attempting to laugh at her.

The hydraulics in the old woman's elbows engaged. She slowly raised her arms and placed her bumpy alligator-skin hands on Rykki's throat just below her larynx and began to squeeze.

The touch was thoughtful, familiar, professional.

She wasn't strangling her, exactly, it dawned on Rykki as a big black dream slid toward her like rain across a lake, but carefully controlling her airflow, gently easing her toward another squall of darkness.

"Ya tink ya know de tune, gwielo girls and boys," the Cat Cultist said as they stepped into the wide avenue jammed with bicycles, weeds and grass briering through cleft cobblestones. Someone shouted at them. They stepped back onto the curb. A jackhammer banged half a block away. Rykki's frizzy uncombed hair was dented on one side. Next to them stood a sunken-chested guy with colorful beads braided into his long white beard. He was selling old British and Russian military stuff ... heavy army coats, watches, and medals densely displayed on an A-frame pair of peg boards. "But wipe it if ya do, mon, wipe it full. Cuz here's de real mel-oh-dee. Here's de top of de cosmic pops. See dat man dere? Look at de way his hand shake like it got a mind of its own. He gonna come down wit de Psychic Furies some day soon, an' dere be nothin' no one can do 'bout it. Cuz ya know why? Cuz he be de Fallen Angel of de Genetic Un. Der. Class. Ain't got de credit gwielo girls and boys come from. Ain't got de xu-ke-zheng. Uh-uh. So his cortex, mon?" They stepped off the curb again and began to locomote. Bikes swerved. A herd of midget bells jingled. "His cortex go all to smash. Maybe his brudder, dat boy's lung

160

spring carcinomatous flower. Maybe his sis, dat girl got herself a little shred of DNA into some fucked-up disturbed sicko shit. Health care system be one fine deaf ear, mon, be it manifest, be it not. Don't like de mel-oh-dee it hear one bit, ya know what I'm sayin'. Employers say fuck ya very much, little bao-chao son of a chromosomally-mashed bitch. Kojaks say dick not wit de Law, cuz we de Mon dat live beyond de Mon. An' so ya hear de real tune, eh? It play de get-out-of-da-way song, the stand-on-de-corner-an'-sell-fuck-off-dead-soldier-shite-like-someone-gonna-buy-dat-crap tune. Only here's de ting, gwielo girls and boys, here's de ting—wait for it—ya *rewrite* dat song, don't ya see?" They stepped onto the curb on the other side of the avenue, into another series of passageways, and passed a row of aged blue-haired Thai meaters in pink micro-skirts and high-platform shoes standing outside a dilapidated Cambodian cybercafé called the Duke of URL. Their bloated legs didn't have any ankles and they stood tentatively, like they were balancing on stilts. Some wore torn fishnet stockings and cosmetic contusions on their arms and faces, and one quickly lay down and struck forensic poses as Rykki, the Cat Cultist, and the rest of the children walked by. Beyond was a series of vendors grilling eels and pigeons on smoky hibatchis. "Every part of ya be a giver, mon," said the Cat Cultist proudly. "Every part be Airdaddy Divine. Cornea, liver, lung. Ya remember dat, gwielo girls and boys. Remember dat good. Cuz ya be saintly, in a manner of talkin'. Ya be de Holy Annointed of Amputation Heaven ..."

Rykki lay spread-eagle on that grubby mattress, sweating exuberantly.

Her eyes pumped like an infarcted heart. She couldn't feel her arms or legs. The room had adopted the misty texture associated with bad fevers.

Every once in a while she heard her brothers and sister mumbling to themselves somewhere nearby, only it sounded like it was coming from inside her cranium. She'd theorize they must all be in some kind of unlit cubular cinderblock cell, but then she'd look up and see clouds sweeping across a nocturnal sky and fathom she was actually in some sort of passage amid an architectural olla podrida. Or she'd

161

assume she was outside somewhere in the middle of a moonless night because she couldn't see a thing around her except thousands of shades of black and gray, but then she'd look up and see wooden planks inhaling and exhaling less than a meter over her head.

The sole thing Rykki *could* be sure of, really, was the disagreeable sensation in her bladder because it had gorged far beyond its normal capacity. It had gorged, in point of fact, to the stage where it had attained a heavy sloshy disposition that made it seem to Rykki there was a tidal sea awash within her.

She unsealed her lips to let someone know she was going to wet the bed, she couldn't help it, but the impetus to express that idea couldn't quite breach the polyurethane membrane surrounding her.

Her bloated organ felt like it was going to burst in her abdominal cavity. It seemed like it was somehow connected with her brain, and her brain would burst too if she didn't do something this very second.

And then she just gave up.

She let out a long fevered breath and let her urethra relax …

And nothing happened.

Rykki opened her eyes.

She tried to raise her head and have a look around, except her muscles wouldn't let her.

In place of the hot nimbic humiliation spreading beneath her, she simply perceived a slight twinge somewhere below her waist and heard this deviant plipping sound commence somewhere around her feet.

She shuddered.

The room breathed.

She found herself faltering down a row of concrete Eastern Bloc-ish buildings, a series of glum gray public-housing flats, with human-sized slabs of stippled surfacing broken on the pavement in plaster explosions.

Asian people with shell-shocked faces the color of calcined limestone waddled around the smashed slabs without acknowledging their presence like others might around canine droppings.

Over a jumble of governcorp bivouacs built on landfill down by the banks of the river, the Thames came into view. It was low tide and the wide strip of olive-brown foil had nearly stopped flowing, falling by the height of a house overnight and from its standard hundred-meters-per-minute to near nil among the sludge piles that rose from its surface like the slick backs of multiple whale pods. The nine-million gallons of crud pouring into it every day over the last thirty or forty years hadn't helped any more than the city's original Victorian sewage system that still spilled over with every heavy rain.

Rusted bicycle frames, car bonnets, tires, splintered plywood boards, and sections of hurricane fencing protruded from the muck. Shiny fish carcasses rocked back and forth in tidal pools along the banks across which mudlarkers slogged, armed with shovels and pales and wide-brimmed floppy hats, digging for the odd Renaissance dagger or Edwardian pram.

Rykki knew if she examined the male fish in those pools, exposed as they'd been to massive estrogen doses from all the women in the area on the pill, she'd find signs of their not being quite as male as they should be. Which would be to say nothing of the effects on them of the pharmaceutical hypermart coursing through their veins, or the chemical plant of lead, plutonium, petrol, detergents, suntan lotions, shaving creams, moisturizers, antiperspirants, aftershaves, toothpaste foam, hair conditioners, mouthwash, nano-spermacides, shampoo, feminine sprays, vinegar douches, bleach, eye drops, fabric softeners, rubbing alcohol, and other domestic, industrial, and military nasties churning in every cell.

In the foreground barges, houseboats, junks and dark-wood wherrys plied their courses around a two-story bubbler injecting oxygen into the waterway to keep at least some of those piscine hermaphrodites alive long enough for them to give a namby-pamby nod in the general direction of reproduction.

Just off the opposite shore hodgepodging with more public-housing flats and what appeared to be a maze of whitewashed mudbrick shanties, a floating-island commons had been grounded when the level of the Thames had sunk so rapidly. The chlorine-blue water from its huge kidney-shaped swimming pool had sloshed over into the tarp-covered area for concerts, and its high-dive tower listed to the starboard.

A water-skier slalomed in and out of a speedboat's wake among all these obstacles, executing pirouettes and flips.

A speck of grit blew into Rykki's left eye. She reached up to rub it with the hand the Cat Cultist wasn't gripping and when she lowered her fist the sky was raining black chips of soot big as snowflakes.

They continued to push on through incrementally more sinuous passageways that wound down toward the shoreline, past a clutch of Indian beggar women who surreptitiously passed a clearly departed baby between them to up their chances of sympathy from pedestrians, and next this rubberbandish buzz of several didgeridoos played by a bored gaggle of aborigines in torn B.U.M. t-shirts, black bikinis, and black leather boots with large silver shin guards.

They footed by a number of families out for early-morning baths and spiritual ablutions just down the strand from a cremation pyre constructed of driftwood, hay, and appliance boxes. A well-dressed Vietbodian clan stood around the blaze patiently, arms folded, chatting each other up in low voices.

Passing, Rykki heard the wet pop of what she hated to imagine was the skull of the corpse.

Ten more meters, and they came to an agitation of boats pulled up along the foul gummy mud. The group aimed for three flat-bottomed sampans. A handful of Cat Cultists climbed in with every two children, except for Rykki, who sat alone with the leader and his henchwoman. As the henchwoman hunkered down between the oars and cracked her knuckles, the leader remembered something, reached into his jockstrap, and extracted an extra derm which he peeled and applied to Rykki's wrist.

Rykki almost instantly felt her optic muscles loosening. Her sight coasted up to the giant holograms over Waterloo Bridge. She tried to force herself to focus, stay alert.

A flux of natural opiates laved through her cortical pleats, bringing on a cool blurry feeling of tranquility. The darkness began sweeping in at her again from the corners of her consciousness, only not before she spied a blipvert spotlighting novelties from the Virgin Dahmer

Collection (silver-plated sledgehammer, gold-plated hatchet, diamond-studded drill bits) and the public service announcement warning folks to take sanitary precautions against the resistant strain of yellow-fever that'd inadvertently been unearthed and activated during an archeological excavation at the old House of Detention over in Clark-in-'Ell last month ...

She sat on her wooden seat in the sampan's prow and felt her chin brush her chest.

She snapped awake, then felt her chin brush again, and understood she wasn't looking up any more, but tumbling weightlessly into hallucination.

A biconcave red disc, she glided through her own circulatory system.

From what she could tell, she had just exited the left ventricle through the dorsal aorta and was speeding up the right carotid.

She felt less like an erythrocyte, though, than an astronaut in an extended forward roll through deep space. She couldn't stop, but the lysergic sense of motion was exhilarating. It reminded her of swimming through *Atlantis* with her sister and brothers in Vachuru Lane.

Other red blood cells swirled around her, colliding and separating, ricocheting off arterial walls and careening by in the cloudy plasmatic solution along with platelets and an assortment of granular and nongranular leucocytes.

The carotid split and split again.

Rykki shot down an arteriole, banked, whizzed along another, and before long was drifting through microscopic capillaries that networked across her neocortex, feeding the dendrites and gray cell bodies of neurons.

But she wasn't a biconcave red disc anymore: she'd transmuted into a nerve impulse, a white ball of energy, flying down an axon far into the interior of her own brain.

Somewhere at the nether edges she picked up the first signs of them ... those permutations in which her cells both remained themselves and yet not quite themselves, coloring infinitesimally off, size almost intangibly irregular ... and then, snap, the first unmistakable traces of tech, just like Magda'd told her that afternoon before Rykki and her siblings had had to leave for good ...

The bots inside her had embraced a swarm aesthetic. They'd reconstituted some cellular clusters into transcellular ones while constructing whole new cerebral ecologies from undiluted silicon. The result was these mean-looking semi-organic tentacles fingering up, kissing, then seamlessly marrying fully organic fabric. And, as Rykki traveled into her subcortex, time beginning to bulge and warp around her, through the corpus callosum, thalamus, and hypothalamus, into the reticular formation and toward the brain stem, she saw those tentacles rooting like blind tapeworms toward their nest, a tangled mass of nuclei, fibers, and silver bundles of metastatic nano-wiring that suggested unimaginable complication and interdependency.

This, it snuck up on her, was who she was.

Jada, Zivv, Tris, and Oran, too.

At the end of the day, they all amounted to this tentacled mass on the inside.

They looked like regular people, they acted like regular people, only they inhabited a territory beyond that inhabited by regular people.

Rykki felt dizzy like she'd just stood up too quickly.

Her siblings and her formed, Magda said that afternoon, snuffling ... well, you could think of it as a sort of bridge, couldn't you, though exactly between what and what was unclear.

That's why that other woman in her head spoke to her. And that's why Rykki had two sets of memories that didn't fit together instead of just one like everybody else. And that's why she learned so fast. And that's why sometimes she heard her siblings and the Mao-Maos speak even though their lips weren't moving.

And that's what that bearded man with the bland eyes in the before time had been doing, wasn't it. He'd been a kind of horticulturist. He'd been planting a silicon garden in their minds.

Rykki hadn't wanted to think about it and so she'd chundered the knowledge out of her thoughts.

Except now it had chundered its way back in again. It was true, wasn't it. Magda had shown her the polychromatic scans.

Meaning Rykki wasn't like her older friend she missed so much right now she could cry. She wasn't like anyone, really, except maybe her sister and brothers, four other people in the whole world, because she was what happened when you crossed something possessing a silicon essence with something possessing a carbon-based one.

"It's a bit of a poser, isn't it," Magda had told her, soft palm on pocked cheek. She glanced over at her large-screen painting-thin Gateway puter console flanked by those fancy speakers. Rykki could see her change frequencies in her head. "I dare say your appearance is comparable to ... well, to the rise of the human race within the animal kingdom. There's no fathoming what might happen next. At least not from our point of view. It's rather like a goldfish trying to read the vidzine the bloke in the easy chair on the other side of the fishbowl's glass is reading on his puter. I mean, the data's right there, isn't it, and the bloke who owns the goldfish might even try to explain a few things to his quashie-headed fish, but in actual fact the quashie-headed fish simply doesn't have the wherewithal to understand, does it, no matter how much it has explained to it."

Rykki didn't feel new, though. She felt sad.

As she watched the tentacles extend through her brain, semi-organic cell by semi-organic cell, spreading out like an array of whitish-gray snub-nosed invertebrates, she realized growing up equaled a growing away ... from your own recollections, from the special places you resided, from those people who one day meant everything to you and the next whose names you had to think about exceptionally hard before they came to you ... if they came to you at all.

Bleached-out recall-traces rezzed up on her faulty mnemonic cinema.

It seemed a cognitive customs agent was unpacking her memory banks, item by item, searching for significant contraband.

Rykki became a very small particle spinning around inside a very large nucleus.

*   *   *

167

She saw the other thirteen-year-old version of herself arrive in a fog of TV pixels.

She began to writhe in the dentist chair in that boutique, send out her small fists, part her lips for the dream scream, and the nurse began to strap her in with those nylon restraints on the arm- and footrests.

The second dose of diluted anesthetic wrapped around her like a heavy black comforter.

She wanted it to hit faster, stronger, but it wouldn't.

"Relax, honey," the nurse said as she struggled, mouth unable to articulate. "Ain't gonna take but a minute here. Little pinprick, is all, and then you'll be on you way."

Hard as she tried to rush to meet unconsciousness, Rykki could still see the Uncle Meat, long dijon-colored fingernails, ears tufted with snowy fur, switch from his work on her cosmetic mastectomy to his work on her right eye.

The hypodermic with the milky fluid containing those seed bots glisked above her face and descended toward her conjunctiva ...

"Bad project design, ultimately, is the thing," whispered the woman whose bald scalp was alive with hundreds of half-formed genetically generated eyes as she lay dying on the arched bridge, aware of the bamboo rods jabbing her spine. "It happens ..."

The hyacinths singing quietly to themselves, fragrance of Magda's psychotropic perfume from Rykki's birthday party ...

"You're a synth, darling," whispered the lab assistant with the knock-off Gucci Kaposi's sarcoma just beneath his right eye.

He was stalking Rykki around the small dead room in the before time.

Hunching behind her potty-chair, Rykki tugged at her yellow nylon tether, trying to put some distance between her and him, but she had nowhere to go.

"You understand me, don't you, darling?" He moved closer. Rykki tugged harder. "Sure you do. You understand me fine. You're a *synth*, you sweet little fuckwit. That makes you a fucking chimp with a fax for a brain ..."

Rykki began to gnaw at her tether. The lab assistant opened his eyes wide and squatted. His knees popped.

"What's that all about, eh? What's that all about?" He sniggered and scratched his nose. "Easy. I'm not going to do anything you don't want me to do. You're looking at a right good Christian here. One of the Pope's Boys himself. Used to shit on the dagos, and then on the ginneys, and then on the Paki's and chop-chops and what have you. Well, that's all behind us now. We've evolved beyond that floor on the evolutionary lift. The ragheads and so forth? They may be a bunch of bleeding brendas, but at least they're fucking *human*, if you know what I mean."

Rykki barked in fear.

The guy's hand streaked out at her, clapped her upside her left temple, and withdrew so fast she didn't have a chance to contemplate ducking.

She cringed and whimpered, tried to back up some more, but found herself pressed against her steel-framed crib. She drew her fists into her chest and tucked in her chin and huddled there, aware of the warm moisture sogging her nappies.

"What I just say, darling? So let's just nark it a bit, shall we? Slip ourselves a bit of the blue angel." He scratched his nose. "Where was I? Oh, right. The ragheads and so forth?" He began undoing his belt buckle. "The ragheads and so forth may be a bunch of bleeding droolers, mentally and culturally speaking, but at least they don't have fucking electronic mozzies for brains, do they? At least they don't eat tin cans and shit puters." He stood, unzipped his fly, and mambaed down his trousers over his wide hips. "Of course not. No. They don't do, do they." He released his plum-purple prick and started kneading it in his palm. "See, here's the thing ... To hell with ethnicity and so forth, darling. To hell with race differentials. Way I see it, us humans got to stick together from now on. It's the species that's got to hang tight these days against the likes of, well … against the likes of *you*, darling …"

He skootched toward her, trousers accordioned around his ankles. His prick pulsed in his fist as he squirmed a Swatch genuine pig-bladder condom on it.

A wide good-natured nurturant smile seeped across his face and a mouthful of high-watt teeth caught the floodlight on the pole outside the open flat window and dazzled.

"Give us a snog, darling," he said. "Come on. That's right. There you go. Give nice Mr. McCoo a bit of that old-time precious …"

"A la brava ése, mate."

"Brava?"

"The bull, mate. Cut it. You know the drill. We slice los niños, check out the merchandise for genetic skrims and biologic shims, and *then* Mu-quin get el crédito. Not before. We play the same old same old. Underprende?"

It was clear the Cat Cultist didn't like the Spanglish guy's tone one bit.

"Ya want me tellin' Mu-quin ya don't trust her product, eh? Dat what gwielo captain want? Fine, mon. Cuz de missus? She take out de weddin' suite in Motel Hell. Call up room disservice an' burn dat captain's ass of yours right cross de Channel ta RobespierreLand, is what she do, dui dui."

The Spanglish guy's eyebrows hiked up in mock surprise between his horn implants.

He looked around at his homeboys, three or four of them two-and-a-half-meter-tall genetic malfs, then at the company of Cat Cultists, then shrugged and produced a flurry of hand signals, just like NorAm urban blacks used to do, only vastly more complicated.

Seemed he was semaphoring the contents of a physics textbook.

"Talk to the hands, mate, cuz the face don't understand … Yo no want you to tell Mu-quin a bloody thing. Ease not a fuckin' question of trust, underprende? Ease a fuckin' question of negocios. Same meat, same beat."

170

Outside the church in the sunshine his face had looked normal enough. Inside, though, the fluorescent bio-paint kicked in, announcing him a member of the City of Dis by revealing a spectral vanilla-ice-cream-white makeup mask, black holes where his eyes should've been, dark outline around that cobalt blue lipstick ... the upshot accenting the manifold-pierced fifty-year-old lips and nose, necklace made from tiny knives also treated with the bio-paint, and devil's-horns implants, ditto.

Which nearly made his ripped carnation-pink webbed stockings and thin jumper, scarf, and shawl comprised of mismatching textures and patterns almost beside the point.

The Cat Cultist's head twitched and his necklace bones chittered.

"Airdaddy got de tune, ya know dat good as anyone, mon, hen jin-ji, only dis be Top of de Universal Pops. Best mel-oh-dee in town. Five-for-one blue-light special, know what I'm sayin'?"

The Spanglish guy knew an incipient rant when he heard one. His hands flustered up into another interruption.

"Same meat, same beat. Same as she do for us, mate. Por qué? You got a problemo with us today? Today ain't like every other day?"

"Nothin's up, mon. Nothin'. Airdaddy ain't got no problem, no problem tall. Uh-uh. Airdaddy got de tune down by heart. He sing *every* note. Only, hey, maybe Carbon Miranda want like a little taste of mista sweetmeat here ta check out de del-ee-ka-see himself, eh?" He nodded to one of his cronies, who pushed Zivv forward. Two steps back, Jada reached up and began rubbing that thing behind her ear. "Nip o' de ol' liver, eh? Oh, yaaaaaaaah. Cuz, ya know, mon, de spleen be mean, but de bladder be radder, and de testicle be one grand-mal festival ..."

Carbon Miranda didn't want a little taste. He just wanted the standard protocol observed.

And he couldn't understand why the Cat Cultists didn't.

So he reentered the biz disco with them while Rykki tried to haul her consciousness back from the brink of that feisty-assed booster derm they'd slapped on her wrist in the sampan.

*　*　*

171

She recalled a couple of things about the last two or three hours pretty clearly ... like, for instance, the Cat Cultist talking to her as they slid across the Thames beneath the waxy yellow sun, henchwoman's steroidal biceps flexing with each stroke of the oars, oversweet fishy taste of decay on everyone's tongue, him chronicling all manner of round-the-bend legend ... as in that junk about those chop-chop babies who purportedly were given the plutonium-enriched river water to drink by their progens and went blind and grew to the size of fleshy ponies and never matured physically and lived in the sewers by means of their radar intelligence... or those little stretches of the river that'd supposedly got it through their minds to start wheeling and dealing on their own, aqueous nano-detritus having reached some phase transition around the entire planet, sneaking up on unsuspecting fishermen late at night and pirañaing right through their ankles, snatching them under the tide before they knew what'd hit them, and schlepping them to underwater lairs beneath the docks far out beyond Wool-Itch, where they hatched bughouse-freaky plans for a microrobotic Pollution Revolution aimed at jumping the human soul and making it all epoxy, PVC, and transistors ...

The sampans had beached in Suthick and the party had hiked up into the Spanglish entanglement called the City of Dis.

An ankle-deep orange-brown smog had developed here as the morning unfurled, product of methane and other atmospheric gunge tying the knot with especially heavy fossil-fuel emissions. Down one mews, barefoot kids were throwing matches into the vapors and delighting in the orange bursts and low thunks of combusted gasses. Pigeons and stray kittens hung by their legs in tapas-bar windows lining the busy squeezed passageways. Guinea pigs squeaked in cages fastened to flaking walls. Rykki remembered glancing up and snatching glimpses of lettuce leaves, carrot tops, and purple-fruited hairy grayish-green aubergine bushes sprouting from low rooftop urbacultural compost beds.

The smog dissipated a few blocks farther on and families began appearing in the doorless portals of their whitewashed flats, tending fires, burning junk mail, zines, peanut shells, alfalfa stems, and raggedy reprocessed clothes in do-it-yourself generators for energy. They languidly wagged paper fans printed with Chinese designs in front of their empty sweaty faces as if stirring up the humidity might help disperse it.

Oran whispered something to Tris, voice still tranked, about how way too many of them were missing body parts ... legs, mostly, but also fingers, hands, and arms.

The Cat Cultist overheard them.

"Whutchew go round wearin' body parts ya don't need for if de black market give ya a shitload of credit for de same, mon, eh?"

"They sell their legs?" Zivv asked from farther back.

"Jus' gettin' by like de rest of us," said the henchwoman.

"Not like dem toffee-nosed silvertails up in de nort keeping Uncle Meat in nickers all de while wit all dat jive-accessory shite. Dey live forever, gwielo girls and boys. Rest of us poor wankers ... rest of us poor wankers gotta do what we gotta do, dong?"

He made a quick turn down an even more squeezed passageway, one where his scrawny shoulders almost scraped the walls, through a medievalish wooden-slatted door into an in-between space with sky and rope-and-plank crosswalks above, and left through an opening that felt more like a structural flaw than the entrance to anything.

They stepped into the fag ends of a shadowy gothic church. Bat droppings spattered the stone floor, wooden beams, and fifteen or twenty rows of pews with Spanglish prayers carved into them that led up to a raised pulpit, similarly vandalized, behind which loomed the warped pipes of a broken organ. On one side of those pipes hung an oil painting of the Pope Himself striking the same pose on his Vatican balcony he did on the cover of *Textual Harassment*. On the other ascended an iron spiral staircase. On the pulpit itself, surrounded by a celestial rapture of votive candles, was a television set looping a vid of the Pontiff in full gear and silver-spiked knuckle rings rapping to "Mugwump."

The Cat Cultists led the children up the iron spiral staircase, single-file, into the plank-floored operating theater in the attic of the church, which is where they stood, listening to Carbon Miranda and the cult leader bicker over whether Mu-quin was going to be paid before or after the kids had been medically disemboweled, one at a time, on that wooden table which occupied the middle of the room and was covered with a large sheet of brown oil cloth over which was draped a blanket and below which sat what looked like a half-sized sandbox with sawdust that'd been turned into a porridge by the last organ-grinder extraction, which appeared to've been performed really recently, given the jar containing the opium powder that must've been knocked over during the pre-surgical struggle and hadn't been uprighted yet.

"First, dough ... first come de tasty trepanning, child," the henchwoman said under her breath in Rykki's ear while the others argued. "Release de evil spirits. Bore couple holes right t'rough de skull, mon, right t'rough, *zzzzzzzzz zzzzzzz*... And ya be lyin' dere starin' up at de ceiling, wonderin' if ya'd ever t'ought Airdaddy have such a good sense of humor ..."

As she became increasingly sensate, Rykki heard a rustling below her and took inventory. Somewhere along their journey from The Collapsed Li-Yung, the Cat Cultists had changed her clothes. She was wearing a cheap off-white paper Azid Reign jujitsu suit. She looked around and realized her brothers and sister were wearing the same.

Next she became aware of the palpable body heat in the place. Curls of wet matted hair had cleaved to her cheeks and temples. Everything smelled like the dust from old heating vents.

"Tree minutes, child," the henchwoman continued. "Whole ting take tree minutes. A one off. Only ting bein', dey be de longest tree minutes in de unabridged version of de universe, know what I'm sayin'. *Zzzzzzzzzz* ..."

Rykki extracted her tongue from her pollution sores and turned to ask the henchwoman to kindly shut the fuck up, she was having enough problems as it was, and caught sight of a louse scurrying into the undergrowth of the henchwoman's dreads just above her forehead.

"Qué los bollocks cares la Inglaterra brown-sliced the sand niggers, mate?" the Spanglish guy was saying. "We got more immediate dances a bailar, underprende? Quién the fuck watches la televisión anyway? Quién the fuck cares what the fuck you care?"

"Airdaddy don't give a piss what you watch, mon. Airdaddy just give a piss whether Airdaddy gettin' paid or whether Airdaddy gettin' laid. Which ya tellin' Airdaddy he be gettin'?"

"You saying yo'm *hoodooing* you? That what you decirme?"

"Ya tellin' Airdaddy you ain't?"

"Hey," up going the hands again, tiny knives clinking. "You wanna know something? You wanna know something good? Well, fuck you, mate. Fuck your pals there. And fuck bloody Airdaddy, too. Underprende?"

A rush of birdbone necklace clackets.

"Fuck *you*, devil mon. Fuck off out of my face, ya little gwielo slut."

Carbon Miranda's eyebrows hiked up between his horn implants, only this time the surprise wasn't mock in the least.

"What you call me?"

The cult leader jutted his twiggy chest forward as far as it would go, which was perhaps an extra centimeter.

"I be callin' ya what ya tink I be callin' ya, ya muthafriggin' granny-jazzer."

The attic got real silent.

The trachelate cables in the genetic malfs started slithering beneath their yellow-brown skin. The henchwoman rose to her feet very slowly as if she was in the midst of a tai-chi number. Carbon Miranda glared at the Cat Cultist who, glaring at a point just behind Carbon Miranda's head, raised his fingerless mitt to his freckle-busy epidermis below his jaw. He opened his mouth to say something Rykki knew would do no one here any good, but Carbon Miranda beat him to the whammy.

"Hey," he said, eyes skidding past the Cat Cultist, "what the *fuck*?"

The cult leader turned. The henchwoman turned. All the genetic malfs and cult cronies turned.

And Rykki turned, too.

Blood was leaking freely from Jada's nostrils, over her lips barely parted in amazement, down her chin, and onto the floor planks at her thonged feet. It formed dark red pop-art designs there. A broad smear crossed her right anemic cheek where she'd tried to rub it away with the back of her hand.

Jada's eyes had tuned in to some destination on the far side of the wall, through hundreds of buildings and passageways, across the Thames.

The hand not wiping absentmindedly at the blood was still rubbing that thing behind her ear. As it did, her arms began to tremble. The small quake moved up into her neck, her head, down into her legs.

Her body stiffened, lurched, and hit the floor with a cumbersome clunk. Rykki heard her sister's vertebrae grate, bone on bone. Her long hair the color of coffee held up to sunshine landed delicately around her.

She was standing there, Jada, screaming inside her sister's head.

She was gone.

16. THE FUTURE OF STATUES

They didn't stop running till the red sun began to bulge over Blackfires Bridge and the tribal drumming commenced across London's parks.

Winded and hungry, they slowed to a jumpy amble along the southern Bankside littered with appliance boxes and meaters, and before long Zivv collapsed on a pile of rubble that used to be part of the low wall hemming the river. He lay back, stretched his arms above his head like a horizontal diver, and shut his eyes. Tris took a seat beside him, pulled his knees to his chest, and steadied his chin on his kneecaps. Oran squatted an arm's length away, pink eyes trained on the Post Tower bayoneting from the urban disorganization to the northwest.

Rykki stood behind him, hands resting on his underdeveloped shoulders, feeling like she was standing at psychic Ground Zero.

No one said anything for a long time.

Rykki listened to the bubble of local silence the four of them created.

Behind her lifted the Beargardens. Nearby a row of blacked-out storefronts were marked, if you looked closely, with round stickers no bigger than bottle caps. The stickers had green phones printed on them signifying those fly-by-night dens where hackers broke into the lines, established illicit connections, then charged others to use them for long-distance calls at substantially reduced rates. Rykki wanted to walk over and ring up Magda and tell her where they were and ask her what to do. She wanted to watch Magda sitting across the table from them in their classroom at the labs and listen to her sweet voice introduce them to the world and make it sound like a seductive place again.

Rykki looked at the dimming outline of St. Paul's across the river. The chunk missing from its dome somehow made her feel that much sadder. Her belly hurt. She massaged Oran's shoulders and he leaned back into her. In front of the cathedral muddled two- and three-story governcorp flats, laundry hanging in doorways and off porches, smoke from private generators fibriling out several dozen chimneys and settling in the playgrounds and empty car parks of cracked tarmac below.

"What's so great about being human anyway?" Zivv said, eyes still shut.

He brought a leaf-brown finger up to his lips, scratched, and lowered his hand to his tummy.

Rykki sensed a physical distance from her own body, like her mind was living in a tiny vacuum-sealed tin within a larger vacuum-sealed tin drifting in an expansive interstellar void that existed somewhere deep inside her torso, and the best she could do was send these staticky messages out to her corporeal being the same way those astronauts on Mars would in the next few years send their staticky messages back to earth, the transmission-delay extraordinary, every fifth word lost to solar flares and cosmic gibber.

"It would've been nice to've been normal, wouldn't it," Oran said.

"Yeah," said Tris, picking at one of his toes, "it would've been."

"I don't know," Zivv said. He opened his eyes and stared up at the sky turning into roses. "Whole thing seems a bit, what … overrated, doesn't it. I mean, what sort of role models are they, anyway?" He sat up and rubbed his nose with the back of his wrist and scanned the governcorp flats. "Isn't like they've exactly made a hell of a meal out of it, is it. Aren't exactly mustard keen on the overachievement business."

Tris raised his head from his cuticle excavation.

"I don't *feel* abnormal," he said.

Zivv's glance brushed over to him.

"You don't feel *ab*normal because you've never felt *normal.* You need to've known what normal feels like before you could've felt other than normal. Which you haven't done."

"How much machinery do you need in your veins before you're not quite normal, I wonder."

"I miss Jada," Rykki said.

Oran peered down uncomfortably at the rubble between his thongs: dirty red bricks, bent steel mesh, a crushed can of Old Speckled Hen.

Zivv rubbed his nose again.

"We all do, Rykki," he said. "That's why we're not talking about her."

Rykki's hands stopped working on Oran's shoulders. Oran reached up and pet them. She looked down at her brother's mushroom-soft neck.

"What ever happened to kids?" she said.

"They bleeding killed us for their mouthwash and dogs' flea collars."

Rykki realized they'd stopped using their vocal cords. She heard Zivv speaking in her head.

Nearby an Indian woman with a shiny pink arm-stub poking from the left sleeve of her formless beige blouse and facial skin like a glazed saddle stepped out of the crowd and approached a Japanese couple, remaining hand extended. A good quarter of her hair had been burned off and what remained in spotty tracts across her corrugated scalp was a shade somewhere between peeled bark and tooth decay. Her butt appeared to have deflated in her formless beige pants collected with black elastic bands around her ankles.

"Combustion," she told the couple. "Walking combustion. I stroll down street one day. I explode."

The Japanese guy reached into his leather flight jacket, scooped out his cloth wallet, unzipped some flap in it, and, trying not to meet her eyes, dropped a couple of coins into her palm.

The Indian woman performed some placatory bobbing and moved off.

"So what do we do?" asked Tris.

The sun expanded over Blackfires Railway Bridge till it seemed a double of the earth. Rykki looked at it directly and saw it wobbling through heatwaves that made it appear London was melting.

"The Chunnel," Oran suggested. "We walk the maintenance tunnel into Paneuropa. Follow the old Exile Route. Two days. Three tops. Disappear in Paris."

"It's rigged," Zivv said. "Isolationists set off that pair of tacticals last year to make sure it stays that way. Bio-contaminates." He processed. "Scotland. What about Scotland?"

"First time we spent a pence of credit," Tris said, moving on to a new butternut-skinned toe, "Aiwa-Benz'd be on their way. Wouldn't have time to walk half a block before wassup luv ..."

As the one-and-a-half-armed Indian woman retreated from the Japanese couple, two other women—one Caribbean, one with a large quantity of Scandinavian genes running through her cellular matrices, both likewise missing appendages and flashing lots of once-semiliquefied skin—approached them from behind.

The Caribbean bumped into the guy hard and immediately sent up a moil of flamboyant apologies. The guy's girlfriend in a squarish blond wig looked on, sincerely discomposed by all the unseemly noise the Caribbean was making. Rykki had just about concluded they must have both been tourists when she glimpsed the dip's white hand with scraggy fingernails disappearing into the guy's flight jacket ... then more bobbing on the Caribbean's part ... and then the activity in that area of the Bankside subsided and eased back into routine.

Zivv rose and began patting himself off. His paper suit was already ripped around the neck and shoulders from where one of those Spanglish giants tried to grab him as he shot down that spiral staircase and into the narrow streets and passageways outside the church. Rykki could see the reddish welts where the giant's fingernails had raked across his skin and the greenish-yellow bruises where he had clipped Zivv on the cheek as he weaseled past.

The sun looked like it would soon set the atmosphere aflame.

"Bri'n," Rykki said.

Everyone turned to look at her.

"What's in Bri'n?" asked Zivv.

Oran recalled first.

"The airport," he said. "The new airport."

"Beijing, you mean," Zivv said, thinking out loud.

"Right," said Tris. "All those people. Everything just on the other side of the rules. It's the perfect place to be lost in, isn't it."

"Only what about the credit?" Oran said. "We've got to have credit to purchase the tickets. Where's that come from, then?"

Rykki calculated.

"I don't know," she said.

"And even if we *could* get us some?" Tris asked. "It'd be like before, really, wouldn't it. Second we spend the stuff, here comes the Chaika."

"Unless," Oran said, "we don't spend it till we absolutely have to."

Zivv took stock of him.

"Till the very last minute, you mean."

"Cuz by then ... we'll be ... what ..."

"A flipping flushed memory."

"Which means ... what?" Tris said, chin rising off kneecaps.

"Which *means*," Zivv said, "we've got one bleeding long bit of the old leg work ahead of us, don't we. Come on."

PART FOUR:
FEAR VELOCITY OF THE
ROBOTIC MYRIAPODS

17. THE INVISIBLES

A bluish-gray lucence accumulated around everything … like in dreams, Rykki thought, as she shadowed Zivv deeper back into the City of Dis and on into southern Suthick.

Suthick unfolded into Lambeth, Lambeth into Stock-It-Well, and Stock-It-Well into Brixton, tight Brazilified passageways opening onto avenues of rundown public-housing towers and single-floor turn-of-the-century cinderblock-and-cloudy-glassed storefronts.

Zivv slowed by a McLenin that had piled its daily rubbish in plastic bags on the street and waited for some older Plugheads who wore greatcoats, brown wool pants, and heavy Army boots to finish. Zivv and Rykki and Tris and Oran then moved in and had some okay luck with a box of semi-moldy buns they found which tasted just fine as long as they picked around the gray-green speckles.

When one of the Ciba-Geigy security cams atop a lamp post caught sight of them and started making some intimidating threats they decided to push on.

Rykki did real well till Strut'em, perimeter of her awareness a far-reaching band of glazed alertness. Only outside a 7-Eleven advertising take-away tests for miscellaneous diseases she noticed Oran starting to lag behind. She figured she'd slow too and give him a jazz-up.

As she did, her lallies got this congested feeling and all that glazed alertness smudged into gray distraction.

Tris suggested they start scouting a place to rack out, which Zivv, not all that on the hop himself, agreed to without even turning around. He cut down the first side street they came to, past a Blockbuster holoporn superstore, a National Westminster fitted with two scary-looking armed ATMs, and launderette. At the end were a few abandoned lots with weeds growing through gravel and, beyond, the commons, an expansive tract of beaten-down grass disrupted by a pair of unpainted football goal posts.

Families had set up small campsites around open fires and cooked in aluminum kettles on aluminum tripods.

Rykki, Zivv, Oran and Tris traversed the commons till they found the vestiges of a genetically fiddled rose hedge in a small public garden and bedded down maybe three meters away from another tribe of teens, most of whom flaunted spraybombed skateboards and matching hair.

Rykki lay with her fingers meshed behind her head, knees cocked. She surveyed the night sky through a fabric of branches as it nuanced toward what you could no longer argue was anything besides the first shades of daylight.

"What do you remember, then?" Tris asked after a while without moving his lips.

"About what?" Zivv said.

He had assumed the same position Rykki had, not twelve centimeters away, except he'd perched his left ankle on his right knee and was rotating his left foot clockwise.

"The ... you know ... Your other past. The one they put in your head."

Rykki investigated her pollution sores. They'd definitely peaked and were on their way toward convalescence.

"My progens and me as a kid," Tris said. He sat back on his heels and brushed his palm over a spiny clump of grass before him. "I remember goldleaf. A whopping chalice. Smoke climbing from one of those Catholic incense things."

"Censers," Oran said.

In the dreamlight, his skin appeared to radiate a cornflower-blue aura. Sleeplessness had tinctured the fleshy concavities beneath his eyes

186

black-currant purple. He lay back and bent an arm across the bridge of his nose.

"Censers," Tris said. "Right. And some kind of liturgy in this really kicking adobe church in the NorAm southwest. And then all this dreadful … *stuff* … happening. An alternative me sprawled on some cold aluminum gurney looking into the faces of all these EMS types working above me. And these … what … flames, like, burning in my veins."

"Glycerol," Zivv said.

Tris, palming the grass, glanced over.

"What?"

"Glycerol. Somatic antifreeze. They were preparing you for cryonic suspension. Doing it while you were alive."

"Do I want to hear about this?" said Oran from under his arm.

Rykki noticed the leaves around them glowed with a very slight blue-green fluorescence like the underwater animals they mimicked. She began rubbing her belly with long slow circular motions.

"Bhopal for me," Zivv said. "Chemical spill. My father was a VP there. I was out playing football with my friends on the street one morning when the fog rolled in. He paid to have me flown to NorAm, med crew doing their freeze-dirty on me the whole flight …"

One of the skateboarders stood, strolled up the hedge, unzipped his fly, and urinated in an unassertive splattery stream. Finished, he reached into his back pocket, tugged out a handkerchief, and lovingly dabbed the tip of his penis dry as if it were a pet.

"This place," Oran said when he was done. "I don't know where it is or anything, only there's this woman, and we've just stepped off a service lift. I try not to think about it much. She lets me go first. We're in a mews. I don't remember any pain … Strange, isn't it."

"Strange?"

"Just this sense of being thrown forward by three hard jolts, like, *kersplat, kersplat, kersplat,* and this feeling of momentum you can't control."

"Someone *shot* you?"

"I wasn't … I don't really know how to say it … I wasn't doing something the way they wanted me to …"

"They?"

"The people in charge. I don't know. I wasn't making them one hundred percent any more."

"So they *snuffed* you?"

"Only, then … it's odd, really. The blokes who whack me? They're also the blokes who have me iced up, I'm pretty sure. Like just in case they might need me someday. Except, well, I guess they didn't, did they." He lowered his arm and sat up, pulled his knees to his chest and looked out across the commons. "What happened to Jada back there—you think it's happening to us?"

"I don't know," Zivv said.

"No one does," said Tris, examining the scratches on the back of his hand and arm where one of the Cat Cultists had gone for him. "Her neural cells just stopped getting along with each other, looks like."

"A one-off wetware crash," said Oran.

"Yeah," Zivv said. "Unless it wasn't."

Tris ceased examining his hand.

"What?"

"Maybe carbon isn't especially bugs about silicon, chemically speaking."

"Must be what most people'd remember about their lives if they could, you know," said Rykki. "The end of them, I mean. The part that counts. Over and over."

"Assuming we're remembering. Yeah."

Oran took his eyes off the commons.

"You're saying we're not?"

"I'm just saying it *seems* we are. But … well, em, what makes us so sure about it? How can you be so positive the electrical-impulse shite going through your head has in actual fact some sort of correlative in the past?"

"Maybe we're experiencing a sort of cerebral short-circuit, you're saying."

"Who's to tell us differently?"

"But … Look," Oran said. "I remember everything. I see the woman. I see the mews. She was wearing a latex glove with fake fingerprints on it … implicate the blokes in charge, keep the heat off her. I feel the shots."

"Do you?"

"Yeah. Absolutely. I do."

"Sure. Absolutely. Unless."

"Unless?"

"Unless you don't. Unless the nano-shite in your head's pulling a botch. Or unless you're hallucinating, us not having slept particularly well in we can't even figure out how long. Plus not to mention being pumped up with god-knows-what kind of simply gruesome meds. What if they put that nano-shite in your head to act just like memories, only it didn't, quite, just to confuse you for some reason we can't even begin to fathom? Or just to give you a false sense of security. Or maybe they put it there so it'd override what in actual fact happened to us back in those bleeding rooms on Hans Crescent, because it's just too ghastly to even contemplate … except, of course, it didn't work. Or maybe it did, and the ghastly memories we presently remember are nish compared to the *really* ghastly memories of what honestly happened. Or maybe They're just having a bit of a laff at our expense."

He reversed his position, perching his right ankle on his left knee and rotating his right foot clockwise.

"Yeah," he said. "You remember. Unless, of course, you don't."

"Our memories aren't our memories?"

"All I'm saying is try to prove it one way or the other and see how far you get."

"So unless two people remember the same deal …"

"You don't have yourself a proper memory, strictly speaking, do you. I mean, what makes something a memory? Sometimes you have this really vivid recollection, don't you, and you could swear it's the real thing, couldn't you, only when you tell someone else about it to corroborate your story because you know they were there and all, they don't remember it. They'll swear blind it never happened. You'll swear blind it

189

did. What's that mean?"

Rykki tried to listen to the sixty-cycle hum in her brain and lose herself in the wonderful scent of Magda's Black Romance ... and almost succeeded, almost flubbed off the high narrow ledge of consciousness ... but, as she leaned forward, something swam up from the obscurity below.

Seemed initially the blackness itself was oscillating ... only then she made out the tremendous flapping black cape ... and the head shaved down the middle, hair on either side moussed into large black wings ... and that rouge-corpse visage resolving right in front of her own startled face, red plastic eye-shells reminding Rykki of something arthropodal ...

"File deleted, darling," Jack the Ripper whispered like a lover trying to work some sort of sexual mojo on her.

Rykki smelled warm electronics.

He leaned forward, his scar-shiny nose no more than a millimeter from hers, and added one more word ...

Crash.

They picked up the A23 shortly after twilight next day and entered an industrial zone of oil-storage tanks braced with crisscrossing iron girders like geodesic bone structures.

Headlights bobbed past, catching in their high beams lengths of dark brick wall, unmanned bullet-proof guard booths, and razor-wire running the length of tall barricades.

The skin between Rykki's toes blistered.

She kept trying to walk but it didn't work, so she sat down Indian-crossed-legged-style on an overturned shopping cart.

Zivv retraced his steps and crouched to examine the damage. He tore off the hem of her trousers, folded the strip into soft rectangles, working mostly by feel in the gloam, and wound the improvised dressing around her right thong nub for protection.

"There," he said. "Try that."

She did, and detected a funny wet-paper-towel smell and paused to suss out where it was coming from. Behind the dampness fermented something metallic and fecal.

Instinctively she reached down between her legs.

Her fingertips moistened with brownish-burgundy menstrual blood.

"Oh, well, bollocks," she said.

Zivv laughed.

"Congratulations, Rykki. You're all grown up."

Oran and Tris overtook them and digested the situation. Tris put an arm around Rykki's waist and gave her a squeeze.

"You okay?"

"The flowers, they used to call it," Oran said. "Flowers ..."

"Flowers my arse," Rykki said. "More like a couple liters of tar inside my belly. Only, well, fuck." She deliberated, trying to put it into words. "It feels like ... like I just haven't gotten used to my own body yet. Thirteen, and I haven't got a clue." She held out her fingertips as evidence. "What a flipping mess."

"Not to worry," said Zivv.

They each contributed their lower trouser legs and shirt arms, and he concocted several paper pads, one of which Rykki slipped down the front of her outfit and shimmied into place.

"Uck," she said.

"Not great," he said, "but not absolutely horrendous, either. Should just do, shouldn't they."

"I guess. Thanks. So. Remind me once more."

"Remind you?"

"Of exactly what all those pluses to aging are, exactly."

"Seem to've lost the combination to that one."

Rykki felt someone flick on the slo-mo switch in her perception.

She expected Zivv to say something more, but he just stood there, confused as she was.

She woke around noon, flesh so sensitive she thought of the translucent bodies of those tiny fish you could see their internal organs through. Her soggy uterus hurt and her constipated bowels hurt and her inflamed breast buds hurt and once, when they were sleeping, Zivv curled back into her, accidentally grazing her left nipple with his elbow, and she had to bite her lip not to poke him in retaliation.

On the other side of the industrial zone the landscape ruffled into hills. Rykki perceived everything like she might if she'd had a really bad cold, hardly noticing the disestablished towns they moved through, or the hedge-lined country roads that commenced cutting off left and right, or how, just past a blacked-out village called Horley, they connected with the dual carriageway of the M23 and things jounced into wheaty pastures.

People began turning up along the roadside, wobbling on bicycles, or pedaling tuk-tuks loaded with Persian rugs and second-hand clothes and caged chickens, or just schlubbing like Rykki and her brothers, some wearing governcorp-issued respirators, some palming handkerchiefs over their mouths and noses, some with children in tow.

Most plowed north, toward the city.

Which made Rykki wonder … till, that is, a carbolic stench of incinerating garbage laced with herbicides wafted in, and a few kils farther they came across RAC rescue service vehicles and road crews burning off a mass attack of superweeds, hacking them back from the motorway which the weeds had tried to cross, fast-growth genes introduced into the agricultural grasses around here having spread into the wild population and gone mental … which reminded Rykki of her own body, how increasingly many of these tender red zits had started erupting across her forehead almost hourly, so raw it seemed they'd grown in backwards.

Passing beneath a halogen-bright flyover where some of the environmental refugees had decided to rest, Rykki realized she was leaking through again. Her flow had been erratic … scarcely anything one minute, a surge the next. She'd already used up all but one of the paper pads Zivv had fashioned for her. And no matter how diligently she tried to contract her muscles down there, she simply couldn't find a way to control it. And now, daybreak beginning to scrub the sky platinum, she felt this warm seepage between her legs and understood if she checked she'd find her pubic hair matted and her inner thighs smeared with slimy mucus and, well, that was it, that was all, and so she came to a standstill in the middle of the verge and began to cry …

Zivv and Oran and Tris gathered around her, embarrassed, fidgety, not quite sure what they'd done, what they hadn't done, what they should've done, only feeling extremely bad for her, which made Rykki feel even worse for herself, especially when Oran tried to hug her and she reflexively wrenched away from him even though what she sincerely wanted most in the world this very second was the hug he was trying to offer her.

She stamped her foot in exasperation, and so Tris tried asking her what was wrong, but Rykki didn't *know* what was wrong, or couldn't even *begin* to articulate it ... and so she just stood there and cried, stood there and wept, and Zivv stood right next to her, gauging, and then decided to take command by reaching out and gently laying his hands on Rykki's shoulders and guiding her in a shuffle down the verge and onto a slip road, slowly, as if they were making their way across a perfectly smooth frozen sea whose ice layer was exactly one fingernail thick.

Half a kil farther lifted the whitewashed broken-glass-topped walls of The Phoenician Arms, a franchised safe-zoned compound themed after a nineteen-thirties Pre-Shudder Hollywood that existed only in the minds of its present-day architects and inhabitants.

Around it grew a henge of palm-tree seedlings encased in green plastic wrap-around shields.

Oran, who'd never seen one before, kneeled to touch a specimen.

In mid-reach, a small raspberry-vested Pekingese with a mouthful of what appeared to be from Oran's angle a thousand enameled thumbtacks sprung from nowhere for his hand, then yakked and stiffened when its choker engaged.

"Heel, Fopson! *Heel*!" shouted the distinguished-looking man in a beige three-piece suit and bowler who incarnated at the other end of the lead.

His skin was the same dark color as Zivv's, but it had been coated with a thin waxy layer into which very fine particles of gold glitter had been set.

"Oh, very much in excess of a thousand pardons, please," he said. "You must forgive my poor canine. He is what do you say ... getting exceedingly far on in longevity. His transistors are sadly not the spring chickens they might be."

Rykki glanced down and, sure enough, poor Fopson was exhibiting those characteristic flank twitches that spelled an old model.

Plus his eyes kept flicking saccadically like he was using most of his energy reserves just to scan the ground point blank in front of his dry peeling-snake-skin nose.

She reached out to pet him and he snarled at her.

His owner re-jerked the choker.

Fopson re-yakked.

"No need to worry in the very least, little boys and girl. My poor canine believes he wants to be what do you say an Alsatian when he matures in bodily dimensions ... don't you, my little four-legged small-pawed angel with interesting breath vapors. But his interior is a full jar of marmalade left out in the ultraviolet radiation too long."

When Rykki touched Fopson's wiry coat he tilted his head at a rigid angle to get a better look at her and she saw the Cartier logo stamped across each eye.

"Sweet dog," she said.

"The day is full of loveliness, is it not? Although I believe it goes almost without commenting upon an exceedingly warm one as well. But warmness is not an unexpected condition in the middle of the summer months. In the middle of the winter ones, either, I am supposing. Forty by noon, they report to me with great earnestness on my radio. An extraordinary thing, is it not, this matter called weather." He appraised the smoky sky. "There is nothing like a conflagration with remarkable chemical fragrances to start one's day. But it can reek hammock on the respiratory system. I must confess to you if I am not being overly graphic in which case pardon me exceedingly much I located a clot of blood on my handkerchief upon my awakening this morning." Then he appraised the kids. Many straight white teeth. "But that is not your foremost concern at present, I am imagining."

"We're on our way to Bri'n, sir," Rykki said. "From London. And, well, we needed a bit of a rest, didn't we," slipping a squiz at Zivv.

"A rest?"

"We're looking for work," Zivv explained.

"Plenty of jobs building the Melt barriers, we hear," said Oran.

"In Bri'n you will most assuredly locate better prospects than in London. There is little more than filth and bodies in that particular great rotting metropolis. This is the wonderful thing about the British citizenry. It is wholeheartedly committed to doing just enough to get by and no more. 'How tiny can we make this item?' they are asking themselves silently on a daily basis. 'Yes, indeed,' they say, with much laudable courtesy in their voices, 'we can always employ a small part less of whatever it is we are employing. We can always perform this function with fewer demanding design perimeters.'" He chuckled. "Small island, small ambitions. The imperial years I am supposing take a lot out of a country. Do you perhaps know the nice thing about cities?"

They shook their heads.

"The perhaps nice thing about cities is how easily you can depart from them. Bombay. Tokyo. But enough. Should you not on this beautiful if admittedly warm day be in your flat with your I am sure loving mothers and fathers, who are most certainly in the process of missing you?"

"We don't have any parents," Rykki said.

"You are saying then what to me?"

"We're … Well. We're sort of on our own."

The man looked startled.

"You are then telling me that you are comprising the poor naked udderclass of street urchins the woman with no eyebrows tells me about on the evening news on a nightly basis?"

"Sorry?"

The man tsked.

He evaluated them compassionately and extracted his gold pocket watch from his waistcoat, flipped it open, and consulted its liquid-crystal display.

"I am making you a little proposition at this moment, if you will be so kind."

"A proposition?"

"Here it is going. I am currently participating in a law-practice establishment located in a southerly direction in the quaint if poorly ventilated town of Cuckfield. My uncle and his third wife, another pair of narratives altogether, were kind enough to arrange this position for me.

195

We are corporate data-theft specialists. This is why you are seeing I left my beautiful homeland which boasts perhaps of a less-than-tactful civil war and many small nuclear devices and journeyed to the renowned Heathrow Airport where miniaturization is a way of existence. I am driving to see the person of my uncle later this morning on an interesting case involving a company that is stealing identities of very good governcorp workers from the Other Side and selling them to very bad governcorp workers in the Big Television. Allow me to treat you to a proper English breakfast rife with cholesterol and a multitude of fatty acids and I will then be in excess of happiness to transport you as far as Cuckfield."

"That's awfully kind of you … really … but, em, we couldn't trouble you any …"

"Call me Mr. Gu."

"Mr. Goo?"

"Not Goo, G-O-O, as in disgusting running matter, but Gu, G-U, as in short for Gujranwala Gwadar Mymensingh. Quite an English mouthful, I am certain."

"We still have a really long way to go and all …"

"I cannot hear you, metaphorically speaking. For let me explain. The drive on the M23 is comprised of exceeding dullness. I am in great selfish need of company to pass my boredom."

Mr. Gu flipped his watch closed.

"Come. My ears are plugged with viscous oils. I am having some brief business on this side of the wall, and then we are off."

He looked at them expectantly.

"Oh, well, yeah, sure, fine," Zivv said. "I mean, it sounds great, doesn't it. Thank you."

"It does," said Rykki. "You're very kind, Mr. Gu."

"Not in the extremely least. No no. You are coming right this way, if you may …"

18. THE PHOENICIAN ARMS

On a cement bench near the front gate sat a skanky flyweight teen with boiled-egg-white skin and a black headband that held five colorless strands of chemo-ed hair out of his nervous eyes.

He'd struck a world-class fake-relaxed splay, long arms hosed over the back of the bench and long legs jutting straight before him, torso resting on its lumbar vertebrae.

Judging by his black and violet Spandex suit, violet super-hightop Gomi Boy techno-sneakers, and awe-inspiringly excessive case of the sweats, Rykki would've guessed he'd just this minute returned from a long-distance run ... only he was so thin and fragile-looking she had the suspicion he'd probably snap his lallies like bread sticks if he actually stood and took even a single step forward.

Everything about him was completely still save those nervous eyes, which shot everywhere at once, and his left foot, which jittered like it wanted to detach from his leg and take its chances solo.

Which peeved Fopson no end.

The Pekingese lowered his head and raised his bum and began barking and tugging at his lead.

Which obviously peeved Mr. Gu, since his mouth kept making these lemon-wedge-sucking flexes as he reached into the same pocket where he kept his watch and pulled out something that appeared to Rykki to be a wad of black-market cash which he balled up in his fist so she couldn't see for sure and sort of inserted it into the skinny guy's palm, which disappeared and reappeared with a vial of some amethyst liquid which went into Mr. Gu's palm so fast Rykki couldn't completely swear she'd just seen a real-life pharmaceutical transaction, except she knew she had, especially because the skinny guy was now staring right at the kids and sweating even more than he had been thirty seconds earlier.

Next he was up and walking away, all his bones miraculously intact, effecting these lunge-like movements which suggested a clanky Gernsbackian robot's approximation of retreat, and Rykki understood this was the kind of guy who was going to go through the rest of his life sweating and sweating no matter what the actual ambient temperature was.

"Not to worry one more throb of the unremitting cardiovascular muscle," Mr. Gu said, moseying up the flagstone footpath toward The Phoenician Arms' entrance, a replica of the iron gates that used to rise in front of Paramount Pictures.

Fopson waddled rat-like, halting for micropulses to shnork at thought-provoking odors along the way.

"I am not what do you say it on the sleeve." He chuckled at the idea. "Exciting with out-of-the-ordinary foreign emotions as that might be. No. I have never if the truth be known even sampled an antihistamine. Such drugs transform my nasal cavities into exceedingly dehydrated forsaken places. I am rather suffering from a Western malady that once made a brief sojourn to my homeland."

"And that's the cure?" Rykki asked, indicating with her chin his pocket where he'd slipped the vial.

"A thousand hopes that it might prove to be thus, but, alas, this is not at all likely. It is rather a symptomatic corrective that works with all the success of a pair of fallen arches on a commanding length of pavement. Have you made the verbal acquaintance of CHRUDS?"

"Chrono-Unific Deficiency Syndrome. Major time malf that hits the brain stem. Lots of cases up in London."

"Those in excess of intelligence at the Centers for Disease Control tell the following tale of misfortune. A poor single mother of Mexiental extraction with the now-infamous-among-my-gentle-countrymen appellative Mai Ri Huana with great unhappiness acquired said malady environmentally in the spectacular metropolitan City of Angles. She bequeathed it to her with every reason to believe otherwise innocent unborn child who she then, filled with terrible remorse and pecuniary diminishment, put into an adoptive condition."

Mr. Gu halted in front of the black slab of plastic set into the whitewashed wall beside the gate and lay his right hand on it. The slab beeped and the lock on the wrought-iron door in the gate ticked open.

A gaggle of surveillance cameras along the broken-glass-topped walls twittered awake and began tracking the group as it moved into the compound.

This time Rykki had no doubt, given that cumbersome military housing of theirs, they were the genuine articles. Tasers, she knew, were about the least of the menu options anyone crossing them would have to worry about.

"Mai Ri's child who maintains the eminent cognomen of Donna Huana," Mr. Gu went on, "carried her heart-breaking abnormality to Anchorage and into the unsuspecting home of her newly-obtained parents, Vern and Vera Vague. Through certain unsightly but unavoidable infantile emissions it is terrible to say she unintentionally infected them. A single month later, Vern and Vera left their presumably still sweet and surely still innocent Donna with Vera's ever-so-kind and correlatively innocent sister, Vanessa, while they not-yet-knowingly undertook a second honeymoon of joy. They traveled to the largely exotic in their minds land of my birth, where also happened to be businessing two music executives. Their names, equally reeking with eminence, were Marco Polydor and Laurie Anasin."

"Air Pyrate Muzzik," Rykki said.

"Precisely. Of Plain Brown Rapper and Kiss My Axe state of famousness."

"Achilles Heal, Viva Bonni Suicide, the Pope Himself."

"I could not have named such luminaries with greater accurateness."

"Everyone who's anyone, really, musically speaking," Zivv said.

"Your correctness is truly overwhelming. I stand before you breathless with full-bodied amazement. How does it come to pass, please, that a poor naked street urchin such as your kind self has knowledge of such important but possibly from my point of view recondite matters?"

The kids got uncomfortably quiet.

Rykki's uterus, which she'd forgotten about since Fopson had almost connected with Oran's hand, began glumping again. She waited till everyone was looking somewhere else, then secretly reached up under her paper top and began rubbing.

"This sure is some place," she said.

The Phoenician Arms was a trim, green, two-hundred-and-fifty acre social delusion.

Each self-sufficient residence impersonated a quaint two-story red-tile-roofed brown-sugar stucco DisCal apartment building from the beginning of the twentieth century. Pink Moorish columns supporting turnip-shaped lintels framed the windows.

The residences had been constructed around a series of what looked like unnaturally blue swimming pools but were, Rykki figured, in many cases solar ponds possessing a layer of highly saline water at the bottom which trapped the sun's heat.

Passing near one, she felt its pump bump to life beneath her, and remembered from her lessons it was sucking the hot salty fluid into some below-ground power station where it would be allowed to evaporate, the resulting vapor used to drive engines that assisted in driving the enclave, while the cool liquid at the top would be sucked out during the milder night and employed tomorrow for air-conditioning.

"And so the Vagues infected Marco Polydor and Laurie Anasin?" Zivv said.

"Through an unmentionable variety of sexual practices which are best not to dwell upon at any length in the vicinity of such good-hearted little juveniles as yourselves assuredly are being."

Other pools farther on functioned as aquaculture farms. Men in blue jeans and t-shirts, hooks and strainers instead of hands attached to the ends of their arms, harvested oysters into large wheelbarrows.

Rykki faded into the things around her.

"So what happened?" Oran asked.

"Mr. Polydor and Mrs. Anasin had come what do you say scouting a new band called with slight morbidity the Pygmy Children, which were themselves on their first tour through a large number of unpleasantly mold-infested clubs frequented by double-headed silverfish and persons without essential bodily limbs."

"*Kujichagulia Guntz.*"

"Here I am catching my breath again."

"Everyone's playing it," Tris said. "It's a great album."

"Well. Mr. Polydor and Mrs. Anasin signed them while being far too engrossed in certain venereal role-playing games extremely popular in Soho establishments some fifty years ago for perhaps their own welfare."

The brownish air was laden with honeysuckle and tangy smoke from the motorway burn. Orange and yellow fruit plumped on upsettingly vivid green bushes sheared into the silhouettes of huge tea pots, ducks, cones. White lawn furniture aggregated here and there though no one but the workers appeared to be outside.

Rykki noticed something large, shiny, and brown moving languidly beneath one of the bushes as they neared.

She focused, but she couldn't get a good look at what it was.

"Which I am in excess of sadness to be recounting brings my tale to me, one unfortunate Gujranwala Gwadar Mymensingh."

"They infected you ..."

"I happened one morning quite by despondent accident to shake hands with a client in Karachi who as it so transpired had engaged the services of the same daily help who were at that very moment ministering to our happy-go-lucky music executives. This small amount of highly regrettable manual gesturing has propelled me into an affliction whereby I am currently being visited by a series of intense memories which may or may not be my own. They involve the nineteenth-century colonization of

201

my beautiful homeland by certain less-than-happy-go-lucky British imperialists with extremely lengthy cannons."

"And so that's why you take that stuff," Zivv said.

"Sadly I must affirm this to be the case."

"And that's why you came to Britain."

"Hence my long if educational journey by air to the renowned Heathrow Airport, and forenoonal dosage of this wonder-elixir produced by the friendly persons at Mainline Pharmaceuticals. They sell it to me as a test version what do you say under the countenance."

"Under the counter."

"Quite so."

A python-sized millipede darted from the shade, flickered and wove across the flagstone path, and disappeared down a thigh-sized hole beneath another bush.

Rykki's frontal lobes produced a mountain range of brain-activity spikes.

Mr. Gu raised his palm like a crossing guard.

"No need to be worrying in the very least. You are simply in the process of having met our guard dogs, metaphorically speaking. Bioengineered by the caring persons at Virgin Protection Limited. They are automatically programmed to recognize your bodily emissions as you are stepping through the gate."

"What if they don't?" asked Oran, several steps behind the rest.

"Ah, well, then things do not proceed in full karmic bountifulness with respect to one's corporeal essence. Suffice it for me to pronounce several extremely unpleasant adjectives and nouns. Steel-like pincers. Contractile motions. Foul-smelling but highly effective neurotoxins."

"..."

"But never to be troubling yourself even at the minimum length of a grasshopper's hind leg. I can assure you that the caring persons at Virgin Protection Limited know what they are doing. We never at The Phoenician Arms have had the displeasure of an unanticipated security adversity. You may kindly rest in peace, please ..."

They rounded a corner.

Mr. Gu interrupted himself and flourished his hand like a game-show hostess presenting a prize.

"Ah, well," he said, "and here we are."

Shops encircled a wrought-iron-fenced garden in the village center.

Men outfitted in the same spiffy beige three-piece suit and bowler as Mr. Gu and women in floppy white hats, austere navy-blue white-polka-dotted dresses and ugly blue Kleenex-box-like handbags swept between storefronts, light green linen pouches hanging loosely from their arms or piled orderly in shopping carts which they trundled behind them.

Young couples with matching slick-backed hair sat beneath the striped awning at an outdoor café and sipped espresso, working at bronze Adolfo laptops inlaid with rhinestones, seashells, and sand.

More Fopsons shnorked at the end of more leads.

Every now and then a polite laugh rose through the matinal clatter.

Around the garden living statues vogued on black pedestals. Instead of clothes, the statues' bodies were covered in thick greasy paint. Each aped a different masterpiece from art history. A plump woman struck the modest pose of the S-figured Botticellian Venus, twenty gallons of reddish flowing hair moussed to connote the well-known wind effect. One guy who made the skanky teen at the gate appear like he had some weight issues to resolve mimed Gauguin's yellow Christ, another the reclining-Adam-with-the-indolent-arm from Michelango's Sistine ceiling.

All of them were crank, Rykki decided as she passed, the way they could hold those positions even in this escalating heat, but her favorite was definitely the Magritte: two inverted merpeople, fish heads and torsos atop human legs, skin the same granular green of the rock on which they sat.

It made her happy knowing someone understood how she felt.

"Do you perhaps as well possess knowledge of such important

matters as contemporary flower-, vegetable-, herb-, and fruit-cultivation?" Mr. Gu asked as they strode by a small brightly-canopied aug stand manned by a blond drop-dead-gorgeous athletic type in flattop haircut and royal-blue thong bathing suit.

His back muscles and flesh had been either genetically or surgically plucked into flying-squirrel-like cartilageous wings.

"We don't," Rykki said. She tried not to gawk. "No."

"In that case let it be my sincerest pleasure to point out that the garden beside which we are at this very instant advancing might twenty-five years ago have exhibited an exceedingly considerable cast of pretty seed-bearing plants designed to be attractive to the optic globes as well as odoriferous cilia."

"Flowers."

"Precisely. Yes. Presently, however, everything you are witnessing is edible in addition to being surpassingly picturesque."

A troop of school children marched single-file behind their teacher, a black woman with white-lipsticked lips, along the pavement on the opposite side of the street.

The children wore identical white kneesocks, polished black shoes, and Klub-Med-tartan kilts.

"Must take a ton of pesticides and fertilizers to keep everything looking so good."

"Far being from it. Unlike our good friends on the M23, we at The Phoenician Arms employ organic products only. Imitation insect attractants being one happy example."

"Pheromones? Like the millipedes ..."

"To interfere with normal reproductive shenanigans comprising the nature of common disagreeable pests by inducing them to mate in a premature state. We are also using insect viruses to be suppressing our verminous friends without leaving unsightly chemical droppings. Bacteria produce a protein very gravely unhealthy for our little leaf-eating companions with homely faces as well. Everything here is simple and perceptually tasteful."

"It's really quite beautiful."

"And may I be adding quite harmless, too."

"You can eat the roses?" Oran asked.

"Most indeed you may be doing so, I am delighted to be reporting to you. They are fiddled to taste of delicious tropical oranges … as are our delicious tropical oranges, though some of those taste also of delicious English cherries and limes. The same might be said with respect to the delicate pink· carnations, except they are tasting of succulent bananas with just a hint of graininess to them that enlivens the palate, and the rhododendrons, which exude the flame-kissed flavor of gently grilled roachburgers, compliments of the ingenious and ever-hard-working people at McLenin Limited, full of healthy protein but lacking in unwholesome carcinogens and fats. Going ahead, please. Endeavor to try one."

Oran reached through the fence for a hydrangeas gathering. He pulled off several pale blue petals and lay them on his tongue.

"Green apples," he said.

"In excess of wowness, yes."

"Thought of everything, haven't they," Zivv said, reaching for some hyacinths.

Rykki and Tris joined him.

"The Phoenician Arms is a semi-natural ecological and industrial system, you will be filled with happiness to learn, which, as an integrated whole, minimizes uncleanly emanations too. Nothing produced by one organism or machine here as waste is not for another organism or machine a source of most fortunate usable material." He pointed across the street. "We are stepping right this way, please."

Still nibbling, they moved by a row of Audis and Vauxhalls troughed at imposture parking meters. Tiny strands of polyester embedded in the cars' finishes iridesced like the wings of monarchs.

On intuition, Rykki looked up. Fifteen or twenty men and women glided above them on the fleshy appendages the guy at the aug stand sported.

They cater-cornered to a Gap store and entered.

It was identical to the tiny uncluttered space lined with

translucent black plastic tube-booths at The Imperial Mallmaze.

"Everything is food for something else," Rykki said.

"I could not have articulated this matter with a greater sense of laconic eloquence. Dead or alive, plant or animal, mineral or vegetable, each thing small and large."

"It's all so ... neat."

"And speaking of this very noteworthy idea, we are at the point in our constitutional to rejuvenate our bodily hygiene. My ears are fully plugged with viscous oils once more. Hop yourselves inside."

"But ..."

"Full aural pluggedness is my present condition."

"Yeah, but we simply can't ..."

"I am not hearing anything whatsoever except perhaps my own breathing. You are, if you may be so kind as to let me remind you, beholding a man without one single beautiful son, daughter, or wife. So please to indulge him for a short while and make him briefly jocund. My face is utterly red with insistence."

There was an icon Rykki hadn't noticed before, three parentheses of increasing size, on the screens inside these tubes which Mr. Gu said the children should push before they pushed the one that would take their measurements.

Rykki did, only nothing much happened except a low hum that grew in intensity around her.

She became aware of a tingling sensation across her exposed skin. It felt as if she was holding a cord with an electrical short. It took her a while to get used to the rills of sound from the ultrasonic shower hitting her, vibrating away dirt and dead cells, but pretty soon she got out of what was left of her Azid Reign suit, crumpled it up by a vent at her feet (the vent inhaled and ate it), cocked back her head, and eased into the feeling.

Three minutes later she flipped through this week's catalog on the internal monitor and tried a few things on the eggplant-purple three-dimensional mannequin-grid representing her body.

Guilty about using Mr. Gu's credit, she decided to go with an inexpensive pair of black jeans, white t-shirt stamped with the large red Chinese symbol for something she couldn't read, black socks, and black shin-tall combat boots with rubber soles.

She hit the ENTER icon and the red-and-blue laser lightshow launched around her.

First thing she saw when the hatch popped open was Zivv who'd also chosen black jeans, except they were those new Gap Morphines with the transparent plastic panes sewn over the buns, usually to highlight tatts there, which Zivv didn't have … plus this gray t-shirt stamped with Wyle E. Coyote's visage and identical pair of techno-sneakers he'd gotten at The Imperial Mallmaze.

He was busy whispering something into a stooped Mr. Gu's ear, but stopped in mid-sentence when he saw his sister. Mr. Gu glanced over and his eyes locked with Rykki's and she could see him get froggy all of the sudden.

"Waiting right here, please," he said, raising a finger, "in cement-like stillness."

Then he was gone, Fopson in tow.

"What was that about?" Rykki asked.

"You ever think about how we spend thirty years of our lives sleeping and seven dreaming and we don't even know why?" Zivv asked.

She refocused on her brother.

"I haven't done. No."

"I was standing there in the tube and the idea just sort of happened."

"So you told Mr. Gu?"

"I told you."

"What did you tell Mr. Gu?"

Oran and Tris stepped from their tubes.

Oran had gone for a pair of shredded backwards bluejean Jim Coach cutoffs, techno-sneakers like Zivv's, and plain black t-shirt; Tris the same jeans as Rykki, a ribbed black tank-top, and bulky black Gap Al

207

Frescos ... as in Al Fresco, the hot football star with the muscle grafts that made his calves look like bean-bag chairs had been glued to the backs of his legs.

"Good taste," Tris said, pointing at Rykki's trousers.

"You too." Then back at Zivv. "So?"

Zivv was busy trying to extract something invisible from under a thumbnail. His attention skimmed up.

"So what?"

"So what did you tell him?"

"Tell who?" Oran said.

Zivv returned to his thumbnail, only Rykki could tell his heart wasn't in it.

"Oh, em, I ..."

And then Mr. Gu was kerfuffling through the door again, light green linen bag in one hand, Fopson's lead in the other.

The Pekingese plonked on the floor and stretched his neck around and began snerking under the miniature toilet-bowl brush that passed for his tail.

All smiles, Mr. Gu offered the bag to Rykki.

"A box of I am blushing to announce unspeakable feminine protection, of which the less said perhaps the better."

Rykki checked out the bag, then Mr. Gu, then Zivv.

"Oh," she said, embarrassed all the way down her spine. "I, em ... Thanks." Back at the bag. Back at Mr. Gu and Zivv. "Both of you. Thanks a lot."

The man and boy exchanged pleased looks, then beamed at Rykki in unison.

"Beneath the ground of our lovely safe-zone enclave is existing a low-pollution-making miniature oil refinery," Mr. Gu said, apropos of nothing, as they slid into their seats around a polished claret-colored table at the rear of the Mimetic Excess.

The place backed with several other rose-trellised shops against the southern wall of The Phoenician Arms. Outside, it matched all the other retro-DisCal buildings. Inside, it was a dead ringer for an authentic British pub … besides the fact, Rykki couldn't help noticing, everything appeared too studied and clean somehow, as if it'd been blueprinted by some Klub Med razzhead who'd never actually set foot in an authentic British pub in his life.

There was no smoke in the air, no nicks in the wood, no stains on the dark red carpet, no dust on the gigantic HDTV screen that was playing, not the requisite darts tournament, but what appeared to be a straight news report having something to do with the Pope.

File footage of the Pontiff striking his patented pose on the Vatican balcony alternated with current footage of the red, white, and blue Lego-like Diacomm Hospital complex in Rome.

Rykki tried to home in on the right frequency to hear what was going on, only the natter around her drowned out the reporter's overdub.

"It is employing waste heat from our solar ponds for its ever so efficient operation," Mr. Gu continued, running his yellow-brown forefinger down the laminated menu he'd freed from between a tomato sauce squeezer and vinegar bottle.

"Everything is food for something else," Oran repeated.

"Beyond a shadow of a lout most definitely. The refinery is selling sulfur removed from its petroleum to a wallboard producer in London in order to replace the gypsum the producer used to employ. Excess steam is helping heat water in our oyster ponds in nocturnal emissions. All of which I am almost ecstatic to announce aids The Phoenician Arms to prosper in an abundance of economic methods." He poked his nose over the top of the menu. "Have you ever sampled the slimy and salty yet fully flavorsome treat of delicious fresh oysters?"

Tris, Zivv, Oran and Rykki shook their heads no.

"Oh, well, you simply must be doing. I will be hearing nothing to the contrary." He removed his bowler and placed it under his seat, then scratched his forehead, careful not to scrape off the waxy finish. "Matter and energy at The Phoenician Arms are truly one, in excess of a thousand thanks to the thoughtful persons at Envirosafe Waste Management. Which reminds me of a tale I am almost forced at this juncture to recite ..."

He carried on, but Rykki monitored her surroundings.

A few customers in the Mimetic Excess were genetically and surgically amped like that guy at the aug stand. They had to go shirtless and had trouble sitting back in their chairs because of their wings, so they effected rigid forward leans.

Many, though, vaunted subtler tweaks which you had to look for pretty attentively to locate ... excessively thick wrist cartilage contrived she imagined to ward off carpal tunnel syndrome, or overdeveloped shoulders and necks for those long hours vultured in front of a puter.

The waitress approaching them, considerable nipples darkly noticeable through her thin cotton sari, showed off knees that faced backwards like some kind of kangaroo. She hopped more than walked and, when she paused before their table to take orders, she eased back onto her haunches enhanced to maximize the time she could spend on her feet.

So this is what it's like being cashed up, Rykki concluded.

She wasn't sure she was all that impressed.

Mr. Gu asked for oysters all around, cider for the kids, and a liquid-oxygen-augmented pint for himself.

The waitress had short blue hair brushed forward like Caesar's and eye sockets smudged blue like a psychedelic panda's. Part of her scalp had been removed on the righthand side of her head and replaced with a cosmetic metal plate with a Haltston logo engraved in it.

On the HDTV screen the Pope had been replaced by aerial shots of the first nano-reef gone dotty in the West Indies, clogging the bay it was manufactured to protect, noshing some boats and boaters and starting to crawl onto the beach where a line of biohazard-suited soldiers with grenade-launchers presently struck fuck-not-with-us attitudes.

An overly grave investigative reporter talked about the latest snuff show, *Duck and Cover,* that began taking itself a bit too earnestly last month, inventing its own reality-based scenarios when viewers' home vids didn't quite live up to the producers' expectations: two kids half Rykki's age gaped in horror as the tether on their bungee-jumping father snapped seconds after he swan-dived off a railroad trestle in the highlands; a female bobby who looked like a waterbug was engulfed by flames as a pipe bomb hidden in a trash bin exploded in her face; the wrenched-mouthed physiognomies of screaming children in the Yorkshire moors bounced around the interior of a runaway school bus whose brakes had just turned to rubbery smoke.

"So how come people don't just eat out of the gardens instead of going into the shops and buying stuff and all?" Zivv asked.

"Ah," Mr. Gu answered. "And here we are beginning to move into the profound realms of philosophy. Our shops, if you kindly see my point, look like shops but do not act like them."

"... ?"

"Let me perhaps to explain." He leaned forward and rubbed at a spot that didn't exist on the tabletop. "Okay. Here we are going. One does not in actual fact pay for the multitude of interesting items gorging our lovely retail outlets. Everything is rather covered by a single monthly assessment based on the aquirements made during the previous thirty-day period."

"A credit plan."

"In the earlier periods, persons did indeed ingest themselves from our becoming gardens, or, if they preferred, had groceries delivered to their tidy doorsteps on a weekly basis by happy be-acned youths."

"Sounds perfect, I should think," Zivv said. "No work, all leisure. Wait for the supplies to roll in."

"Except for an unexpected outcome you are one-hundred-percent right. The paradigm tended to deplete the act of social intercoursing while excelling the state of unpleasant to the extremities personal isolation. People became planked."

"Bored, you mean, I think. So they needed ways to fill their time?"

"Many at The Phoenician Arms otherwise simply listened to their credit rate growing merrily. Yes. Presently, however, they are buying without really buying, shopping without shopping. In order to be weaving themselves into the larger and more beauteous social fabric. They are

211

meeting their mates at the pubs for a hearty boisterous guffaw over many warm pints, developing leisure-time diversions in superfluity, putting the whisper on each other's surprising extramarital enterprises. In many other words, they are taking the perhaps disagreeable duties of the middle-class and making them into euphonic to excess artwork."

"I don't follow."

"One hundred years ago, persons were defining as unpleasant such time-engorging tasks as shopping and cooking. The keen-witted persons at The Phoenician Arms have redefined these acts into pleasant intellectual and imaginative challenges. Are you familiar with one shockingly famous Mrs. Martha Stewart?"

"I'm not, no."

"A very great NorAm who fully transformed laboriousness into a pleasurable middle-class sport. The Phoenician Arms hired her to reconceptualize our constructional model. Please be beholding."

He indicated plaster casts hanging on either side of the fireplace. Death-masks, Rykki saw, of a heavily-creased woman's face whose eyes chaperoned everyone in the room.

"Our patron saint," Mr. Gu said reverently.

"But how can anyone afford it?" Zivv asked. "There's nothing middle-class about it. The whole thing must cost a fortune."

The waitress returned with their food.

On each oblong plate glistened twelve half-shelled oysters atop a bed of crushed ice.

Mr. Gu rubbed his hands in open felicity, garnished the first with a dab of red cocktail sauce and a spritz of lemon juice, lifted the bivalve mollusk to his mouth, tipped the shell forward, and slurped it between pursed lips.

He shut his eyes and relished the moment, then followed it with a quaff of dark brown lager.

Tris and Zivv warily imitated him.

"Slup, sluuup, slurgle, slurgle," Oran said.

Rykki couldn't bring herself to touch what appeared to be piles of pigeon droppings on small wedges of rock so she unobtrusively reached for the hunk of bread on her side plate and started picking off hot plugs.

Everyone ate noisily.

"The upper-class must be exuding great financial abundance to live like the profoundly middle-class used to," Mr. Gu said. He chewed. "Are these not plentiful taste treats, I am asking you?"

"They're great," Zivv said. "So things aren't as simple as they look, you're saying."

"From the mouth of babes great geysers of wisdom spew."

"You have butter on your chin," Oran told Rykki.

"The outward aspect of simpleness is depending on vast complexity. Enclaves such as ours flourish due to the key being that we are moving information, not persons. They generate value and prosperity without consuming vast and greatly unwieldy physical resources, time, and emotional wear and tear. We are in the past creating an artificial middle-class."

Someone across the room rose and turned up the volume on the HDTV.

All at once an Egyptian official glaring into the camera was loudly denouncing Britain, claiming recent intelligence from hacker raids on the British Telecom Network revealed the meteor that had leveled most of Cairo had been diverted more than a decade ago from its normal course near Uranus toward earth by three nuclear detonations set off by a cabal of Egypt's most fierce enemies.

"We consider this an act of terrorism," the official said, "and our governcorp will take appropriate countermeasures."

"Go wobble your bleeding mumsie's bottom," a hairless guy with a constellation of jewels implanted across his head said from the bar. "You lost the bloody war. Now bag your face."

"In the middle of the twentieth century," Mr. Gu said, paying the disturbance no attention, "to relieve London from its then already-expanding overcrowdment, the architect and planner Mr. Ebenezer Howard was advancing the concept of building self-sufficient satellite communities being separated by luscious to the point of heartbreak

213

greenbelts connecting by railways. Two dozen such communities were constructed between 1946 and 1991 ... Milton Keynes, Redditch, and so forth, each platted on open fields and each, like the unsettlingly lovely Phoenician Arms, highly self-contained."

The Pope appeared back on his balcony on the sheet-wide television screen.

"Nearly three-fourths of the enclave workforce are residing locally. We are waving over our metaphorical shoulders at the sad to say great rotting metropolises as they recede into the inclement weather of cultural forgetfulness ..."

"Hey," Zivv interrupted, pointing at the HDTV. "Look. The Pope's sick."

Footage cycled of an ambulance arriving in the middle of the night at the Diacomm Hospital complex in Rome amid a convulsion of flashing blue and red lights.

The Pontiff had fallen ill yesterday shortly after retiring for the evening. A search of his chambers uncovered more than fifty gamma-ray-emitting pellets scattered under his mattress, beneath the carpet around his reading niche, and throughout his wardrobe closet. From the look of things, he'd been poisoned over a period of several months by the isotopes. It was unclear, said the chief surgeon at an early morning press conference, how close to success the assassination attempt had come. All he could say at present was the Pope was gravely ill.

A man with a coif so perfect it seemed he was wearing an orange rubber wig asked the world to pray for the Pontiff ... and see it in their souls to purchase his plasma-wrench album (which was as of three hours ago climbing the charts like it had been released yesterday) as a sign of spiritual solidarity.

The report scattered into a televisual university blipvert reminding college-bound students their genetic profiles and MRI/PET scans were due by August fifteenth for fall admission.

"This is very bad," Mr. Gu said, turning back to the kids and his plate of mostly empty shells. "Very bad in the high-end of badness."

"Who'd do something like that?" Zivv asked.

214

"There are many who would like to see such a very great leader fall into species extinction."

"His music was so pretty," said Oran.

Mr. Gu sighed.

"Indeed you are obese with accuracy. There are so many unwell feelings in the world outside the walls of The Phoenician Arms. Religious militants who are debating who are the Chosen and who the Discarded. Unscrupulous often less-than-fully-bathed persons who wish to see their never-very-handsome faces on the six o'clock news."

"He'll be all right," Rykki said.

"You know they're flying in the best Uncle Meats in the whole world right this second," Zivv said.

"If anyone can make it, he will," said Tris.

"Such sadness," said Mr. Gu.

"Maybe we can buy a copy of his album on our way to Cuckfield," said Oran. "It'd be really good to listen to again."

Mr. Gu looked from one child to the next.

Slowly, his teeth began to regroup.

"You possess an excellent idea, little boys and girl. Yes. Precisely. These great men with fine minds and corpulent bank accounts are doing all they can, are they not?"

"Bang on," Zivv said.

"His Holiness is in an excess of good hands."

"The best," said Oran.

Mr. Gu raised one finger to indicate they should hold on a sec, then extracted his gold pocket watch from his waistcoat, flipped it open, and consulted its liquid-crystal display.

"And so may I respectfully point out that it is time to be bringing to a close this most wonderful if also at the end of the day quite mournful social interlude."

"We're ready when you are," Zivv said.

"Good. Good. Then let us then nip along smartly," he said, pushing back from the table.

* * *

215

Rykki stepped outside into a cloud of delicate paper butterflies.

Some were large as her hand, some smaller than her pinkie, but all had shiny bodies that iridesced like those cars at the imposture parking meters in the village center.

Astonished, she stopped in her tracks.

Fopson was tied to the fire hydrant, right where Mr. Gu had left him, only he was lying on his side in a big letter C.

The skanky flyweight teen with boiled-egg-white skin and nervous eyes stood above it, holding what seemed to be a transparent green plastic water pistol with a shower nozzle attached to the tip.

Rykki recognized the military burst-gun cooked up to blind enemy troops with short laser discharges.

Walking toward them across the lawn was one of the giants from the City of Dis. He had a remote-control panel in his hand. What appeared to be a chum of his was lowering himself over the southern wall of the compound.

The skanky guy, it looked like, hadn't noticed either of them.

"What is being the meaning of this?" Mr. Gu asked behind Rykki.

The skanky guy raised the burst-gun at her, aimed, grinned, and eased his finger back on the trigger.

"Hold still now, luv," he said. "Wouldn't want to damage the goods any, would we. This man what I knew ..."

Then the butterflies around his head began exploding.

His torso clomped to the pavement.

The guy on the lawn began jogging. His chum hit the ground and sprinted toward the Mimetic Excess. The mechanical screech of millipedes animated the brownish sunshine.

The air turned into a galaxy of popping flashbulbs.

Tris's body fell to the flagstone footpath like all the bones in it had been extracted. Oran gawped at his dead brother, eyes wide, and then over at his sister.

"Flowers ..." he mouthed, and his head shimmered into ignition.

19. TWENTY-FIFTH HORSEMAN
OF THE APOCALYPSE

Someone grabbed her, but Rykki just started kicking and punching. She bit a hand that curled around her from behind, dropped and rolled across the flagstone path, careful to protect her head with her arms, bounced up, and was racing across the lawn.

Only she was racing right at the Spanglish giant who had just come over the wall and veered to cut her off. He was carrying something that looked like a high-powered telescope under his arm. It wasn't till he braked and lifted the contraption to his shoulder Rykki realized it was a portable rocket launcher.

It was pointed directly at her.

"Deténgase!" he shouted from behind the scope. "Deténgase, you little cunt!"

Which Rykki did, maybe ten meters in front of him, panting like mad, at the very second the first millipede struck. It smashed into his right leg, all couple hundred kilos of it, and his right leg bisected at an unwholesome angle.

The rocket launcher tilted skyward and the missile discharged from its maw in a rush of white smoke and orange flame straight into the flock of squirrel-winged gliders gathering above the commotion.

Rykki saw the burst of canary light and then felt the thunder.

Bodies slugged the earth around her.

Something inside her came to a standstill as the reality of what'd just taken place struck her. One blink: people were alive. The next: they

217

weren't. And somehow there was nothing in between those blinks, even though she was right there the whole time, witnessing.

So she took off again, trying not to pay attention to the Spanglish giant's shrieks as a dozen more millipedes caught up with him, and, five quick breaths after, with his friend, who had snared Zivv by one of the belt loops on the back of his Gap Morphines and was trying to haul him in.

The millipede whipped the lower three meters of its bulk into the second giant's knees, which made a wet popping noise before his upper torso fell off them like a chainsawed tree.

Then the thing went for his face.

His blatting sounded like mating cats in a burlap bag.

Rykki swerved toward the southern wall of the compound and put on speed.

She barreled across the grass and shinnied up the rose trellis on the side of one of the shops. Spiky vines ripped at her fingers. That metallic flavor flooded her mouth again. She couldn't be sure whether it was from the guy whose hand she'd bitten or herself.

Just as she prepared to throw her left leg onto the roof of the shop and hoist herself up, someone locked onto her combat boot.

She peeked down under her armpit, ready to start kicking again, only saw it was Zivv. He was trying to give her a boost. His pupils were dilated. A trickle of blood unhurriedly pointed from his right nostril toward his upper lip.

Her look coasted up, over her brother's head.

Two writhing piles of razzed millipedes fed on the lawn. Some of the gliders who'd been brought down by the rocket were littered nearby. A crowd huddled in the doorway of the Mimetic Excess, taking stock of the battlefield, the corpses of the two boys, the dog, and the teen in the fancy jogging suit.

Among them stood Mr. Gu.

Even at this distance, Rykki could see the sorrow the angle of his shoulders suggested. Maybe he even saw her looking at him, because just then he raised his fist in front of his gold-flecked face and slowly spread it open.

Waving goodbye.

Rykki and Zivv lifted themselves over the wall, plunked to the ground on the other side, and scorched through the baby-palm henge into the open fields beyond.

At sunset, they emerged into a rest area.

Heat rivulets washed across the orange-aired car park busy with Nissans, Peugots, Fords, Fiats, Citroëns, Hyundais, Renaults.

Next to a rotted picnic table stood a woman with auburn ringleted hair. She wore a pink latex one-piece mini-dress and spiked dog-collar necklace, and was connected by a silver chain to a matching spiked dog-collar necklace worn by her shirtless boyfriend in black latex pants.

The pair stood hand in hand, observing the last of the titanic sun's slick head quaver behind a landscape crosscut with the lineaments of powerline towers.

The boyfriend had the four horsemen of the apocalypse tattooed on his chest. While the gold-crowned bow-and-arrow-wielding guy on the white horse was no doubt into his work in a pretty obsessive way, the sword-wielding guy with fangs on the red horse was surely less than merry, and the tubercular one wielding the scales on the black horse was downright nasty, it was Death Himself (pigmentally challenged skin peeling from purple-red muscle, protruding comic-strip bloodshot eyes, jaw flopping off loose hinges) on the pale horse that was the honest-to-godless wild-arse incubusal incarnation of fear and loathing.

Twenty-four more, just like me, read the jagged red letters beneath him.

Rykki and Zivv hurried past, knowing it was never a great idea to get mixed up with one of those Brotherhood of Dada jokers, and halted by a GTE oxygen booth that aped an old-time bright red British phone booth. Inside sat a genderless person about Zivv's age in a gray jumpsuit and cateye designer sunglasses. His or her head was lowered and she or he seemed to be speaking into a clamshell diaphragm case. He or she was crying.

Neon lime and yellow stickers peddling sex trashed the booth's tiny square windows. One of the larger ones displayed a grainy photo of a female Ozone Baby with a sexy leer …

ALWAYS●LIVE●&●UNIQUE
!TALK WITH HOT NYMPHO FREAKS!
LOBSTER GIRL

ALSO:
BAT BOY
WORM PRINCESS
EXOTIC MIDGETS
RUBBER TOYTOTS
BI SIAMESE TWINS

0181.LUV.FREK

Zivv squeezed Rykki's shoulder and signaled across the car park.

At the far end, beneath a row of halogen lights swirling with insectival planetary systems, droned the colossal bio-diesel engine of a three-story five-carriage land barge packed with thousands of sparkling mountain bikes.

The kids aimed in its direction.

Approaching, they saw the pilot and co-pilot standing beside a chain-link ladder leading up to the control cabin on the top story.

Both were bulky in an unhealthy bangers-and-mash embolismic way. The one Rykki guessed was the pilot had a number of ringworm-sized impressions on his face where melanomatac patches of epidermis had been removed. He flourished a large silver ring with a day-glo winking green holographic eye in place of a stone on each finger of his right hand.

The co-pilot was shaped like the Michelin Man. Caterpillarish

220

white spittle gathered at the margins of his mouth. When he talked his tongue got involved somehow, like it was trying to attract more attention than it really deserved.

They were doing a deal with what appeared to be a one-third-scale-model of a beetle-backed Chinese geriatric.

The Michelin Man passed him three black-market bills.

The beetle-backed one-third-scale-model geriatric returned two and a handful of purple rectangular tablets.

"Keep up all night, all day. Come from great yào-diàn. Guaranteed. Drive lorry Bri'n back eight million time before tired."

Rykki glanced over at the oxygen booth.

It was vacant.

A fretful bird noise spooked from a clump of amped weeds skirting the car park and sank beneath an excitable sportscar engine.

"Be a good chop-chop now and fuck off, mate," said the co-pilot, divvying up the goods with his boss.

An inordinate amount of unctuous bowing ensued.

"Guaranteed," backing away. "You see. Best leapers in British Isles. No fung pi ..."

The pilot and co-pilot had already forgotten the supplier, though.

They were hoicking themselves up the ladder toward the control cabin, eating the interestingly shaped drugs as they went.

Rykki and Zivv nestled among the mass of bikes on the first story of the first carriage, inhaling the carcinogenic scent of mats lining the floor. For a while they just watched the scenery creep past. Communications towers. Emu herds. A white steeple. Zivv sat with his chin on his fists and his fists on his knees. Rykki wondered how she'd feel if she could ever enter her body again. A forest-green sign with white lettering and yellow route numbers announced the exit where the A23 peeled off toward the residue of the defunct Gatwick. She thought about how she and her brother were the last members of a short-lived life form. Suburbs began encroaching on farms. The ratio of farm-to-suburb decreased. A red-paint-on-aluminum sign saying MAKE OFFER was nailed askew to the side of broken-down Airstream trailer next to a low crumbled brick wall. Farms disappeared altogether and were replaced by a rumble of villages. Kids sifted through a town dump by candlelight. Rykki looked over at Zivv and saw he'd fallen asleep. His head bobbed flaccidly. Black blood flakes granulated on his upper lip. The strangest thing was Rykki'd never felt like part of a species. She'd always just felt like Rykki. The land barge, voluminous engine laboring, cruised past a shockingly-lit AJ's family petrol-and-restaurant enclave shaped out of some kind of gray cementish stuff into an open-mouthed closed-eyed human head studded with red, white, and blue mosaic tiles surrounded by harsh floodlights. Of course, every member of a species had to feel that way. Every member had to feel like it was an individual. That's what made you part of a species: the illusion you weren't. If you thought differently, if you really *were* an individual, you wouldn't be all begging for it, reproduction-wise, wouldn't let your cells and trace elements boss you around so much. Rykki examined the lines in her palms for clues. There were none. She raised her eyes. British Petroleum. A strip joint called Fifty Beautiful Girls and Three Ugly Ones. You wouldn't have to. There'd be no need. Chalky patches of erosion crossed the advancing hills which, in this washed-out light, appeared to be darker shades of gray superimposed on lighter shades of gray. Rykki was stunned there were so many kinds of ambiguity. She reexamined the lines in her palms for clues. There were none. The last pterodactyl must have felt this way, too, mustn't it: lonely, anxious, unfulfilled, frustrated, blown out, with a sort of queasy sense way down deep that evolution had passed it by. Except pterodactyls had existed for how many millions of years … and she and her brother had only managed—what?—a couple of months, really. A couple thousand hours. Jada, Tris and Oran less. Knowing this, Rykki's breasts began to hurt. Someone had bought and sold her mind. Her speech was merchandise. Her memories. And now they wanted her flesh. They wanted her organs. She wondered who she'd been before she had a name. She reached up under her white t-shirt stamped with the large red Chinese symbol for something she couldn't read and rubbed her

222

abdomen. Pyecombe. Patcham. The last witness of JFK's assassination would die in 2074, Woodstock six years later, Vietnam two years after that. She remembered Oran's achromatic skin. Corporeal space had become something new for her. It was like touching someone else when she touched herself. Maybe in Beijing things would be different. Maybe in Beijing she would reenter her own body. Only a little while, and she'd be moving through the digital advert sparking inside her brain ... the long lush boulevard ... the treed median ... the bluish-gray haze of skyscrapers ...

Zivv snorted in his sleep.

Rykki raised her eyes: over the next billow of hills, the pink-gray glowing nimbus of the airport.

Zivv's hands dropped. His head snapped sideways. He woke, evaluated his environment murkily, sunk back into sleep again, tucking his fists under his jaw for safe keeping.

Rykki shut her eyes, too, trying hard to sense herself penetrating her own destiny.

Instead, she penetrated a dream that may have been hers, or may have been a dream of the other person sharing the inside of her head.

She was lying in darkness so black it was heartbreaking.

She smelled her own periodic breath.

When she reached up to continue rubbing her abdomen, her knuckles cracked against the lid of the coffin in which she lay. She tried to wriggle her feet, but the narrow box wouldn't allow her.

The odd thing was she didn't feel like panicking. For some reason, she knew this was what was supposed to happen and felt comfortable enough knowing it. She wished she could bend her arms or raise her head, but these limitations were something she could live with. They were something she could, in time, get used to.

She would spend the rest of her existence here. She could think of worse. She was impressed, for instance, by how much air there still was to breathe.

So she decided to enjoy it, aim her consciousness at the simple pleasures associated with respiration ... except then she perceived the moisture touching the fingertips of her right hand, and another smell entered her sensorium: calcium oxide.

Quicklime was percolating into her coffin, seeping through her cellular membrane.

She stared up into complete negativity, feeling her body turning into stone, nucleus by nucleus. She thought about how much she would come to weigh over the course of the next few months, how much trouble she would cause those who came after her when they tried to move her remains.

Everything flashing by.

A change in velocity woke her.

The land barge was easing off the motorway, crunching to a stop on the verge.

Headlights ripped past. A tacky heat enlivened with salt-spray flowed in around her. The night was rich with sardines and defoliants.

Rykki instantly became attentive.

Zivv had already crawled to the edge of the barge and was craning to see what was going on.

Rykki canted forward.

The engine choked off. That slow incessant vibration which had been leeching through her so long she'd come to ignore it arrested. The control cabin hatch banged open. The chain-link ladder clanked down the barge's side.

Then the man Rykki thought of as the pilot was descending.

Only he was having serious trouble. His feet kept missing rungs. He'd slip, dangle, curse, brace himself, and try again. A labored whistle wheezed in his throat. His scarred face was shiny and greenish with perspiration.

Rykki figured he was snootered from those pills he'd been popping.

But it wasn't just that.

There was something really off here. Rykki contemplated him.

Those pills were supposed to be leapers and leapers weren't supposed to make you act like that.

"You all right, mate?" the co-pilot shouted from the control cabin.

The pilot wasn't okay.

He stepped back into air and fell the last meter to the ground.

Almost simultaneously, he vaulted to his feet again like some rodeo clown, brushed off his elbows, and stared straight ahead into the overgrown weeds along the roadside.

He sat down circumspectly and crossed his legs like a monk.

"Bleeding chop-chop poisoned us, didn't he," the co-pilot shouted. "He bleeding *poisoned* us. What were we thinking, then? What was going through our bleeding *minds*?"

The pilot reclined in stages till he was flat on his back. He clasped his hands over his belly and unfocused his eyes. It seemed to Rykki as if he was trying to relax his internal organs, like someone who knew he was about to vomit but didn't want to.

"Bleeding geriatric put that bleeding nano-shite on our bleeding paper, didn't he," the co-pilot shouted. "Fuck the wanking youth, was his bit, wasn't it. Fuck the whole bleeding tri ..."

A jet of fire blasted out the control-cabin hatch.

The co-pilot's burning body lobbed into the darkness, wheeled once, and pile-drove into the gravel two meters from his boss.

Zivv reached the pilot first.

He hesitated, looked back at Rykki, looked at the pilot, and began rummaging through his pockets.

The pilot didn't seem to mind. His eyes focused briefly and slid over the boy who had just stepped into his event horizon.

Then he unfocused them and parted his lips.

An orgone-blue flame licked out his mouth.

Rykki, who was running to join her brother, paused.

From where she stood, she could see the skin on the back of the pilot's hands ripple and blister. Little yellow welts speckled his forehead

225

and cheeks. They plumped, split, and started making a sizzling noise like grease in a frying pan.

Then the guy strobed into a human torch.

Traffic on the motorway set about braking.

Metal ground into metal.

The blaze crackling through the control cabin picked up momentum.

Zivv raised the pilot's ebony cybercash slab and ID in his right hand and key chain in his left for Rykki to see.

Rykki turned to head for the co-pilot.

Something in the control cabin exploded.

A glare of white light paralyzed the verge, the motorway, the nearby field.

Shadows jumped back.

Rykki froze. Her lungs cramped. She held her position, aware of options emptying around her.

20. DOOM PATROLS

"You okay?" Zivv asked.

He dismounted his mountain bike and rolled it toward the metal racks sunk into the pavement outside the first row of security bunkers on the perimeter of the airport.

"Sure," said Rykki.

"Sure?"

Hot acidic dawn fog clung to the grass, almost obscuring the tiers of zigzagging razor-wire fences.

Columns of compact automobiles crept into access tunnels where they'd be sniffcd by razzed dogs before being allowed to enter the underground car parks.

"I feel really bad about going through the pilot-guy's pockets. I mean, he was just lying there."

She stopped walking her bike and looked at him.

"It wasn't like you could've done anything for him."

"I guess. Except ..."

He popped his bike into the nearest rack and kneeled, pretending he was locking it just in case one of the guards in the bunkers or vidcams hovering in the area was checking.

Rykki copied his actions.

They stood and joined the pedestrians passing into the airport. The muscle-grafted guards, Ludovico-9 machine guns suspended over their shoulders, hardly noticed them. These guys were looking for the really big news, the obvious weapons and profiles.

Rykki and Zivv collected with hundreds of other people on a clean aluminum-and-cement platform.

"You ready for this?" Zivv asked.

"*Please mind the gap,*" an AI's voice said, sounding like it was speaking from the bottom of the ocean. "*Please mind the gap.*"

The phrase was repeated twice each in Chinese, Japanese, French, Russian, German, and some form of maybe Pakistani.

The next maglev monorail swished up. Its unpleasant electric burring put Rykki in mind of a low-resistance connection. The doors hissed back and the throng pushed forward all at once. Rykki thought of rush-hour in Beijing. She couldn't have changed her direction or speed if she'd wanted to.

"Let's do it," she said, more afterthought than anything else.

"*Failure to stand away from the doors may result in loss of limbs,*" the AI announced.

A tenth of a second after the first Russian version of the phrase had been enunciated the doors clamped shut with unbelievable force and the monorail kicked into motion.

Everyone inside shot around nervous shufties, steadying themselves, careful not to meet other people's nervous shufties.

The train raced above the initial line of defenses.

"Remind me," Rykki said, unable in the crush to even raise her arms from her sides. "Why are we doing this again?"

She wasn't moving her lips.

Outside, turf-covered bunkers and razor-wire yielded to a one-hundred-meter-wide barren expanse flanked by four-meter-tall cinderblock walls highlighted with guard towers.

No grass, no weeds, no obstructions ... just sandy gray soil Rykki knew was doused with herbicidal showers every day to prevent growth ... and those nefarious movement-sensitive AI-guided laser nests.

"For Jada," Zivv said. "For Tris and Oran."

She watched wasted landscape blap by.

"So it all comes down to remembering."

"If you don't have that, you don't have yourself, do you."

"And if you *do* have that?"

"Good question," Zivv said, attention gliding out the large rectangular windows toward the eerie view below. "What do you suppose you have then?"

Beyond the barrens bobbled more grassy slopes, now artificially green and tufted with sinuous pink, white, and yellow flowery shrubberies and almond trees, and, next, the airport swirling up all around.

Designed by Hugo Furst, with the backing of the Disney-Virgin people, the sprawling arrangement was fabricated fewer than four years ago to impersonate the Royal Pavilion in Bri'n's city center, only on a much grander scale. The original had been fabricated starting in 1787 by Henry Holland as a little neoclassical seaside getaway for George, then Prince of Wales, so he'd have somewhere to hang out near Mrs. Fitzherbert, the foxy lady he'd secretly and illegally married, but over the course of the next thirty years the place accreted through John Nash's deranged touch into a vast indic-oriental tribute to what had become the grotesquely whopping, gout-ridden, edematous King George's excessive taste and corporeal profusion.

Reserved ionic columns seizured into an exotic pin-cushion of spires, arabesque domes, and decoratively spiked concrete pineapples.

Bri'n Airport, though, made Nash's original seem a bit unassuming. It prickled in every direction as far as Rykki could see and was alive even at this early hour with travelers flowing through clear-tube bridges, monorails skiing along at various strata, and low-flying security copters buzzing among the organic architecture like mechanical hummingbirds among fiber-glass blossoms.

The notions of interior and exterior vanished.

Rykki and Zivv's monorail bolted among spires and was all at once skirting the domed ceiling of some stupendously vast banqueting room with red drapes and a thirty-meter-wide chandelier made out of glass daisies and a three-dimensional king-sized green-copper-scaled dragon levitating magically, holding that chandelier up, red tongue flicking … and then, before Rykki could establish a sense of perspective, into pale-yellow haze, which might have been natural light and then again might not have been … glints of aerospace planes, skins titanium-silicon-carbide fabric, dirigibles moored to the tarmac like immense shiny silver sausages … and through a windowless gallery, much closer to what felt like ground-level, walls vivid azure overlaid with a trellis of cut-out strips of paper, block-printed in imitation of bamboo, double-doors grained to simulate teawood and framed by semi-round wooden columns resting on fake marble bases, staircases leading nowhere … and slowing, the AI speaking again in that spooky oceanic voice, monorail burring parallel to another platform, this one carpeted, red, and opulent.

The doors shushed back and Rykki and Zivv were carried into an echo of the airport-pavilion's music room. Lit by a series of lotus-shaped chandeliers, it glowed in honey-and-rubicund luminescence. More flying dragons, now carved silver, supported blue silk-satin window draperies fringed with gold tassels. Thousands of gilded cockle shells studded the domed ceiling.

Along the crimson velvet walls embossed with gold images of ancient Chinese villages stood what looked like rows of old-fashioned, pre-armor-plated ATM machines.

Rykki and Zivv approached one as a well-dressed businessman in a dolphin-gray Gucci exoskeleton stepped aside.

Zivv reached into his back pocket, slipped out the ebony cybercash slab, and inserted it into the slot beside a red LED. The screen rezzed up with the Virgin-Disney logo.

When he touched it, the logo dithered into a series of instructions.

Zivv and Rykki scrupulously worked through them, providing false information whenever the machine let them, giving correct information from the pilot's and co-pilot's ID cards whenever it didn't.

They knew they'd have long taken it on the creep by the time anyone back north got around to tracing them this far.

Confuse the system a little, give it one or two additional dots to connect … less than an hour, and they'd be aboard the next luxury flight to Beijing.

Ticking ensued. The balance on the cybercash slab spun down to almost zero. Zivv prised it out of the slot.

Two boarding passes marked FIRST CLASS clicked into a plastic tray.

Rykki scooped them up and tucked them into her black jeans.

A glass escalator lifted them through an exhibition called Dr. Haze's Fabulous Mutant Taxidermy Display, where glass human eyes formed a necklace down the back of what should've been a stuffed Labrador Retriever, except its head, which was really the head of a python with two jaws, jutted from its ribs, and it had eight legs like a spider, and it wore several of its organs on its hips like dried greenish-blue seaweed bladders.

At the top of the escalator Rykki and Zivv joined something that came close to resembling a queue.

They shuffled down a plush corridor through a pat-down and a saliva check for viruses.

On the other side, they ducked into the congested clone of the anteroom to the king's apartments and spent the last of their credit on two Virgin Colas.

They sat in black-and-faux-gilt elbow chairs at a black-and-faux-gilt table. Low-definition public sounds immersed them. Over the hoax fireplace roosted a hefty mantel clock. On either side were bronze figures of Cupid and Psyche. Three long micro-mosaic political allegories which Rykki couldn't understand, but which in at least two cases involved naked nymphs with Margaret Thatcher's face cavorting with naked pixies who were dead ringers for Tony Blair, were set into the walls and wired for audio. One periodically broadcast arriving and departing flights, one paged passengers, and one recited the news.

Every so often the things Rykki thought were tiles reconfigured and the allegories changed.

She watched them, taking unconscious drags on her straw, and then two women air-kissing each other on both cheeks in the entrance.

"What if the problem isn't having too little memory but too

231

much?" she asked.

Zivv, who'd been scanning the other patrons, turned his attention to her.

"How so?"

"What if it doesn't all come down to remembering in the sense of not enough, but remembering in the sense of too flipping much? If you have an excess of recollections, you don't have yourself either, do you."

The headlines began to cycle on the micro-mosaics.

The Pope's condition had deteriorated. Further symptoms of radiation sickness had materialized: nausea, intense headaches, diarrhea. His red and white blood-cell counts were dropping. The chief surgeon called for more prayer, and reminded everyone afresh that a purchase of the Holy Father's *Textual Harrassment* was a purchase of hope.

"There are too many of you, you mean," Zivv said when the news reader moved on to the next item.

Rykki considered.

"I'm coming to think the true first-person pronoun is the plural. It feels like my RAM's all blocked up."

"Maybe data storage is the relic of an old technology. Maybe the real job of computerized intelligence isn't retrieval but revelation. So it's not about long-term memory anymore, but short-term ... abrupt, multiple, discontinuous, powerful, evanescent."

"Amnesia as an active process. Knowing as distraction."

"Forgetting might just be good for your health. Sure. Maybe the most important feature of your hard drive becomes its ability to be indefinitely rewriteable."

A woman's voice tossed above all the others in the anteroom.

"Slut's like a piece of bubble gum," it said. "I could chew her all night."

It submerged again.

"And certain emotions," Zivv said. "Those dependent for their being on an understanding of the past—devotion, say, or revenge, or hope, or despair—they don't exist anymore."

"Can't." Rykki took a long sip. Playing with her plastic white straw, she said: "I'm not sure I like it."

"Without my memories, I wouldn't know you."

"You'd know me differently."

"Not in the ways that count. Not as part of this long write-up we've been living through. You'd be someone different every moment I looked at you."

"Hey ..." She consulted the clock on the mantel. "Time to get this thing over with."

Zivv followed her glance.

"Time to cut the rug," he said. "Get down and juke."

They'd told the ticketing machine they were traveling to Beijing to meet their wealthy parents and they'd never been out of the country before.

That and those first-class boarding passes, and the flight attendants treated them like rock stars. A nice man with a pink string of scar at each corner of his mouth led them from the waiting room down a long ramp, the ceiling lowering as they went.

The impression they were still in the Royal Pavilion fell away into institutional gray and white. They rose ten stories in a spotless glass capsule and crossed into the plush interior of the airship.

It reminded Rykki of photos Magda had once showed her of late nineteenth-century cruise liners. Everything was mahogany and bronze. The maroon carpets were so squashy it seemed to her she was already airborne.

The flight attendant pointed out interesting things as they strolled along. He escorted them by a diamond-blue swimming pool fashioned after a Roman bath. Wrinkled men and women with wide middles and thin arms stood hip-deep in steaming water, talking. They visited a dining room that was comprised of many smaller dining rooms, each duplicating the elegant white-table-clothed ones in country estates, and the flight attendant told them they'd already paid for the privilege of eating in any of them at any time during the week-long trip.

Some passengers congregated around a green-felt snooker table covered with red balls in a dark pub, smoking cigars and sipping sherry, while others worked out in the extravagant gymnasium, pedaling high-wheeler bikes, pumping dumb bells, thrusting up and down on step-machines made of polished wood trimmed in brass, VR rigs bulky on their heads.

The passengers weren't so much experiencing nostalgia, it crossed Rykki's mind, as they were the nostalgia for a previous generation's nostalgia.

Only it was those people reclining in the chaise longues along the observation deck that really unnerved her. They all wore thong bikinis and the women went topless and they all had this creepy translucent green skin. Plus they lay smack in the sunshine splashing through the picture-window portholes ... and Rykki couldn't detect the oily sheen of sunscreen on any of them.

"What are they doing?" she asked. "They could hurt themselves, couldn't they?"

The flight attendant bent almost in half and whispered so the local passengers couldn't hear.

"Homo photosyntheticus, madam."

"What?"

"Chlorophyllors to you and me. Products of The Benevolent Venereal Disease."

"The Benevolent Venereal Disease?"

His scar strings twitched.

"You know about the old, em, what you call it, parallel parking, don't you?"

"Parallel parking?"

"The, em, you know, madam ... the jack in the box ... playing the old night baseball ... if you take my meaning."

"Sexing up?"

They started walking again.

"Of course you do, madam. Well. These ladies and gentlemen have introduced a symbiotic algae into the gentlemen's, em, privates."

"What for?"

"How I understand it, the algae moves into the reproductive bits

234

and then mixes around."

"They're changing themselves into *plants?*" Zivv asked.

"Gonadally-Osmosed Plant-Like Entities, I believe is how they prefer it. GOOD & PLENTIES, they call it."

"But what *for?*" Rykki repeated.

"Something of a new religion. Able to manufacture their own food right out of the air and sunlight around them. Ecologically correct, you could say. They get high on the radiation, is how they explain it."

"And they like it that way?"

"Bloke down in surgery? He tells me you give them a couple generations, their mouths are going to seal right over. Nothing to say, nothing to eat. Water them a bit, keep them in a well-lit place, and they'll be happy as a dog with two tails ..."

He halted in front of a door at the end of a muffled corridor, reached into his jacket pocket, and produced a plastic key. He inserted the key into the slit above the doorknob. A tiny light blipped on.

He swung the door open with a flourish.

"Your cabin," he declared, with the same pride as if he'd designed and built it himself.

The carpet, foil wallpaper, four-poster bed, stuffed chairs, and davenport were powder blue. A crystal vase with watercolor-rich flowers fanned open on a lace-fussy coffee table across from an armoire whose surface, Rykki had a feeling, was holographic.

The entire hull was a porthole, the entire rectangular border of which was a fish tank alive with yellow tangs.

When Zivv thanked the flight attendant and closed the door after him, the wall-sized mirror at the foot of the bed trembled into a huge HDTV screen filled with images of more yellow fish, these ten times their natural dimensions.

He laughed.

"All we need's a bit of music, and we're on a good wicket, aren't we."

The room heard him and, based on the profile generated by his answers to the ticketing machine's questions, saturated the cabin with a track from the Dead Girls' second album, *Lampshades*. An angel's dreamy vocals sculled deep within a miasmatic mix of wavering rhythms, minor chords, shifting tonalities, and a steady drone of semitonic sludge.

Rykki recalled seeing a vid by them back at ABNORMAL. The lead singer, Glenda Glandular, wore her liver outside her body in a jar hanging off a shoulder strap like a handbag.

"I can't quite believe it," she said.

"It's like finding your flat's been constructed on one of those polystyrene-and-cellophane mountains in a theme park. We're on a dirigible pretending to be an ocean liner in the guise of a holiday resort pretending to be a dirigible." He looked around the cabin. "You hungry?"

"Famished."

"I'm sure there's a fridge here somewhere. Let's see if we can dig something up ..."

Rykki's stomach started feeling funny as she popped the last cracker spread with Brie into her mouth.

She'd stretched out beside Zivv on the powder-blue bed, dusting of crumbs across her chest and tummy. They'd been surfing channels on the huge telly, and had already hit two hundred and fifty seven of them without finding one that looked even vaguely appetizing.

"What's that?" she asked.

"What?"

"*That*. That feeling."

She wiped her hands on the front of her t-shirt and turned toward the porthole. The perspective out there had modified. The airport spires and bulbs were contracting at a peculiar angle beneath them, shrinking, collapsing into distance.

"We're on our way."

"We're not."

"We are," Zivv said, sliding off the bed and padding barefoot toward the view. "We're airborne."

Rykki put down the knife she'd been using and trotted over.

Far off, the whir of engines.

The geography shifted heavily below as the airship came around into the wind and leisurely gained altitude.

"We just did it," Rykki said, tasting how the words felt in her mouth. She looked at Zivv. "We just *did it.*"

Zivv gazed out the porthole.

"We have it knocked, don't we," he said.

The dirigible swung over housing projects packing the hills north of the old city and hundreds of windmills pumping water out of the low-lying areas near the Melt barriers.

The Palace Pier with its amusement center swelled up, pink-tan pebble beach, turquoise railing, slate-green water reaching out toward the yellowish horizon.

Zivv slid his arm around Rykki's middle and they stood indexing the span below them.

Swirls of gnat-sized brown-white seagulls. Eighteenth-century beachfront buildings. White foam along the shoreline. Redundant oil rigs outfitted as power platforms.

Then the wide skew out over the Channel ...

Part of Rykki knew she would always be a patchwork girl.

This wasn't the shape of endings.

And part of her felt anxious, and part hopeful, and part simply experienced a surge of microperceptions ... the exact texture of the air in this cabin, the precise color of the sea below, the buoyant feeling of optimism rising through her thorax.

She hugged her brother, wondering why everyone everywhere didn't already understand ... the end of the world was already behind them, had come and gone, and they were still on the mystery tour ...

Next thing Zivv was kissing her, and she was coasting into the waterfall of sensation, and his familiar tongue was slipping into her mouth, like words made flesh.

PART FIVE:
BEAUTIFUL MUTANTS, LIMITED

21. HYSTERICALLY BLUE

"What?" Rykki said, opening her eyes.

Zivv took a step back, face raided with terror.

He peered down at his hands as if he'd never seen those weird things before. They fluttered up to his chest.

"*What?*" Rykki repeated.

He parted his lips. A bloody ladybug crawled out his left nostril. He looked at Rykki as if maybe she could explain it.

She reached out for his shoulder and his eyes snicked off.

He sunk to his knees like he was in a china shop and didn't want to disturb any of the merchandise around him. Eased forward onto his hands and knees, studiously tucked his right arm beneath him, and rolled onto his side.

Rykki heard the sound of the plastic key in the lock before she could think.

The door opened quietly like the person opening it didn't want to disturb anyone inside.

A horrendously old, horrendously fat man who looked like Saint Nick in a peach-colored analog-cotton zoot suit limped in.

He halted by the bed, inhaling and exhaling with effort, and rubbed the side of his bearded face which didn't work, loftily contemplating the furniture, the fish on the telly, the fish in the plastic hull, the yellow-blue sky out the porthole, and, after a while, the brown boy on the floor who had ceased moving and the black girl with the terrified methylene blue eyes glistening with tears staring back at him.

"Hello, Rykki," he said. He freed something invisible from his lower lip and examined it between his thumb and forefinger. "You must be quite tired after all this."

"Help him," she said, gaping at her brother, palms in front of her like she was ready to receive a large serving bowl.

The man contemplated the body at her feet some more.

A dispassionate smile germinated in the cumulus of his whiskers.

"Oh, it's rather too late for that, I should think. The oysters have been working on him for, what ..."

The petabyte nano-puter that was his peach-colored silk tie spoke in a high lilliputian voice.

"Twenty-two hours and forty-six minutes," it said.

"Quite a while. Toxins have set upon every cell by now. Best to let him take his leave gracefully. He's been through a lot, just like you."

Rykki was in motion before her brain knew her body was aiming at the door.

She trampolined off the bed, hit the carpet half a meter in front of him, pivoted left, and plowed smack into Dante Allegro's arms which flew out from behind the doctor to intercept her.

His citrus soap enveloped her.

She struggled, but his muscles constricted with pythonoidal strength.

"Still got her knickers in a twist, doesn't she," he said. "You want I should pop her a shot of the barbs?"

"A little calmative might just work the magic, Mr. Allegro," the old man said, rubbing. "Dr. Hung-chang? Dr. K'ai-chuh? Would you please join us ... and shut the door behind you, if you'd be so kind ..."

"Straightaway, Dr. Mizzle-Sluggbury," Rykki heard a diffident Devin say from the hall.

Rykki heard the door clap and the bolt clack into place. She felt herself rise into the air and plunk down on the powder-blue bed dusted with crumbs. A syringe pricked her thigh and withdrew before she could react.

When they let her loose, she clambered off and huddled down beside Zivv.

His skin had tinted purple. She could see the whites of his eyes where the lids had slit open. The bloody ladybug had made its way across his cheek, down his jaw, and along his neck, where it had begun to stain his gray t-shirt.

"This must be a lot to take in, Rykki," Fiona said gently as she stepped up beside Devin and the others. "It's hard for us to imagine what you must be going through."

"You need to go off the boil a bit," Devin said, reporting what he heard from his forefinger, which he'd inserted to the first joint and a half in his ear. "Put your head together. We're here to help."

"You're supposed to be dead," Rykki told the ancient man.

Dr. Mizzle-Sluggbury laughed.

"I am," he said. "Was. But, well … it's all rather a long story."

Rykki took Zivv's left hand and held it between hers. It felt like a surgical glove, it was so cool and rubbery. She didn't want to cry, but she couldn't control the sadness forking through her chest.

"Please help him," she said, voice solid even as the tears started sliddering down her cheeks. "I'll do anything you want."

Dr. Mizzle-Sluggbury raised his eyebrows.

"Well, that's the thing, Rykki," he said. "You will anyway."

He sounded truly concerned she didn't understand.

"Rykki?" Fiona asked. "Do you happen to remember your lessons about the Gulf War? Those afternoons with Ms. Karter …"

Rykki wrinkled her nose.

"Magda …"

Dr. Mizzle-Sluggbury's tone faded into tenderness.

"She had rather an extensive set of complications during the landing phase of her lunar shuttle flight."

"Ka-*boom*," said Dante beside him.

His discolored teeth gathered.

"That's enough," Dr. Mizzle-Sluggbury told him.

243

Dante's head retracted into his shoulders. His pale contacts dropped to the carpet. He put his full weight on one foot, then the other.

Rykki stared at her brother, fingers combing through his hair, trying to erase the rest of these people from the cabin.

"How," Fiona said, "after the fact, the NorAm soldiers complained of an array of symptoms the governcorp came to think of as a cluster of illnesses ... a syndrome ..."

Dante, instantly bored by the stench of education in the breeze, checked in with the Sony watch implanted in his wrist, and barged over to the bed, conspicuously scratching his bottom.

He released a punctured tire of air from his lungs and picked up the clicker and snicked off the telly and sound system. The electron fish turned back into the mirror and Alternatives to Enthusiasm came up short in the middle of a cover of "Hysterically Blue."

He gazed straight ahead, licking his lips, the vaudevillean who'd just been conked on the head with a baseball bat but whose brain hadn't quite passed on the inside dope to the rest of his body.

"Everyone thought the whole affair was about chemical poisoning," Devin explained. "The fatigue, the rashes, the miscarriages and birth defects ..."

"But it wasn't," said Fiona.

"Not at all, in actual fact. Saddam wasn't simply continuing R and D on a weapon that had already existed for years."

"No. He was, much to everyone's surprise, trying his hand at a completely new weapon ... one that came, I suppose it goes without saying, with the blessings of his backers on the mainland ... who were themselves quite busy planning for the imminent turn-over of Hong Kong, and hence redesigning their own defensive capabilities and economic infrastructure."

"Nano-tech," Devin said, "in a word."

"That's how it all began, really," Dr. Mizzle-Sluggbury said. He limped over to the sofa and sat down with a long suspiration. He freed a piece of lint from his trousers and held it up quizzically to the light.

"First experiments into the potential infective and reconstructive powers of the stuff, you see."

Zivv gurgled deep in his throat.

His body bucked, once, went still.

Rykki bent over and hugged him, crying softly.

"Poor Saddam, however, gink that he was," Fiona went on, "couldn't get very much right if his life depended on it. Hence the results were less than resultful. But he did succeed in setting the stage in Britain, NorAm, and China for some rather serious governcorp investigations into a realm that previously had been thought science fiction. Got everyone up to scratch in actual fact."

Devin took a seat in one of the powder-blue chairs opposite Dr. Mizzle-Sluggbury and rubbed his freckled scalp.

"New atom bomb, really," he explained. "Only an atom bomb that works from the inside out … rewiring and rethinking cells in any part of the body …"

"Just imagine," Fiona said. "A governcorp could take over a whole country without firing a single shot."

"Which is when," Dr. Mizzle-Sluggbury said, "things started getting interesting."

"And complex."

"Very complex. Right." He coughed, clearing his throat. "You see, it was just about this point when the idea of geographical borders became rather, em … what …"

"Iffy," Devin offered.

"Iffy. Thanks. And certain economic rather than political entities moved toward the cultural fore. Tech began to seep out of governmental centers and diffuse into corporate ones."

Rykki got the feeling they'd forgotten her. They were celebrating a job well-done, composing a history not for her but for themselves.

Fiona walked over to the fridge built into the armoire, opened it, withdrew a bottle of champagne, and walked back to her seat. Devin found glasses in a cupboard disguised as wall. The airship bumped into some turbulence and out again. Things around the cabin rattled and settled.

Fiona popped the cork and poured.

"Some of which centers," she continued, "like the one the good Dr. Mizzle-Sluggbury here is associated with, were also involved with research into cryonics and life-extension."

"Others somato-enhancement," said Devin, passing around the drinks.

"And still others the reintroduction of illicit drugs into the general population. Thank you."

"Drugs to end all drugs." Dr. Mizzle-Sluggbury frowned like a bearded bullfrog, swallowing. "Imagine the possibilities ... a pharmaceutical you inject into your body once, and once only ... a serum charged with nanobots which accrue in your neural grid, nest, sidle up to unsuspecting cells and give them a bit of the old wink, and, when those unsuspecting cells give them a bit of the old wink back, well, they just hop aboard ... merge ... adjust ..."

"The ultimate perpetual high."

"A multiplex inside your skull which you can't tell is really someone else's. An amusement park of the mind. A holoporn boutique ... a video arcade ... an endorphin factory ... all at once ... all instantaneously addictive ... and all, it almost goes without saying, shockingly lucrative."

"Literally mind-altering."

When Rykki tried to sit up straight again and wipe her nose, she discovered her arms wouldn't work. Her pupils were dilating, she could tell, letting in too many photons. The cabin hovered in fuzzy overexposed whiteness.

"It's hard to grasp how much credit you'd need to pour into such an enterprise to make it succeed," Dr. Mizzle-Sluggbury went on. "And yet it's even harder to grasp how quickly venture capitalists from around the world—and off it—began swarming out of the new geopolitical woodwork to volunteer their services. But who wouldn't want to be able to make the subject of choice into anything one might fancy ... sculpt a new personality ... keep the proverbial mass consciousness content ... send blipverts into its cortex telling it who to vote for, who to love and hate, who to trust and fear, which religion to choose, which products the economy needs it to purchase this week?"

"An artist kept alive in a tank off the coast of Scotland," Fiona said, "caught wind of the endeavor early on and was first to offer his rather extensive resources in a bid, among other things, to reenergize the sagging rock'n'roll market."

"Klub Med was eager to reenter the venerable family trade," Devin said.

"Missionary zeal returned to certain elements at the Vatican."

"And everything became, well ... entertainment."

"Just like that."

"Heavily encrypted messages arrived from the Virgin-Disney people, the NorAm governcorp, the Knesset, the Environmental Protection Agency ... even the Global Space Administration, interested in creating cheap expendable cyborgs capable of performing everything from combat to deep-space travel."

"In a word," said Devin, "a new species."

"A new species," said Fiona, pleased with the term.

"Which didn't initially realize it *was* a new species."

"Couldn't."

"Programmed precisely as those in the box seats felt it should be programmed. Designed to begin breeding with the general population at the earliest possible opportunity."

"Homo ductilis. Malleable man." Dr. Mizzle-Sluggbury coughed again. "Pardon. We gave them pasts. Little hobby of mine ... uploading memories from some of my cryonic patients when their bodies and credit accounts were all gone to smash."

"Except," said Fiona. She drank. "Except things didn't exactly... take the biscuit."

"Bad wiring," Devin explained.

"Gray Goo Problem at the cerebral tier."

"Organic and inorganic didn't chum up as we might have

hoped."

"Our subjects began to experience … psychic episodes … unintended hallucinations," Dr. Mizzle-Sluggbury said. "Memory incongruities."

"But we're working through those problems."

"Doing up the fudges."

Rykki felt shot. Her face was clammy, her feet and hands numb. She wanted to lie down and close her eyes. But she fought the urge, kept trying to flinch herself awake.

"Turing meets Darwin," said Devin.

"They shake hands," Fiona said. "Have themselves a nice night on the town."

"Over time artificial evolution can codify and combine the behaviors of the most effective subjects in a system to breed an even fitter population of subjects."

"We predicted we would find examples of parasitism, symbiosis, and many other phenomena familiar from the biological world."

"And we were right."

"Man," Dr. Mizzle-Sluggbury said, "becomes the sex organs for machines, permitting them to evolve into higher forms."

"Klub Med has already begun distributing them on the street."

"First hit's free, lads, isn't it."

"Slightly more complex serums have been circulating on Erewhon One for three years."

Rykki shut her eyes, thinking she was blinking, only when she opened them again the room had rearranged itself. Dante was pouring himself a lager by the fridge. Dr. Mizzle-Sluggbury was still talking, but in a different register. Devin and Fiona were kneeling next to her.

She herself was leaning against the cool wall-wide porthole, unable to move, bright yellow fish flitting at the edges of her vision.

"We induced a catastrophe curve that transformed you into… you," Dr. Mizzle-Sluggbury was saying, "thereby introducing a fairly sudden discontinuous change into a fairly stable continuous system. We can't predict the precise effect of that catastrophe, but we can use this model to help ascertain the conditions most favorable for its manifestation."

"If the nineteenth century was a photograph," Fiona whispered into Rykki's hot ear as she crossed her arms on her chest and eased her back onto the padded carpet beside her brother, "then the twentieth century was an x-ray."

"And the twenty-first, a hologram," whispered Devin, tightening his grip on her ankles.

"We've produced, you see, a revolution on an individual scale," Dr. Mizzle-Sluggbury said. "Now it's time to provoke the same on a global one."

Devin said to Fiona: "Ready?"

"Ready."

"Right. One ... two ... and *three.*"

Rykki rose in the air and bumped down on the bed. Her face was anesthetized. The air felt too chilly. Fiona attentively arranged her head on a duck-feather pillow. Dante belched.

"Which brings us, in a sense, to the beginning of my story," Dr. Mizzle-Sluggbury said. "They occasioned my heart attack by spiking my food with a pharmaceutical usually used in cryonic preparation. Ever the sense of humor." He coughed. "Pardon. And, half a year later, your pedagogical friend at ABNORMAL ..."

"Ms. Karter," Fiona said, brushing Rykki's hair out of her face.

"Right. Ms. Karter let the human mice loose in the urban maze, thinking she was doing so by means of an act of beneficent free will ... a charming notion that doesn't quite bring home the bacon like it once did."

"Chemicals," Fiona whispered as if she were whispering a nursery rhyme to Rykki. "Probabilities."

"Do you by any chance remember your inoculations?" Dr. Mizzle-Sluggbury asked.

"I don't believe she's in the answering mood," Devin said.

"No," said Fiona. "She's not."

Dante barged over and, peeling a Cadbury's chocolate bar,

leered down at Rykki with his blue-milk lenses like he might at a bad accident in the street.

"Homing device in the brain stem," Dr. Mizzle-Sluggbury spelled out. "Just had to sit back and watch the beta test administer itself. At the end of the maze, for those who worked quite hard and managed to survive, waited another cage."

"I believe she's leaving us," Devin said.

"Is she?"

"Misreplication," Fiona whispered as Rykki watched the big black dream slide toward her like rain across a lake. "Program mutation, data malfs, transcription errors."

"Welcome to your new home, Rykki," Dr. Mizzle-Sluggbury said kindly from somewhere very far away. "Diacomm's Airborne Laboratory Incubation and Experimentation Node."

"Your nest from this day forward ..."

"A place you'll always be comfortable ... always part of the plan."

Rykki groaned.

"We'll always be with you," said Devin. "We'll always be at your side."

"You're not the end of anything," Dr. Mizzle-Sluggbury explained. "That's the whole point, you see. You're the beginning of everything. You're our, em, what ..."

"Our mother, really, in a way," Devin said.

"Our queen bee," said Fiona.

Rykki closed her eyes.

Phosphenes spattered her view.

"Sleep well," Fiona whispered, stroking her hair.

Devin stooped and kissed her lightly on the forehead.

"When you awake," he whispered, "the sights you'll see ..."

"Everything'll be right cushy, like," Dante added. "Soft as easy street, i'n'it. Sleep right well, my little pretty. Yeah. That's it. Have a good one on us ..."

* * *

Rykki felt something warm and rough against her face and broke into a dream in which she was breaststroking through shoppers in a jammed Beijing side street. An erhu twanged. Pedestrians who sounded like they were being goosed haggled with vendors behind bamboo-and-plywood counters selling legless chickens, soggy black-market vegetables, and worthless shellacked boxes. Zinc-gray smoke gauzed the alley, smelling bitter and carrying the dull greenish olfactory backbeat of puke and wet puppy. In another universe, Rykki felt perspiration gather above her lip. Someone applied a cool moist face flannel to her forehead. She heard her own voice say the words *inarticulate brilliance of the garden.* She stopped in front of a man skinning a cobra. Pink-white muscle appeared between flaps of yellow-brown scales. On the back of the snake's hood was a white mark that looked like a pair of spectacles. The man was working so quickly Rykki had trouble following the movements of his hands. It reminded her of the chefs who sliced and diced sushi as though they were working under the influence of amphetamines. Bluish-green organs fell out of the cobra's belly. The man, short and bald except for the black-hair jets spraying from his nose, hooked the carcass to a rusted shower-curtain ring fastened to the booth's bamboo frame. Eight or ten snake carcasses already dangled there like belts in a closet. In another universe, someone above and to the right of Rykki muttered to someone above and to the left that they should begin. A caged bird squawked. Rykki caught a glimpse of herself in a shard of mirror hanging on a whitewashed wall. Her head, she saw, wasn't a head. It was a television set attached to her body. The skin on her neck blended imperceptibly into smooth black plastic. Her own face was on the screen, only it was super large. Her televisual eyes were big as her mouth in real life. Her mouth was the width and height of a forearm. She saw her tongue nudging among her shiny white teeth like a blind mollusk. She looked scared. She raised her hand to confirm she really had a telly growing in place of her head and her fingers collided with brittle plastic. As they made contact, her face wobbled into other images. Magda extended her hand to touch Rykki's cheek but her face warped into a grimace and her shoulders crowded around her ears like Dante's and she coughed, hard and soggy, freeing up a perfect red rose from her esophagus, which hovered in front of her lips. Rykki felt something tug at her ankle. She didn't know which universe this was happening in. The Chinese man in the booth went about his business as if Rykki was no longer there. The perspiration on her upper lip accumulated. A male bedbug seen in alarming closeup on the screen, reddish-brown, oval, and flat, mounted a female bedbug and punctured her abdomen with its sharp beak, releasing his sperm into her copulatory wound. Sweat slid between Rykki's lips. She heard herself sleeping, long full breaths with the smallest allusion to a snore at the end of every third inhalation. The Chinese guy reached under the counter and pulled out another cobra carcass and started in. Rykki was thirsty. Her tongue felt porous, like she could feel each taste bud. The tugging at her ankle became more pronounced. Rykki understood, congruous with nothing, there was no life form on the planet without some kind of membrane separating it from every other life form on the planet, a kinetic semi-solid lockup, and the best you could do was bump your jail cell against someone else's jail cell if you wanted to communicate. Only now the membranes were gone. The camera ballooned up and suddenly was gliding through the Vatican library, past row upon row of allegedly lost manuscripts ... Rykki could read the titles on the spines ... the disappeared books of Aristotle, Sappho, Aeschylus ... a whole floor-to-ceiling shelf of demo tapes ... the Beatles in Hamburg, Viva Bonni Suicide in Scotland, The Dying Pope Expresses Grief Musically. Rykki saw all of this upside-down. She felt like her tongue was bullying her teeth and gums out of the way. The tugging at her ankle became more pronounced. She tried to sit erect. The Chinese man hooked the carcass to a rusted shower curtain ring fastened to the booth's bamboo frame and reached under the counter for another snake. The gabble of overlapping conversations fell away. The erhu went still. She glanced down and saw rats chewing through her left leg. They'd already shredded her jeans and torn through flesh and muscle right to the bone, which didn't look much like bone anymore, but more like a bloody ivory woodcut. The rats weren't rats. They seemed more like they'd been designed for exhibition in Dr. Haze's Fabulous Mutant Taxidermy

Display. They sported anemic human skin instead of fur, supernumerary frog legs sprigging like flaccid wings from their vertebrae, and small pinched human faces with sucker mouths spiny with piraña teeth. Their bellies exuded a silvery jellyish trail beneath them like oversized slugs and their feet were bird feet with talons. One wore Dante's face like a mask. Another wore Dr. Mizzle-Sluggbury's. One of them was Fiona and one Devin. The faces were all squashed and constricted, but she'd know them anywhere. Magda was working diligently on her right ankle, and Petrina Bogg was there, and the Cat Cultist (who still wore his miniature bird-bone necklace), and Mu-quin in a toy-version of her wheelchair, and even that nice flight attendant who probably wasn't a nice flight attendant at all but a lab technician. Rykki staggered and her legs buckled, tendons tattered, and she fell to the ground in front of the Chinese guy's booth without any sound except for the soggy ones associated with good appetite. The rat things skittered over her. More joined in, flooding out from beneath the guy's booth. Rykki felt nipping at her wrists, her tummy, her breasts. The people in the alley walked around her politely, eyes averted. A bicycle swept past. No one was riding it. A pack of especially hungry rat things began to exert themselves on her neck. Her legs had already dissolved to the knees. Her fingers were gone. Her breasts that had ached so much recently were raw concave hollows.

"Hiya, sweetie," a bantam version of chubby Mao Zedong in a clown's nose and drab jacket said in a New Jersey accent on the screen. "Pleased to meetcha."

One rodent struck her jugular.

Her blood pressure plummeted.

In another universe, something velvet and rubbery entered her mouth and probed toward the back of her throat.

She began to gag.

Her point-of-view swapped ... she was above the alley now, discarnate, watching her other self lie there on the dirt. Channels sputtered so fast on the face of the Rykki on the ground that the Rykki in the air couldn't follow the pictures. Snowstorms bloomed across the screen. Ghosts flared and died. Double images rolled.

One of the rats was albino. Its skin was lavender-white. From this angle, through the smoke, squinting, Rykki could barely make out Oran's squinched face.

The one next to it was Jada.

There was Tris, too, scurrying from a hole in the base of the Chinese guy's booth, and there—the last one to emerge—was Zivv. His mouth was open like a pollution sore. Rykki lay there in the alley, cathode-ray head too heavy to raise, channels flipping across her countenance, pedestrians wending their way around her.

She listened to hundreds of tiny jaws chattering.

She couldn't smell the smoke anymore.

Her abdomen was a meaty hole.

As she waited, an arm appeared on the TV set. Nothing but an arm. She could see each magnified hair follicle, though she couldn't identify whose arm it was.

It reached back into the screen, into Rykki's head.

She felt it pushing parts of her brain aside to get at what it was searching for.

And then it just clicked her off.

LANCE OLSEN, Philip K. Dick Award finalist and Pushcart Prize recipient, is author of more than a dozen books, including the acclaimed speculative novels *Tonguing the Zeitgeist, Time Famine*, and *Burnt*. He teached in the M.F.A. program at the University of Idaho and lives near McCall with his artist-wife, Andi, while residing digitally at Café Zeitgeist (www.uidaho.edu/~lolsen).

FREAKNEST is #23
in the Wordcraft Speculative Writers Series.
For other titles, visit our website at:
http://www.oregontrail.net/~wordcraft
email: wordcraft@oregontrail.net

Support small press. Order direct.

WORDCRAFT SPECULATIVE WRITERS SERIES

#1: Prayers of Steel, Misha,
ISBN: 1-877655-00-7 $5
#2: The Magic Deer, Conger Beasley, Jr.,
ISBN: 1-877655-01-5 $5
#3: Lifting, Mark Rich,
ISBN: 1-877655-03-1 $7.95 (limited supply)
#4: The Liquid Retreats, Todd Mecklem & Jonathan Falk,
ISBN: 1-877655-01-3 $6.95 (OP)
#5: Oceans of Glass and Fire, Rob Hollis Miller,
ISBN: 1-877655-04-X $7.95 (OP)
#6: The Seventh Day and After, Don Webb,
ISBN: 1-877655-05-8 $7.95 * (OP)
#7: Pangaea, Denise Dumars,
ISBN: 1-877655-08-2 $7.95 (limited supply)
#8: The Raw Brunettes, Lorraine Schein,
ISBN: 1-877655-12-0 $6.00 (limited supply)*
#9: Scherzi, I Believe, Lance Olsen,
ISBN: 1-877655-11-2 $9.95 * (OP)
#10: Ke-Qua-Hawk-As, Misha,
ISBN: 1-877655-13-9 $9.95 * (limited supply)
#11: The Eleventh Jagaurundi..., Jessica Amanda Salmonson,
ISBN: 1-877655-14-7, $9.95 (OP)
#12: The Blood of Dead Poets, Conger Beasley, Jr.,
ISBN: 1-877655-15-5, $9.95
#13: Unreal City, Thomas E. Kennedy,
ISBN: 1-877655-17-1, $11.95
#14: Burnt, Lance Olsen,
ISBN: 1-877655-20-1, $11.95
#15: The Book of Angels, Thomas E. Kennedy,
ISBN: 1-877655-23-6, $12.95

#16: The Din of Celestial Birds, Brian Evenson,
ISBN: 1-877655-24-4, $10.95 (limited supply)
#17: The Explanation & Other Good Advice, Don Webb,
ISBN: 1-877655-25-2, $9.95
#18: The Winter Dance Party Murders, Greg Herriges,
ISBN: 1-877655-26-0, $13.95
#19: Shadow Bones, David Memmott,
ISBN: 1-877655-28-7, $10
#20: Red Spider White Web, Misha,
ISBN: 1-877655-29-5, $12
#21: Splitting, Brian Charles Clark,
ISBN: 1-877655-30-9, $9
#22: Contagion & Other Stories, Brian Evenson,
ISBN: 1-877655-34-1
#23: Freaknest, Lance Olsen,
ISBN: 1-877655-35-X
#24: Smoking Mirror Blues, Ernest Hogan,
ISBN: 1-877655-37-6 (forthcoming early 2001)
#25: Realism & Other Illusions:Essay on the Craft of Fiction,
Thomas E. Kennedy,
ISBN: 1-877655-38-4 (forthcoming 2001)